TWISTED LOVE

ALSO BY MAYA ALDEN

SERIES: ONCE UPON A TIME

The Temporary Wife

An Age-Gap Arranged Marriage Romance

Inspired by the fairytale *The Little Match Girl*

An Ugly Love

A Slow Burn Unrequited Love

Inspired by the fairytale *The Ugly Duckling*

SERIES: GOLDEN KNIGHTS

The Wrong Wife

An Arranged Marriage Romance

Bad Boss

An Office Romance

Not A Love Marriage
A Second Chance, Surprise Pregnancy Romance

Golden Promises
A Single Dad Instalove Romance

Twisted Hearts
An Enemies to Lovers Romantic Thriller

A Golden Christmas
An Age Gap Romantic Mystery

Twisted Love
A Serial Killer Romantic Thriller

TWISTED LOVE

MAYA ALDEN

Copyright © 2024 by Maya Alden

All rights reserved.

No part of this publication may be reproduced, distributed, or transmitted in any form or by any means, including photocopying, recording, or other electronic or mechanical methods, without the prior written permission of the publisher, except as permitted by U.S. copyright law. For permission requests, contact [include publisher/author contact info].

The story, all names, characters, and incidents portrayed in this production are fictitious. No identification with actual persons (living or deceased), places, buildings, and products is intended or should be inferred.

ISBN: 9798865963028

Content Warnings

Twisted Love is different from the other books in the *Golden Knight series* or any other book I have ever written. This is a straight-up romantic suspense, police procedural, serial killer mystery wrapped in one. So, in this book, expect a dark and intense journey into the psyche of a serial killer and the complexities of a high-stakes investigation.

This novel contains graphic depictions of violence, murder, and physical and psychological torture. It also includes themes of sexual assault, trauma, and psychological manipulation. The narrative delves deep into the disturbing actions and mindset of a serial killer, which may be distressing for some readers. Strong language and adult situations are prevalent throughout the story. Reader discretion is advised, particularly for those who may find such content triggering or overly disturbing. This book aims to explore the darker aspects of human nature and criminal psychology in the context of a gripping thriller. It is intended for a mature audience comfortable with these themes. Your mental and emotional well-being is essential.

"Beware, for I am fearless, and therefore powerful."
Mary Shelley Frankenstein

"We are all broken. That's how the light gets in."
Ernest Hemingway

"The past is never where you think you left it."
Katherine Anne Porter

CHAPTER 1

Sunday, October 1

They recited poetry when they worked.

"As lady from her door, emerged; a summer afternoon," they crooned to the woman lying on her stomach on the metal table, her legs and hands tied down with ropes, her body arranged like Vinci's Vitruvian Man.

The caterpillar before them was immobilized, but could still make sounds. They'd gag her, but then they'd miss her transformation from caterpillar to butterfly. She was their first caterpillar and thus special. She had silky, milky white skin. They stroked her back, and she whined.

"Please don't. Please don't," she begged.

They chuckled. Did she really think that they'd go to all this trouble and then not do what they were meant to do—help her become what she was destined to be?

At least she'd stopped screaming for help because that shit had gotten old real fast.

"Her pretty parasol be seen, contracting in a field," they continued as they dipped the tattoo injector into black ink. They put the injector on the caterpillar's skin. She screamed. They smiled as they assisted in her transformation.

The butterfly was whimpering softly by the time they were done. In the past, the Butterfly Killer used to end with a flourish—showing off their calligraphy skills as they inscribed the words of Emily Dickinson: From cocoon forth a butterfly.

But this time, they would dedicate this butterfly to a caterpillar they knew would make the most beautiful butterfly of them all. The Butterfly Killer had only gotten a quarter of the way through last time with her, but this time, oh, this time, they'd go all the way.

The caterpillar on the table sobbed.

Ungrateful bitch.

They were giving her a chance to be so much more, and she was whining and moaning. Just like their mother. Always complaining.

The moon cast a ghostly glow over their studio, where shadows danced like specters. They moved silently, a wraith in the darkness, their breath a measured hiss. The garrote, a mere whisper of wire, was already singing its silent song of death in their hands.

They slipped the garrote around her neck, the wire biting into her skin with a lover's caress turned lethal. Slowly, slowly, slowly, slowly—they saw her transform, rise beyond the earth, and become a glorious creature. She gagged and gurgled, her body clamped to the table, danced in desperation, and oh so gently, she became a butterfly. Her gasps became ragged whispers, and then those whispers disappeared as she soared and ascended.

Then, silence.

Next time, they'd want to see her eyes as life left her. Next time, they'd do things just a little differently so the butterfly would be theirs and theirs alone.

They stood over her, the wire now a crimson necklace in their hands. Their heart was a drumbeat of triumph and terror. Feeling that sexual rush and throbbing between their legs, they found their release in the quiet of the night as they tattooed on the butterfly's back: Sweet Caroline, are you ready to become a butterfly?

Chapter 2

Sunday, October 1

She wasn't sleeping peacefully.

He knew why, and he hated that her demons found her while she was in slumber.

"Shh, shh." Aurelio pulled Vega into his arms. "I'm here. Come back to me."

Was there anything more debilitating than seeing the strongest woman you knew whimper in her sleep? To hear her begging a monster to stop hurting her?

Vega woke up suddenly, as she always did after a nightmare, shaking, moaning. He did what he'd done several times before. Helped her to the bathroom, where she'd throw up violently.

He sat next to her on the bathroom floor of her luxurious high-rise apartment in downtown Los Angeles, wiping her face with a wet washcloth.

She looked at Aurelio and shook her head. "Why are you still here with me? I'm such a mess."

He smiled calmly at her, even though furious rage coated his insides. If fucking Jacob Soller was not already on death row in Dallas, he'd kill the man with his bare hands, which was a testament to his anger. Because Aurelio was not a violent man. He was a farmer who nurtured.

Watching Vega go through this was brutal. Especially since he knew she had to do this alone when he wasn't around. He lived in Golden Valley near Fresno, where he ran his family's farm, and only made it to Los Angeles a few times a month.

Vega was a corporate lawyer with a high-power job, so she couldn't just mosey on up to California's central valley so they could hook up.

He wanted her to move in with him in Golden Valley. But he knew if he mentioned that, he'd lose his head because she'd fucking bite it off. She wasn't ready to live with him, she wasn't ready to commit, she wasn't ready to lower her guard.

He was a farmer. He'd wait patiently for her feelings to grow.

"Come on, baby, let's get you in the shower." He knew that after a dream, she felt a strong need to immerse in boiling water and cleanse herself. Her body continued to tremble and shiver, even amidst the warmth of the cascading water.

She put her head on his chest while he simply wrapped himself around her, the water hammering down on them. She was crying and Aurelio felt as helpless as he always did when he was with her on a night such as this.

"I hate to put you through this," she whispered.

He kissed her hair. "I hate that you have to go through this. I hate that I'm not with you the nights you have to do this alone."

She looked up at me, her eyes sparkling. "What makes you think I'm alone, honey?"

He smiled again. Since they'd gotten together nearly a year ago, there had been no one else, not for him and not for her. Oh, his southern beauty could honey him from here to Sunday, but he wasn't alone in how he felt. She was just as fucked as he was when it came to this relationship, just as tied, just as enchanted.

"Do tell, darlin', about all the other men you've had in your bed," he chuckled, turning off the shower. If she was well enough to crack jokes, she was well enough to get out of the shower and back to bed. She could probably catch a couple of hours of sleep before she'd drag her ass to the Knight Technology offices where she was the General Counsel. Aurelio would tuck her in and leave for home earlier than that, even though he didn't want to. But he had responsibilities he couldn't shirk off.

He previously made the long drive from his family farm in central California to LA. However, recently, he'd adopted the less eco-friendly but more convenient method his brother Alejandro and sister-in-law Maria preferred: chartering a helicopter. Now, he took off from the Westin Bonaventure Hotel Heliport, reaching home in just thirty minutes, bypassing the exhausting three to four-hour drive usually hampered by the notorious Los Angeles traffic.

But this night, she was more needy than usual, and he intended to deliver, be whatever she desired him to be, for as long as she required. Aurelio texted his pilot to let him know he was going to be late. He lay in bed with her, and she hugged him close, her thigh between his, her arms tight around him.

"Baby, I wish I could take this away from you. I wish I could carry this for you." He felt tears burn his eyes.

She hadn't given him details, just the Cliff Notes of what had happened in Dallas to her and why she'd left her job as an Assistant District Attorney in Dallas and turned to corporate law.

"You probably think I'm plumb crazy."

She was trying to lighten the mood, but how could she? His Caro had been brutalized, and even though it had happened seven years ago, the wounds within were still fresh.

"I think you're one of the bravest, smartest, and most beautiful women I know," he whispered, kissing her forehead.

"Aurelio?"

"Yeah, baby."

"Am I drivin' you away?"

He didn't blame her for that question either. They'd been on again, off again—more on than off. But for him, for the past three months, it had been on.

His feelings for her baffled him. He usually liked his women quiet and timid. Hell, the last time he'd thought he'd met the one, he'd gotten engaged, and she was, as his sister Isadora put it, "boring as hell."

Jenn Whelan had been bland but sweet. She was the daughter of Barnaby Whelan, who owned a large cattle farm, and Barnaby had been more excited about Golden Valley and Whelan Farms becoming related to one another rather than about Jenn marrying him. It had been a colossal mistake, one he'd quickly moved to fix.

The truth was that Jenn wanted to become Mrs. Santos. She wanted to quit her job as a successful accountant and become a fulltime housewife. He didn't know what that meant because he lived in a house in Golden Valley, where he had a cleaning crew that came to fix up the house on a weekly basis. His mother, Paloma, made sure her elves did the laundry and stocked up his fridge. When he'd tried to get Jenn to explain what keeping house meant to her, she'd gone off in the direction of motherhood, and Aurelio had ended the relationship. She'd gone around insinuating that she'd dumped him because he cheated on her, and he let her. If that helped her feel better, he was all for it.

But even when he'd proposed to Jenn, which had been lackluster—we should get married since we've been dating for six months without a single fight and your father is being pretty insistent—affair, he'd not been in love with her. He'd never said the words to her or any other woman who wasn't his family.

He'd met Caroline Vega—who went by Vega at work and with her friends in Los Angeles and Texas—a few months after his engagement had ended. It had been at a bar in San Francisco. She'd been like a sledgehammer. They'd ended up fucking all night and into the next day. In the beginning, he'd thought that sex with Jenn had been so average that Vega's heat and passion enamored him. Still, now, nearly a year later, that passion and heat hadn't cooled one bit—and he knew it wasn't just about sex. Aurelio Santos was in love with his Texan honey. He'd admitted it finally when he'd watched his sister get married in Scotland, with Vega sitting next to him in an old church. He knew he was with the woman who he'd marry. If he'd told Vega that, she'd have run after kneeing him in the nuts.

Knowing her fear of commitment came from, he'd have been frustrated—but the scars she carried ran deep within and on her body. Every time he stroked her back, he felt the slight bump of the partial tattoo of the butterfly that a monster had left on her skin. He'd asked if she wanted it removed, and his brave woman had said, "It's a scar. Can't go around fixin' every scar, honey; they make us who we are."

He nuzzled her, soaking her in. She was worried she was driving him away? Where the fuck would he go? Where could he go?

"Baby, I'm not going anywhere."

Her hand stroked his stomach and slid down to where he lay semi-hard against her. Whenever she had a nightmare, he was sure he'd never get it up again. But then she'd touch him, and boom, he'd be hard enough to hammer down fence posts.

"Do you have to leave right away?" she asked, her eyes vulnerable as she shifted so she could look into his eyes.

He was getting hard in her hand, and his breathing was already becoming choppy. "Not right away," he said huskily and pulled her against him, relieved that she'd recovered from the nightmare.

He knew she needed to connect after the dreams assailed her. She wanted to feel loved, even though she'd say something crass in that Southern accent of hers, like, "I just wanted to get my rocks off, honey; it's as simple as that."

They were past getting their rocks off—this wasn't just sex; it was love, and he hoped that sooner than later, she'd allow that into her pretty little head.

He flipped her so she was beneath him.

"I haven't kissed you yet," he whispered, lowering his mouth to hers. He loved kissing her. He'd kiss her all day, every day, if they both didn't have to go to work. She was so fucking responsive and so sweet. If he told the people she worked with that his Caro was sweet, they'd think he had lost his mind.

When she was Vega, a no-nonsense lawyer, she intimidated the fuck out of everyone. Not him. Oh, never him. He was smitten, madly in love, ready to fucking die for her if she wanted it—but he wasn't scared of her.

He kissed her mouth and then slowly traveled down her body. She had the most luscious fucking breasts. He loved seeing his dark hands against her lighter skin. The contrast was erotic, and when he suckled her, she writhed, which made everything hotter between them.

He smelled her arousal and felt the desire and satisfaction race through him. She was his. No matter what happened, no matter how horrible the nightmare, she wanted to wake up to him and with him.

"Aurelio," she whispered when he slipped inside her.

"Yes." He moved languidly in and out of her, feeling his release build at the base of his spine. Nothing had ever felt this much like home as being inside her.

"Tell me."

"I love you, Caro," he replied, and she cried out her release as she always did when she heard him confess what was in his heart. She tried to pretend she was some badass who didn't need the words, but she sure as hell needed them to orgasm.

When she came down from the high, he looked into her eyes. "You want me to say it again, baby?"

Chapter 3

Monday, October 2

The apartment felt empty after Aurelio left just like it always did. Vega knew he wanted her to move in with him. She knew he wanted her to tell him she loved him. She knew he wanted her just the way she was, no matter how screwed up she was, and she was *plenty* screwed up.

It wasn't always this way.

Caroline Vega was once a happy, well-balanced, ambitious woman, in love and engaged to a wonderful man. Then, as the lead prosecutor in the case against Jaco Soller, a.k.a. The Butterfly Killer, her life blew apart.

Now, if she looked at her life objectively, she was in a damn good place. She made nearly ten times more money than she had as an Assistant District Attorney in Dallas as the head of legal for Knight Technologies. In the past six years since she'd been working for Declan Knight, the CEO of Knight Tech, she'd not seen one single dead body, hadn't interviewed one single rape victim, and had not been sexually assaulted, tortured, or tattooed by a crazy man. She had friends—fucking hell, she had women friends; go figure. There was Esme Knight, Dec's wife. There was Maria Caruso-Santos, Aurelio's sister-in-law. There was Daisy Knight, Hollywood producer and wife of Dec's cousin, High Court Judge Forest Knight; and last but not least, Raya, one of her closest friends, Mateo Silva's wife.

None of her friends knew what had happened in Dallas and why she left. Mateo knew she'd been sexually assaulted. She didn't hide it. She just didn't offer details. She saw a therapist. She worked out five days a week. She ate healthy. She only drank on weekends. For the past year, she was in a monogamous relationship with Aurelio Santos.

When she'd left Dallas and come to Los Angeles, she had no friends, worked twenty-four-seven, drank every night until she fell asleep, and then woke up in the morning and went right back to work and did it all over again. She had not been able to have sex.

She refused to have the single, half-wing of the butterfly tattoo on her back lasered off. To her, it was a survivor's badge, a symbol of her enduring resilience. Yet, despite this emblem of survival, she often struggled to feel like one. On nights when haunting dreams converged, and the fear and pain clawed at her with palpable intensity, she felt like a victim.

Her phone beeped as Vega sat at the head of the polished mahogany conference table. The morning sun cast a golden hue over the skyline of Downtown Los Angeles, its rays filtering through the expansive windows of the Knight Technologies high-rise.

Her posture was impeccable, exuding an aura of controlled power. Her blonde hair was styled impeccably into a loose chignon. Her power suit—a blend of femininity and authority—complemented her tall, statuesque figure. She favored Saint Laurent and Galvan London now that she could afford it. As an ADA, she'd shopped at Macy's and worn Calvin Klein and Tahari on sale.

"Morning, Vega," her executive assistant and lifesaver at work, Jada Matthews walked into the meeting room. In her mid-forties, Jada had been a holdover from the previous general counsel. When Vega had started, Jada had told her point blank, "I know you think you need your own people, but your own people will be as new as you, and I know where all the bodies are buried."

"Excellent," Vega had replied, "Let's go dig up some of those bodies."

And since then, they'd been working together very well.

After the events in Dallas, Vega moved to LA, having already passed the bar in California due to her involvement in a case with federal jurisdiction. Being licensed in California, a state known for its extensive federal court activity, had been essential for effectively handling the complexities of that case.

Vega had wondered how she'd make the shift from criminal to corporate law. The change was not just in the type of law practiced but in the very ethos and rhythm of the work. With its labyrinth of contracts and negotiations, corporate law seemed a world away from the gritty, high-stakes environment of criminal law she was accustomed to.

But it worked out.

A lawyer she'd worked with on a case in Texas, Cyrus Allen, had helped her make the right contacts in Los Angeles. She'd landed a job at a prestigious tech company where she climbed the proverbial corporate ladder. A few years later, her career hit a high when Dec Knight offered her a position on his leadership team.

Now, she worked mergers and acquisitions; HR issues; patent law. Not a dead person in sight. It was fucking fantastic. Or rather, it should've been. But she missed her old job, *not the pay*, but she'd loved helping bring justice to victims and their families. Now it was all about money.

Vega grew up in San Antonio, the daughter of a lawyer. Her mother, a homemaker, tragically died in a car accident during Vega's teenage years. An only child, Vega found her relationship with her father growing distant after he remarried and started a new family. They used to meet for Christmas, but even that fragile connection faded after the incident with Jacob Soller.

The ordeal with Soller had left an indelible mark on Vega. He hadn't just assaulted and tortured her; he had shattered something fundamental within her. A part of her humanity had been extinguished in that harrowing experience, forever altering her identity. She didn't view herself as damaged or weak, but as irrevocably changed. Sometimes, she regretted having been rescued, wondering if it might have been better to have died like Soller's other victims. This rare thought emerged only when she was deep down the rabbit hole of emotional pain. She had managed to keep it at bay with the help of therapy.

"Good morning, Jada." Vega held up her coffee cup as a toast. "How was your weekend?"

"Excellent," Jada grinned. "Joe took me to n/naka for dinner."

"Nice."

Jada handed Vega a manilla folder and opened her laptop. Before Vega could open the folder, her phone buzzed. She smiled when she saw it was from Aurelio.

Aurelio: How are you?

Vega: Good. Thank you for last night.

Aurelio: I love you.

Vega felt her throat closing up as it did whenever he said those three little words. Why couldn't she just say them? Because the last time she had, it had meant little. Jamie had not been able to stay with her after she'd come back from Soller's murder room. Her father had been close to wringing Jamie's neck. "A real man would hold his woman and care for her, bring her back from the hell she's been through."

"Then I'm not a real man, John. I can't do this."

Jamie had always been a weak man, a fact she knew but hadn't mattered until strength was required of him. During her numbness and struggle with recent trauma, it took several months for her to fully realize that Jamie had abandoned her when she needed him most, even though she couldn't express that need at the time.

Now, those words didn't come easily. Affection didn't come easily. Vulnerability didn't come easily. Somehow, though, Aurelio, her farmer from Golden Valley, the most unlikely man she'd thought she'd be with, had managed to get through all her walls and defenses.

Getting here hadn't been easy; there had been push and pull. Once, when he suggested they see other people, she had thrown a drink in his face. Another time, when she declared she was done, he refused to leave her house until they reconciled. Several similar incidents occurred over the past year, but something changed after their trip to Scotland for Aurelio's sister's wedding. Now, both were calmer, more settled in their relationship, believing it was indeed real and that, for now, there was no need to fight it.

Vega: I miss you.

She couldn't say those three words, but she could say other words that she knew he'd make do with...for now. Eventually, he'd want more; he'd already said as much. "Giving you all the time, you need, querida, but one day you'll have to give in."

"Or," she'd asked, "Or what?"

She'd waited for him to say, then he'd leave her; instead, he said, "There's no *or*. You *will* give in."

She'd told him he was cocky as hell, and he'd shown her how cocky. He wasn't going anywhere he'd promised her. But promises meant little to Vega; she wasn't sure they ever would again.

"Joey running late?" Vega asked about the new counsel she'd hired three months ago to manage M&A because Dec and Mateo were on a binge, acquiring companies left, right, and center to grow Knight Technologies.

As soon as Vega said the words, the conference room door opened, and in walked Joey Mann, whose string of impressive accomplishments belied her youth. She was in her mid-twenties and had already worked on two significant cases at a law firm in Arizona, from where she'd moved to Los Angeles a few months ago when she got the job at Knight Technologies. She had an eager sparkle in her eyes, attentive to every word Vega spoke.

She was a tall brunette, nearly five feet eight or nine inches, and had a commanding presence. She was on the masculine side and her voice reminded Vega of the infamous Elizabeth Holmes of Theranos. Unlike Holmes, Joey was easygoing, humble, and eager to learn.

Jada cleared her throat, bringing the meeting to order. "The acquisition of Solarix Technologies is on the table today. They're a key player in enabling solar energy with their software, and this acquisition could significantly boost Knight's portfolio in the renewable sector."

Vega nodded, her Southern drawl adding a distinctive melody to her businesslike tone. "Thank you, Jada. Let's delve into the specifics. We need to ensure this acquisition is seamless and beneficial on all fronts. Joey, you've been reviewing the contracts. What's your take?"

Joey leaned forward, her voice steady but with an undercurrent of enthusiasm. "The contract is solid, Ms. Vega. Solarix's assets are a perfect match for Knight's long-term goals. However, there's a minor clause about the intellectual property rights that we might want to renegotiate."

"Good catch." Vega's blue eyes flickered with approval. "We don't want any loose ends, especially with IP rights. Solarix has some innovative patents that are critical to this deal."

Jada interjected, "Should we schedule a meeting with Solarix's legal team next week?"

"Yes, but let's keep it informal for now," Vega replied. "We don't want to show our full hand just yet. And make sure Mateo is at that meeting—he can speak tech jargon and scare the lawyers."

Jada grinned. Joey just nodded. No smile. She needed to loosen up, Vega thought. She'd get there. She was new, everything was more serious than it needed to be at that age.

Throughout the discussion, Joey's contributions were precise, her insights sharp. Yet, there was something about her—a glint in her eyes, perhaps, when discussing strategies or probing for weaknesses—that could appear a touch too intense for a corporate legal negotiation.

As the meeting drew to a close, Vega's phone buzzed. She glanced at the screen. "Dec wants me in his office right away."

"Let's hope there's no shit hitting the fan this week. We simply don't have the time," Jada warned.

"I hear you. I'm fixin' to focus on Solarix all week. Jada and Joey, thank you both. Let's proceed as discussed."

CHAPTER 4

Monday, October 2

Detective Drago Horvat left Vice because he was sick of working undercover. He'd moved to Homicide, and now he wasn't sure if this was much better. It was easier than working with a rape victim and harder as well because the person was dead, and no real justice was possible. No matter what you did, a person's life was taken and there was no way to bring that back.

Sakra! Damn! He'd seen some shit in his days, but this was…well, this was something else. The body was on the rooftop of a skyscraper that had stopped construction during the pandemic and towered over Figueroa like an eyesore, with plastic sheets fluttering around the seventy-story monolith of steel and concrete. The setting sun cast long shadows, turning the incomplete floors and exposed rafters into a labyrinth of dark and light.

Drago pulled out latex gloves from the inside of his suit jacket, where he kept them for situations just like this. A patrolman brought him Tyvek boot covers that he also slid on so as not to contaminate the crime scene.

The body had been spotted accidentally by a drone. Kids trying out their new toy. Now, those fifteen-year-olds would probably need therapy for the rest of their lives.

Crime scene technicians, clad in white suits, moved methodically around the site. Their flashlights and camera flashes piercing the encroaching dusk, capturing every detail of the grim scene.

The body lay face down, a discarded marionette at the edge of the rooftop. Drago's eyes, hardened by years in Vice before Homicide claimed him, studied the scene with a practiced detachment.

"Cozy place for a crime scene," Drago remarked, his voice carrying over the sound of the wind.

Dr. Emily Chen, the Medical Examiner, looked up from where she knelt beside the victim. Her expression was inscrutable behind her glasses. "If by cozy, you mean cold and desolate, then yes, absolutely."

"Hey, Doc," Drago greeted and turned to the patrolman who was first on the scene. "Well, Lambert, what do we know?"

"Two teenagers saw her from their drone and called 911. We got their statements, nothing much to say except they were half excited and half scared shitless."

"Youth today," Drago sighed.

Lambert grinned. "No kiddin'." He looked through his notes as he continued, "We don't have ID on the victim. Crime scene guys are looking around the rooftop to see if they find anything."

"You got anyone to canvas here?" Drago looked around. The abandoned building was right across from Staples Center (he refused to call it Crypto Fucking Dot Com) and LA Live.

"There's a security guard, but he saw nothing. My partner is with him."

"What was he securing?"

Lambert chuckled. "Rad Periera was securing a blowjob, Detective from a hooker last night in his car. We're trying to find the hooker, but he was light on the description. Said she had big tits and wore red lipstick."

Drago grunted.

"He has a prior."

Drago's eyebrows rose.

"Sexual assault. According to him, he hit on a server at a bar, maybe got handsy. He was drunk. According to the police report, he had his nonconsensual hand up her snatch. She kneed him in his nuts, and then they arrested him."

"Insult on injury! I like it. You think maybe because of the charge, he confessed about the hooker with the big tits and red lipstick?"

"Yeah," Lambert agreed, "he didn't want nothing to do with this body."

"Thanks, Lambert." Drago walked up to the body and crouched, noting the ligature mark around the victim's neck. "Classic garrote. Efficient, silent, personal. Our killer's old school, huh?"

Dr. Chen adjusted her gloves. "Or unoriginal. But the precision is almost surgical."

But it wasn't the garrote that drew his or anyone else's attention. The butterfly tattoo on the victim's back was a striking and macabre piece of art, a chilling fusion of beauty and morbidity. Spanning the entire breadth of her back, the wings stretched from shoulder to shoulder, the tips reaching towards the lower ribs. The detail was exquisite, almost lifelike, as if a giant butterfly had momentarily alighted on her skin.

The wings were a kaleidoscope of colors, predominantly shades of orange and black, with hints of iridescent gold that shimmered under the harsh crime scene lights. The intricate patterns on the wings resembled delicate stained glass, with each section a meticulous mosaic of hues and shades. The colors were vibrant against the pallor of her skin, creating a startling juxtaposition.

In the center, the tattoo artist had skillfully shaded the body of the butterfly for a three-dimensional effect, adding to the realism of the design. It was as if the butterfly's body slightly protruded from the skin, poised to take flight at any moment.

The edges of the wings were fringed with fine, black lines, mimicking the delicate veining of a real butterfly's wings. These lines were interwoven with subtle swirls and flourishes, adding an elegant complexity to the design.

Below the wings, an inscription was written in a flowing, cursive script. The words: *Sweet Caroline, are you ready to become a butterfly?* were inked in a deep, glossy black, stark against the skin.

"The tattoo work is exceptional," Drago observed, his voice low. "How old is it?"

Dr. Chen shrugged. "The ink is barely set. I'd say less than twenty-four hours."

"These whackos are getting whackier by the minute," Drago groaned as he rose, looking around. "Lambert said no ID."

Drago noticed that her wrists and ankles were chafed. Fuck me! She'd been tied down.

"Rope burns?" he wondered.

"Maybe I can get some fibers." Dr. Chen rose as well. She was a petite woman who came to Drago's shoulder, and most of the time, she looked small enough that he could tuck her into his pocket. She was known to be one of the best MEs on this side of the Mississippi. He'd worked with her on a few cases since he'd moved to Homicide a few months ago and enjoyed her professionalism.

"I'll run her prints. Maybe we'll get a match on AFIS."

The Automated Fingerprint Identification System (AFIS) could quickly compare the prints to millions of others from criminal records, employment records, and other sources.

Dr. Chen turned to face Drago. "She doesn't look like she was on the street. Her teeth have been well cared for, so we'll run her dental as well."

If that failed, Chen would go the DNA route and compare it against CODIS and other databases.

"Send pictures to Ybarra at TID."

Ybarra was one of the best technicians he knew at the Technical Investigation Division and had helped identify victims from time to time with the department's sophisticated facial recognition software, which was especially handy when you walked into a drug house with ten dead gangbangers.

Ybarra would run the victim's photo through a variety of databases, including mugshots, driver's license photos, and others.

"This doesn't feel right," Dr Chen finally said and then shook her head, smiling when Drago gave her you've got to be kidding me look. They had a dead naked woman with a fucking butterfly tattooed on her back with a cryptic message to someone named Caroline, who was sweet. "I mean someone who is this methodical...you know? It feels ritualistic."

"Yeah, I know." Drago had shivers running up his spine as soon as he'd seen the body. This didn't look like your standard pump and dump.

A technician, young and eager, called out from a corner of the rooftop. "Detective Horvat found something! Fabric, caught on a nail."

Drago strode over, his suit jacket billowing behind him like the dark wings of some avian predator. He examined the fabric—a piece of black cloth with a unique texture. "Fancy. Let's hope it didn't come off a Halloween costume."

I went back to Dr. Chen. "Your Elf found some fabric."

"His name is—"

"You change them every month; I can't fucking keep remembering everyone's name. Hard enough to keep straight the people I know."

She chuckled. Her interns never lasted long, but lately she'd told Drago it had become ridiculous. Apparently, doing autopsies of people who were brutally murdered took a toll on you when you'd just finished the slog of medical school and were trying to find your specialty.

"You wish you'd stayed in Vice?" Dr. Chen asked with a solemn tone.

"I don't know. This is fucking insane, but then maybe it's better than breaking open a sex trafficking ring and finding kids stuck in basements, you know?"

"It's all relative," Dr. Chen agreed. "You sometimes wish you'd found another line of work?"

"Fuck no." He winked at her. "I love my job."

She laughed when his phone buzzed. It was his old partner from Vice.

"Fucking Esper," he groaned.

"You've got to let your old Vice friends go, Horvat," Dr. Chen picked up her medical bag. "We're going to take the body to the morgue."

Drago walked to the end of the rooftop, answering the call. "Horvat. Make it quick; I'm standing on the edge—literally."

The voice on the other end, a relic from his Vice days, was hurried. "Drago, buddy. I got some bad news."

Drago gazed out at the sprawling cityscape, the lights flickering to life like fireflies in a dark field. "Give it to me," he said, the wind carrying away his words, as he listened to his old partner tell him about how one of his old CIs who'd gone missing had been found dead.

"She was getting high on her supply," Esper remarked. "Took some heroin laced with fentanyl."

"I told her to stay away from DeSantis—fucking drug dealing pimp. Tell me, you got him?" He felt frustration rise through him. Gemm was a whore to support her drug addiction. She didn't deserve this.

"I'm sorry, man. DeSantis is in the wind. We find him, we'll talk to him, but you know he's slick, we got nothing to charge him with. Where you at?" Esper asked. "Darina was wondering when you'll come by for dinner this Saturday night."

Darina was Esper's wife and mother of his three children. They were one of the most balanced couples he knew. Many married cops fucked around—not Esper.

Fuck, if he were married to someone who looked like Darina, he wouldn't fuck around, either.

"I caught one. Once I clear it—"

There was silence on his side. He never turned down dinner, especially when it was a summons from Darina. "It sounds bad."

"Like you won't fucking believe it."

Inside the bustling bullpen of the LAPD headquarters on First Street, Drago navigated through the organized chaos typical of a late afternoon. The room buzzed with activity; desks cluttered with files and coffee cups formed a labyrinth in the ample, open-plan space. The hum of conversation, the clack of keyboards, and the occasional burst of laughter created a symphony of city policing in motion.

Detectives, in various attire, ranging from crisp suits to casual shirts and jeans, were huddled in groups or pinned to their phones, discussing cases with intensity. Monitors displayed maps of Los Angeles, blinking with real-time crime data. On the walls, whiteboards were scrawled with case notes and timelines, evidence of the relentless pace of their work.

At the far end of the room, Drago's boss, Lieutenant Eduardo Gomez, waited by his desk, which seemed to barely contain its mountain of paperwork with his no-nonsense attitude. Beside him stood a young woman, her posture rigid with a mix of excitement and nerves. She was as tall as Gomez, so around five nine, hundred twenty pounds, give or take, mostly muscle. Her brunette hair was tied away from her face in a ponytail. She wore no makeup except for some eyeliner that made her blue eyes pop; maybe she'd flicked a wand of lip gloss on her lips so they would shine, wouldn't remain that way, considering how she was nervously chewing on them. She wore jeans, sensible black shoes she could run in if she had to, and a high-end designer blazer that showed off her badge but concealed her weapon. She wore a watch, antique. A man's Rolex. Daddy gave her a family heirloom as a graduation present, which tempted me into thinking she was an only child or at least she didn't have a brother. Sure, that was sexist, but a lot of people were sexists and gave masculine family heirlooms from father to son.

Ah, fuck me! Gomez was going to introduce him to his new partner. He'd been expecting it since his previous partner, Pat Clurman, had retired.

On cue, Gomez said without preamble, "Horvat, meet your new partner, Detective Nikki Wasco. She's sharp, graduated top of her class, and she's your headache."

Drago offered her a hand, his expression unreadable. "Wasco. Related to Monique Wasco?"

Her back straightened. Oh yes, an only child who hates to be thought of as a nepo kid. Deputy Chief Wasco was the commanding officer of the Detective Bureau.

"She's my mother." Her grip was solid, but she was not trying to use it like some other assholes like me would do to show who's boss.

"Welcome to the hurricane, Detective Wasco." Drago turned to Gomez. "I need to update you on the Figueroa body. I feel this is whacked enough to not be personal or isolated." He would not use the S for serial word until he had to.

Drago walked up to the blank whiteboard and wrote with a marker: Unidentified Victim. He updated Gomez and Nikki.

"A fucking butterfly tattoo?" Gomez shook his head. "What the fuck?"

Nikki's expression shifted subtly, her eyes narrowing slightly as she transitioned from listening to deep thought. Her face was remarkably expressive, a canvas of her internal processes. But in this line of work, such transparency could be a liability. To coax confessions from hardened criminals, she'd need to master the art of concealing her thoughts behind a more guarded demeanor.

She raised her hand as if they were in a classroom and, realizing that awkwardly put her hand down.

"Do you have a photo of the butterfly?" she asked.

Drago pulled out his phone, and her eyes flashed. "This is The Butterfly Killer's work. He's a serial killer from Texas."

"Fucking Texans coming to California and fucking our state up," Gomez muttered.

"I think Californians are moving to Texas, not the other way around," Drago countered. "Pull up the case file," he instructed Nikki.

She nodded and started to pound on the keys on her computer.

"There is only one problem," she mentioned as her fingers flew over the keyboard, "Jacob Soller is on death row in Cooke County Jail in Gainesville."

She pulled up the case file on ViCAP, the Violent Criminal Apprehension Program database managed by the FBI was specifically designed to allow national access to case files pertaining to violent crimes, including murder and especially serial killers.

"Fucking hell," Gomez said coolly when he saw the photos of one of Jacob Soller's victims in Dallas. The butterfly tattoo was identical. The only difference was the message. On all of Soller's five victims, the inscription was From Cocoon Forth a Butterfly.

"From Cocoon forth a butterfly. As lady from her door emerged. A summer afternoon. Repairing everywhere," Drago whispered.

Gomez stared at him like he'd grown horns.

"Her pretty Parasol be seen contracting in a field," Nikki added.

"You wanna explain the weird shit you both are saying?" Gomez looked at Nikki and Drago.

"From Cocoon Forth a Butterfly is a poem by Emily Dickinson," Drago explained.

The bullpen around them continued its relentless pace, a backdrop to the unfolding drama. The clatter of activity and the buzz of conversation faded into the background as Drago flipped through the files on Nikki's computer.

"Fucking hell," Drago muttered and ran both his hands through his dark hair.

"The ADA," Gomez noticed it as well.

"Yeah," Drago felt his heart constrict, "Caroline Vega. She's not in Dallas. She's here, Loo. She works at Knight Technologies." She's dating my best friend's brother-in-law. Talk about a small fucking world.

"Sweet Caroline," Nikki whispered.

"Fucking hell," Drago repeated in frustration.

Chapter 5

Monday, October 2

The sun was already high in the azure sky, casting its warmth over Golden Valley Farms, a sprawling expanse of lush greenery nestled in the heart of California's Central Valley. Aurelio loved to manage this vast organic operation. He stood amidst rows of verdant crops, his gaze sweeping across the fields that stretched to the horizon.

Around him, the farm was a hive of activity. Workers moved between the rows, their hands expertly selecting ripe produce. In contrast, others tended to the irrigation systems that snaked across the fields, a lifeline for the crops in the arid California climate. The air was filled with the earthy scent of rich soil and the faint hum of tractors in the distance.

Aurelio, dressed in rugged work clothes and wearing a wide-brimmed hat to shield him from the relentless sun, walked purposefully through the fields. He stopped occasionally to inspect a plant, his hands gently examining the leaves and fruits. His knowledge of organic farming was evident in his attention to detail, understanding that the health of each plant was crucial to the farm's overall success.

Managing Golden Valley was a massive undertaking. The farm was not just a series of fields but a complex organism that required constant attention and care. Aurelio's day-to-day responsibilities ranged from overseeing crop rotation plans to ensure soil fertility to coordinating with department heads about harvest schedules, logistics, and the distribution of produce to markets.

In one farm section, Aurelio paused to discuss crop yield projections with a team of agronomists. They stood over a digital tablet, analyzing data that informed their decisions on planting schedules and harvesting. Technology played a vital role in the farm's operations, allowing them to maximize efficiency and output while maintaining strict organic standards.

Beyond the fields, greenhouses dotted the landscape, housing a variety of herbs and delicate produce, requiring more controlled environments. Aurelio made his way towards them, greeting each worker he passed with a nod or a word of encouragement. His leadership style was hands-on, and he was well-respected among his team for his fair approach and deep understanding of organic farming.

Aurelio examined the hydroponic systems in the greenhouse, ensuring they were functioning optimally. Integrating these systems was part of his initiative to modernize the farm, making it a leader in sustainable agriculture.

As the day progressed, Aurelio's tasks took him to the administrative side of the operation. He met with the finance team to discuss the farm's revenues and expenses. Golden Valley was a significant player in the organic market, and its financial health was crucial to its ongoing success. Aurelio's role was to balance the demands of running a profitable business with the ethos of organic and sustainable farming.

The sun dipped towards the horizon, casting long shadows across the fields. Aurelio stood for a moment, looking out over the land. This farm was more than just a family business; it was his life. There was no way he could leave this. And there was no way Vega would leave her work in Los Angeles, and why should she? She was damn successful. Maybe they could do what Maria and Alejandro were doing. His brother was CEO of Golden Valley, and Maria was the CEO of an investment banking company in LA. They did a split sort of thing, though they spent most of their time in Golden Valley because of Silvano, Alejandro's son.

My phone rang, and Aurelio sighed. "Mama."

"Don't 'Mama' me," she muttered. "You go away all weekend, and now you text me that you can't come to the house for dinner?"

Aurelio's parents lived a good fifteen-minute drive from his house, which was how he wanted it. All his siblings had homes on the estate in Golden Valley. Alejandro was closer to our parents. Isadora and her husband Gordon were building a house near a lake, which would also not be within walking distance from the main house. Raya and Mateo, who'd become family, were also planning to build on the estate. Still, like Alejandro, they didn't want to be too far from the main house. To each his own.

Aurelio loved his mother, but his introverted soul needed space.

Actually, Paloma was not his biological mother. Alejandro and he lost their mother when Aurelio was a baby. When he was ten, his father met Paloma—and their lives changed. They'd immediately became a family.

Paloma became Mama, and now Alejandro and Aurelio thought of her as their mother. He couldn't remember his own, who died a year after Aurelio was born, but it wouldn't have mattered. Paloma's big heart was impossible to resist.

Isadora, his sister, was born three years after Arsenio and Paloma met, and Aurelio was sure if he counted the months; Mama was pregnant before the wedding. Isa was their adored baby sister. He'd changed her diapers, bathed, and held her when she cried along with his brother Alejandro. They were a close-knit family. And sometimes the closeness was fucking claustrophobic.

"Mama—" Aurelio began.

"Dinner is at seven. I expect you here at six thirty. Don't argue with me, Aurelio. I haven't seen you in two weeks. I miss you."

Aurelio growled. "No one does emotional blackmail as well as you."

"I have mad skills," his mother acknowledged.

Dinner was always raucous in the Santos household, and this night was no different. It was also a full house with Maria and Alejandro, their son Silvano; his sister Isadora and her husband Gordon.

"I didn't see you all day." Alejandro held out a glass of wine for him, probably because he could see his brother looked like he needed it.

"In the fields." Aurelio took the glass, not caring what red liquid was in there. He just needed to loosen muscles that were tightened up. Going back and forth from Vega's resulted in him not getting enough sleep, which made the long days longer.

They were always busy at the farm, but in the summer, everything ramped up until they hit the fall. They were continually planting and harvesting; it was the rhythm nature had set for the various fruits and vegetables that they grew.

But things were busier now, and Aurelio knew he couldn't spend as much time in Los Angeles as he used to. He had suggested that Vega could work from Golden Valley, like Maria and Gordon, but she had resisted, just as she had resisted spending time with his family. She kept a distance, likely leading his family to perceive her as somewhat cold, which was far from the truth. Vega was vibrant and lively, yet also a woman recovering from old trauma. After seven years, it still lingered... would it be with her for life? And if so, Aurelio wondered whether he would stay. Damn it! He knew he would. His life might have more friction than he preferred, but he couldn't imagine living without Vega. She was his best friend, lover, and confidante. She understood him. She balanced him.

"This baby inside me is driving me nuts," Isadora bellowed as she went to the bathroom.

Maria grinned, stroking her belly.

Both Maria and Isadora were going to have a baby real soon. Once Maria was pregnant, Alejandro decided they were going to get married right away. Isadora helped plan their winter wedding in Golden Valley right after Gordon had planned hers in his hometown in Scotland.

Aurelio wondered as he sat at the dinner table if he wanted to get married. How would he and Vega do it? Probably in a courthouse. Or maybe she'd like to marry in Texas, where her father was, the only family member she had whom he had not met.

Damn it! Couldn't he have fallen in love with a woman who wasn't quite so contrary? But the heart wants what it wants, and Aurelio wanted Vega.

"You okay?" Paloma leaned toward her son.

He realized he looked more pensive than usual. He was an introvert, and his family accepted that he liked to keep to himself, but he was normally a little more verbose during family dinners.

"Nothing," he replied as was rote. Vega's nightmare was still weighing on him, and he'd not shrugged off that darkness yet.

"All okay with Caro?" she asked.

He smiled. She always knew, like mothers do, what was bothering him. "I don't know," he said honestly. He was reluctant to tell his family about Vega's past. This was her story; he had no business sharing her dark pieces with anyone, even his mother.

He put his hand on his mother's, stopping her from asking her next question. "I can't talk about it, Mama."

Paloma nodded. She'd been a social worker all her career and even now volunteered at women's shelters. There were no horrors that she had not seen, and Aurelio knew if he told her, she would only show compassion, but how could he tell her something he knew so little about? All Vega had said to him was that she'd put a serial killer in prison. He'd gotten free and taken her. He kept her with him for thirty-three hours while he raped and tortured her before she was rescued. The tattoo was part of his modus operandi, his final desecration of his victims before he killed.

The rest Aurelio had figured out on his own. The tattoo had been instrumental in his Google search efforts. He'd found plenty of information about Jacob Soller, who had been nicknamed The Butterfly Killer by the media because he tattooed a butterfly on the backs of his victims, along with a line from an Emily Dickinson poem.

Like Bundy, Soller possessed a charming demeanor. Like Gacy, he had a family—a wife, a daughter, and a son. Similar to Hansen, he was well-respected in his community as the owner of a sports and outdoor retail store in Frisco, a suburb of Dallas. He owned several properties for rental or business use, except for one warehouse. Officially listed for storage, it had actually served as his murder room. He used a similar property when he took Vega, which ultimately led the police to her.

It had been chilling to read about Soller and his four...no five—including Vega—victims. His targets had nothing in common; the first worked in a diner, the second in a post office, the third had been an entertainment podcaster, and the fourth a yoga instructor. He had a physical type: blonde, blue-eyed, average height, and slender, just like Vega. They'd probably picked her to prosecute the case because of how much she looked like Soller's victims to rattle him. It had been nearly fatal for Vega.

He'd tried to talk to Vega about it, but she was tightlipped. "I only discuss this with my therapist," she'd told him. Aurelio was glad that she saw a therapist because, without one, he wasn't sure how she had any chance of healing. He wondered what her therapist said about her nightmares, the ones that woke her screaming and crying, making him feel like the most useless fuck in the world.

"Aurelio, you still haven't told us if you and Vega are joining us in Oaxaca in August?" Isadora, the planner, asked of a family vacation she intended for all of us to take. She ran the Golden Valley Inn and the ski resort, making both coveted destination wedding and event locations.

Aurelio had asked Vega, and she'd told him she couldn't do August. If he'd told her the holiday was in September, he'd have gotten the same answer. It was almost as if she didn't want to get too close to his family, just in case they didn't work out.

"Yeah, we'll be there." Fuck it, he'd drag her with him if he had to. He'd talk to Dec Knight, her boss to make sure she had time off then. He'd convince her. His family was important to him. She was vital to him. He wanted her to meet them, not just in a distant social way but as family.

"Really?" Arsenio, Aurelio's father's eyes lit up. "We'll get to spend time with your Caro?"

"I'm so glad Vega agreed," Maria added.

"Well, she hasn't, so say nothing to her. I'll make this—" His ringing phone cut him off. He looked at the caller ID and frowned. He only knew Drago Horvat through Maria, as he was one of her closest friends. Drago, he knew had also become close with Isadora when they'd been stuck in a snowstorm in the Golden Valley resort, along with a murderer and a couple of dead bodies earlier in the year.

Paloma had a strict rule about no phones at the table, which suited Aurelio just fine. He'd call Drago after dinner, he decided, setting his phone aside.

Maria's phone buzzed then. She raised her hand when Paloma growled. "It's Drago."

Aurelio felt the first frisson of fear race up his spine, and it spread when Maria looked at him. "Drago wants you to call him ASAP. It's urgent."

He grabbed his phone and called Drago. "Caro okay?" he demanded.

"Yeah," he heard the LAPD detective's gruff voice, "where are you?"

"Golden Valley."

"How soon can you get here?"

"To LA? What the fuck, Drago?"

"I'm with her at her place. She's physically fine. But I had to give her some news that upset her, and she's right now chucking up her dinner. I don't think she should be alone," he explained.

Aurelio rose slowly from his chair, his heart thumping against his ribs. "What the fuck happened?"

"We have a body. It's Soller's MO. There was a message on the body for Caroline."

It took Aurelio a moment to process what Drago said. "Give her your phone," he said when he found his voice.

His whole family was looking at him.

"I'll call the pilot." Alejandro was already making the call as he spoke.

Paloma came up to him and put a hand on his shoulder, offering comfort.

"Hey, baby," he breathed when he heard Vega's whispered hello.

"I need you," she said for the first time in their relationship.

"I'm on my way."

When she gave the phone to Drago, he barked, "You stay with her until I get there. If you can't, you get Mateo there. Okay?"

"Mateo is in Sydney," Drago muttered. "Raya is in Orange County and it's going to take her a while to get to LA. I can get a constable to—"

"I want *you* to stay with her. She doesn't know the fucking constable."

"Okay. My partner and I'll stay until you get your ass here," he agreed. "Get the fuck back ASAP so we can go catch this guy."

CHAPTER 6

Monday, October 2

Vega looked at shivering hands that were wrapped around the cup of coffee Drago's partner Nikki had made for her. She sat on a couch in her living room, looking at the sprawling twinkling City of Los Angeles spread in front of her.

Drago had shown up with his partner in the early evening. She'd been surprised when the doorman called to tell her Detective Horvat was here to see her.

Drago had reached out to her another time as a rapist she'd convicted in Dallas had been arrested in Los Angeles. She'd thought it was another such case—all those rapists and criminals coming to California from Texas, who would've expected it, considering how expensive the Golden State was.

She shook hands with Nikki Wasco, his junior partner, and asked them to come in. They sat in the living room; she was on the couch, and they were across from her in matching armchairs.

"I'm so sorry to bring this to you," Drago began, "but we have a murder victim we need to talk to you about."

Vega nodded, still not expecting the blow he delivered.

"Someone killed a woman who we have now identified in the same MO as Jacob Soller," he said and watched her as he did.

It was a gut punch. All the air left her lungs. She felt the blood drain from her face. She clenched her fists because her hands had begun to shake.

"Did he escape?" she asked, her voice hoarse, barely a whisper. The last time Soller had escaped, he'd come for her. The last time he'd escaped, he'd destroyed her.

"No." Drago came to her and took her hands in his. "No. He's still on death row in Gainesville."

Vega nodded and stared at his hands holding hers. She wanted to pull away, but his hands were warm, and she was so very cold. The warehouse Soller had kept her in had been chilly. He'd tied her up naked, spread-eagled on a metal table.

She took a deep breath and pulled her hands away from Drago. ADA Caroline Vega clicked into place. "Tell me about the victim. Where did you find her? What are the similarities? I'm assuming she has a tattoo on her back?" Like the one he'd almost carved on hers.

"Yes," Drago said softly.

"Okay."

"There is one difference," Nikki said, her voice was calm.

Vega waited because she knew this was not going to be good news.

"It's the inscription, Vega," Drago took over. "He left a message for you."

Her head felt light, but she wore the new mask she'd become adept at wearing, the one she'd worn in that miserable warehouse where she'd spent thirty-three hours with Soller. The mask that didn't show him fear or pain, no matter how many times he jabbed her with a prod, no matter how many times he choked her into unconsciousness, no matter how he violated her.

"You're a pathetic wimp. You asshole. This is the only way you can get a woman," she'd taunted when he attempted to penetrate her. He got off on fear, and when she showed him defiance, he couldn't continue, his penis would become flaccid. So, he'd hit her, jab her, choke her, and use a bottle to violate her because he couldn't do it himself.

She cleared her throat. "What did the message say?"

"Sweet Caroline, are you ready to become a butterfly," Drago whispered.

Vega rose then, not sure why or even how, because she couldn't actually feel her extremities. "Show me," she demanded.

Drago nodded at Nikki. She came to Vega with her phone and held it up to her. Vega stared at the beautiful tattoo; she had a quarter of a wing on her back. Same wing. He was consistent you had to give him that. And artistic. It was a beautiful tattoo. Under the tattoo where on his other victims there was the sentence, from cocoon forth a butterfly, on this poor woman's back, the asshole had left a message for her. It was for *her*. There was no other Caroline that Jacob Soller would leave a message for.

That had shattered her mask. She'd rushed to the bathroom and thrown up. Drago had come, but she'd asked him to leave her the fuck alone, and he had.

When she returned to the living room, he was on the phone. "It's Aurelio," he murmured, handing the phone to her.

She stared at it blankly. A part of her wanted to scream at Drago for dragging Aurelio into this ugliness, but a bigger part of her was comforted as she'd never been before. She'd whispered hello, and then when he spoke, she said the only thing that came to mind, I need you, words she'd spoken before with ease but not since Soller. But they had slipped out of her smooth as butter on warm grits.

Even though he told her he was on his way, she wasn't convinced; she wouldn't be until she saw him, touched him, and hugged him because the last time she'd been in love with a man, he'd abandoned her when she broke, breaking her even more.

"Raya is on her way as well," Drago mentioned.

"Tell her not to bother," she sighed. "Please."

"Vega, you shouldn't be alone."

She smiled weakly at him. "I'm not. I have you and Detective Wasco here, and Aurelio is on his way."

He's on his way, Vega. Just hold on until he gets here, and then you can fall apart. Then you can let go.

"Who's the victim?" Vega asked, surprising Drago and Nikki.

"We're waiting on ID."

"Who's your ME?"

"Emily Chen," Nikki supplied.

Vega nodded. She'd heard of only good things about Dr. Chen.

"She had rope burns," Nikki said, and Drago groaned.

"Wasco, not now."

"It's fine," Vega asserted, "Rope burns? Soller didn't use a rope. He used leather straps. He had an autopsy table, just like the fucking ME, and he'd fitted them with leather straps, the kind you find to restrain patients in the nut house. Did he use a garrote?"

"Yes," Nikki told her.

"Fuckin' hell," Vega spoke softly. When she'd been with Soller, she'd feared the garrote, of dying slowly and painfully.

Nikki opened her phone and began to type furiously, taking notes. Drago was old school, and his notebook was small Moleskin, and he used a Pilot pen.

"I'd like to see the ME's report."

Drago sighed. "Vega, come on, you know—"

"She used to be an ADA, Horvat, and she knows the killer up close and personal," Nikki gushed and then stopped as she realized what she'd said, "I'm sorry...about the up close—"

"Don't worry about it." Vega felt her blood pump. She missed this. She missed working cases. Sure, in her current job, she never saw a dead body, but she also never had her adrenaline rise quite like this. "Drago, I want in."

"You're a fucking civilian, Vega, and if something happens to you between Maria and Paloma, I'm a dead man."

Vega smiled despite herself. She'd met Paloma a couple of times only, tried to stay away from her but she knew from Maria and Raya that Paloma wanted to get to Aurelio's girlfriend. But Vega didn't want to insinuate herself into the Santos family, especially when she was staying away from her own. She didn't want those ties. She ended up hurting people who cared for her.

Then what are you doing with Aurelio, honey? He cares. Hell, he's in love.

"I can help you," she said. "If this is a copycat, then the first victim is probably a server from a restaurant or a diner. Low end. Your next victim will work at a post office. And the third...then fourth, and I guess I'm still reserved to be the fifth?"

Drago's gaze lingered on her; his eyes flickered with a mix of confusion and intrigue as if he were attempting to reconcile the composed figure before him with the memory of the woman who had been helplessly retching in her bathroom earlier. Vega, aware of his scrutiny, thought wryly to herself that she had an arsenal of masks at her disposal. She could always don a fresh one whenever another fell to pieces.

"Did you find out why he chose these women?" Drago asked.

"You mean, besides body type? He likes them blonde and skinny. He prefers women who are around five five-six height. His autopsy table was set up for that. He gets off on fear. He doesn't wear a condom, which is why once we had him, we had DNA."

Vega's phone rang then, and she grabbed it, the shakes back. "Where are you, goddamn it?" She choked out. She didn't care if it made her weak. She didn't care if it made her stupid. She needed him with her.

"Five minutes, Caro. I'm five minutes away, baby. You hold on."

Chapter 7

Monday, October 2

He'd barely walked into the door when she came to him. Aurelio wrapped Caro in his arms, holding her tight.

"Oh, baby," he whispered.

She was shaking as she burrowed into him, holding on for dear life. He nodded at Drago.

"Nikki Wasco, I'm Detective Horvat's partner," a tall brunette said to him.

"Hi, Nikki." He put his chin on Caro's head, nuzzled. "You need her?"

"Not right now," Drago said.

He didn't wait to see them leave. He slid one hand around her neck and the other at her knees and carried her. "I'm so sorry. But I can't do this alone," she whimpered.

"You don't have to do anything alone ever again. What do you need?"

"Just you. Can we go to bed?"

He helped her get naked, which wasn't easy because she clung to him. No way was he going to let her go. He got them both undressed and into bed. She put her head on his chest and then broke. She simply broke. He felt her tears on his skin, as she held him tighter and sobbed.

"It's never going to go away, is it?"

"Yes, it is. We'll make it go away."

It took a half hour, until she fell asleep, exhausted. The emotional toll of going back to a place she was trying to forget brought on a tiredness, he knew, she hadn't been able to escape.

He tucked her in and watched for a while to make sure she was sleeping restfully, for a while at least. He put on his clothes and walked into her living room.

His phone had messages from his family. He sent a group text, telling them Caro was okay, and then called Alejandro.

"I'm not leaving her," he told him.

"Okay."

"You get Turturro to take care of things on the field, and you're going to manage the rest of the...I can't leave her."

"You want to talk about this?"

Aurelio walked to the tall windows and looked at the sprawling city before him. "You know she used to be an ADA in Dallas?"

"Yeah."

"She...ah...she put away a serial killer. He...." He couldn't go on; his throat constricted. He couldn't put into words what she'd gone through. How had she survived what he could barely talk about it?

"Aurelio? Estás bien?"

"No. I'm not okay, man. She cried herself to sleep. You met her; she look like a weak woman to you?"

"No, she doesn't. Just a minute, Aurelio." He heard rustling noises. "Duquesa, head to bed; I'll be there with you soon."

"Maria okay?"

"Yeah," Alejandro said with satisfaction, a sense of delight in his voice. "You want us to talk to Drago instead?"

"No...I mean, sure, you can talk to him."

"Lighten your heart, brother."

Aurelio closed his eyes and took a deep breath. "She didn't tell me a lot. I pieced it together. She put this creep Jacob Soller away for killing four women. He'd rape, torture, and then he'd tattoo a butterfly on their back with some fucking poem."

"Deep breaths, Aurelio. You want me to come to you? I can—"

"No." He knew his brother could hear the tears in his voice. "He was convicted, and he escaped. And while he was out, he took her."

"Ah, fuck. Ah, fuck."

"Yeah. He had for thirty-three hours before they rescued her."

"Fucking hell. Oh, damn. I'm so sorry."

"She has nightmares. Seven fucking years and she still has nightmares. It's so bad that she throws up and I can't do anything for her. You know? I keep thinking what she does when I'm not there." Tears flowed down his cheeks. Assholes who say that love makes you stronger were full of shit.

"That's why you've been spending more nights with her?"

"I'm trying, but...you know, I got the farm." He brushed off his tears. "I don't have details. I needed to take care of her. They have a body here in LA, the same MO as Soller. He tattooed a message for Caro."

"We need to get security on her," Alejandro declared. "What did the message say?"

"I don't know. I'll call Drago and see if he can come by."

"What do you need?"

"Time."

"It's yours. What else?"

"I don't know, Alejandro." I felt something crack inside me. "I don't know how to help her."

"You're there with her. You're helping her."

He checked on her after he ended his call with Alejandro. She hadn't moved from where he'd left her. Sitting next to her, he texted Drago: I need more information.

He got back immediately: I'm on my way home. If you give me a drink, I can fill you in.

Aurelio: Deal.

He kissed Vega's forehead, and she shifted, burrowing toward him. She did that often. When she was asleep she knew him, knew how she felt about him—it was when she was awake, her walls came up.

It was nearly midnight by the time Drago got to Vega's apartment.

"She okay?" he asked as they sat at Caro's dining table with one of her best whiskeys.

"She's sleeping. But she may wake up. She still has nightmares."

Drago leaned back and stretched his legs. "You know what happened to her?"

"Some."

Drago picked up his backpack and pulled out a folder. He set it in front of Aurelio. "Read. I'll wait."

It took him thirty minutes. Thirty excruciating minutes of reading the case file of ADA Caroline Vega's abduction. Drago poured him two fingers of whiskey when he was done. He downed the whiskey in one go.

"Fucking hell. How does someone get through that?"

Drago sighed. "Because your girl is one tough woman. You remember that. And you remind her of that. She never backed down with Soller."

"She didn't laser the tattoo off."

"She wouldn't." Drago smiled. "We found a body today. Same MO as Soller."

He held his phone up for Aurelio.

Sweet Caroline, are you ready to become a butterfly?

Now, Aurelio felt like throwing up. It was macabre, the artwork, the message, the whole fucking thing.

"So, this is what in the movies they call a copycat?"

Drago smiled somberly. "We call them that in real life as well. Yeah, we think it's a copycat."

Aurelio slumped in his chair. Alejandro was right; they needed to get security on Vega. Or maybe he could get her out of Los Angeles while Drago solved the case. He could take her to Golden Valley and tuck her into his house. She'd be safe there.

Drago rose and stretched. "I got to hit the hay. I'll call Vega tomorrow."

Aurelio went to bed after Drago left.

He didn't care if it would wake her; he pulled her into his arms. He needed to hold her. He'd just read something that sounded a lot like an episode of Criminal Minds, where the woman he loved was a victim. He needed the comfort.

CHAPTER 8

Tuesday, October 3

"You don't have to stay with me," Vega told Aurelio while they had coffee. He was looking through emails on his laptop.

"Okay," he said mildly, his fingers typing away.

"Aurelio," Vega called out.

He looked up. "You're going to say, hey Aurelio, I had a weak moment, and now I'm fine, you can go. I'll say, fuck no, I'm staying. And we'll fight, and I'll end up staying. Can we skip all of that? I need to get through some emails before Drago will show up here like a bad penny."

Vega folded her arms. "I don't like this."

"No shit," Aurelio muttered, his focus on his laptop screen. "Serial killers are leaving notes for you on dead bodies; it'd be weird if you liked it."

"Are you being cute?"

Aurelio grinned. "I was born cute, baby." He rose and came to her. Put his hands on her hips. "You want me to leave?"

He had an effect on her that no one had ever had. It had been there the first time she'd met him at Bourbon & Branch, a bar on Jones Street in San Francisco. He kept an apartment in the city she'd learned when he'd gotten her into his bed. She's teased him that it was his fuck pad, and he's not denied it, but he'd also given the vibe of a man who was discerning about who he had sex with. That was over a year ago. Since then, there had been no one else for either of them. On or off, their relationship had become all-consuming, and Aurelio had declared that this was the last relationship either of them would be in. He was comfortable saying the three little words to her—she hadn't mustered the courage to tell him what he already knew, what she knew she felt.

"I don't want to disrupt your life," Vega acknowledged.

He kissed her nose. "I love you, baby, and you are my life. Even if you listen to country music."

She sighed. He disarmed her with stuff like this. Who went around saying things like, baby, *you're my life*? No one in real life...well, except Aurelio, who somehow managed to not sound cheesy when he did.

"What's wrong with country music?"

"Where do I start?" he teased.

She chuckled and relaxed. "When did you talk to Drago?"

"Last night. Caro, give me an answer. Do you want me to leave?"

She shrugged. "If you want to stay—"

"You have to say the fucking words, baby."

"Why?" she asked, feeling the walls close in.

"Because I'm scared shitless that you're going to let your lack of trust in me take over, and I'll lose you."

She leaned her forehead against his. He was so honest. He was so vulnerable and fucking open about how he felt it made her feel childish for not letting him in, for making him work every time. It had taken a brutal murder for her to ask for him, to lean on him.

"You won't lose me," she assured him. "I don't want to go through this alone."

He smiled, kissed her forehead, and went back to his laptop.

"What did Drago tell you?"

He sighed, closing his laptop. "Come here." He held out a hand, and when she got close to the dining chair he was sitting on, he pulled her, so she ended up on his lap. "I don't believe in lying or hiding things from you. He let me read the...he let me read your case file about what happened in Dallas."

She stiffened. He'd read it! All of it? She tried to pull away, but he wouldn't let her. He held her tight. "Tell me why you want to run right now?"

"I don't. I'm just not comfortable sitting on your lap and—"

"Caro, baby, tell me what you're feeling. Please."

"Embarrassed. Ashamed. Afraid."

"Why afraid?" he honed in on the thing that was bigger than all the others.

"That you'll look at me like I was someone to pity. Like I'm broken or something," she whispered.

"Every time I look at you, I see the strongest woman I know." He brushed wisps of hair off her face that had escaped her braid. "It hurt to read how the woman I love was brutalized. It crushed me. But you're not broken. You're a fucking warrior."

She leaned into him and laid her head on his shoulder. "You say the most perfect things, you know that?"

"Yeah. Because I am fucking perfect."

"What else did Drago tell you?"

"He told me about the current case. This morning, he sent me a text saying that he had the MEs report and wanted to run it by you."

He let her stand up.

She tucked her hands in her suit slacks. She'd dressed for success today. It was something she'd learned from her mother. When you weren't feeling your best, you wore your favorite dress, put on some red lipstick and high heels. She chose a blue Stella McCartney power suit with a cream-colored shell. Chin up, tits out, honey, and now conquer the world.

Paired with nude Yves Saint Laurent heels, the pantsuit made her look lean, mean, and good, inside, and out.

"Are you going to work?" Aurelio asked.

She nodded. "I have some meetings starting around eleven. Aurelio, what will you do while I'm working and...it makes no sense for you to waste your time here with me."

"It's my time to waste, baby. I'm sure you have a spare office at Knight Tech I can use. I have some meetings I can take on Zoom."

"You run a farm; you can't run it remotely," Vega said, exasperated.

"Why don't you let me run my farm the way that I feel is best and not worry your pretty head about it?"

Her eyes narrowed even though she could see the amusement in his. "Pretty head?"

He grinned. "It's a damn pretty one, baby."

"I don't know what this is...this murder," Vega finally admitted, "I don't know what this will turn out to be. How long will you stay here with me?"

She wasn't sure if she was asking him when he'd leave or begging him to get her through this, whatever this would be.

"As long as is needed," he said, giving her the exact words, she needed.

They'd just gotten into the Knight Tech building when Drago called.

"Hey, I spoke with Loo, and we'd like you to, if you're comfortable, come to the morgue," he said tentatively. "You're the only expert we have on The Butterfly Killer, and if this is indeed a copycat, we could use your help."

"When do you want me there?" she asked calmly despite her pulse pounding. Could she do this? Could she be the old ADA Vega again? The one who didn't think twice about putting on a Tyvek suit and walking into a bloody crime scene. The one who poured through gory ME reports and even sat through autopsies.

"What did he want?" Aurelio asked as they entered Vega's office.

She told him and was surprised by his response. He was fucking furious. "You want to go into the fucking morgue and see this dead woman? Is that really what you want to do?"

"Yeah. You know this used to be my job, right?" she countered.

He shook his head. "Baby, you have nightmares, you...come on, Caro."

She shrugged. "I was having nightmares even before all of this."

Aurelio dropped his backpack on her visitor's chair and stood at the windows, looking over Bunker Hill. "This is going to make it worse. You know that, right?"

She touched his shoulder, and he turned to look at her. "Yes, I know. But maybe it'll be the closure I need. I ran away after...and...even though I've talked to a therapist, I don't feel I've processed it all."

"This is one hell of a way of getting therapy, baby." Aurelio covered her hand with his and then pulled her into a hug.

They stood there for a long moment. When they heard a discreet clearing of the throat, Vega extricated herself from her lover. She saw Joey at the door with her laptop and files in hand.

"Hi, Vega." Joey's eyes danced with amusement.

Vega knew why. She'd never seen her boss like this, an ordinary woman with a boyfriend. "Joey Mann, meet Aurelio Santos. Aurelio, Joey is a junior counsel who joined Knight Tech a few months ago."

Aurelio shook hands with Joey, and she grinned, looking at Vega, her silence saying, wow, nice catch.

He was a nice catch, Vega thought. Tall, handsome, rugged, and with a dry sense of humor—and strength—a lot of strength that allowed him to stay with her and hold her even when he knew she was resisting him. Objectively, the man was handsome with none of the arrogant assholery that some men had because they knew they looked good.

"Baby, can you find me an office or a cubicle so I can set up?" He picked up his backpack and slung it on his shoulder.

Vega felt a flush rise at being addressed as baby. She didn't look like the kind of woman men called *baby*. She was a badass woman who ate iron nails for breakfast. She was intimidating and daunting, a persona she'd developed. And here was Aurelio, all but pinching her cheeks and indicating Caroline Vega was feminine and cute.

Vega straightened, walked to her door, and called out for her assistant. "Jada? I need some help."

Jada looked Aurelio up and down like he was a tall glass of something cool and delicious. Even though Vega and he had been dating for over a year, she'd never brought him to the office or any work engagement. She'd kept her relationship with him private.

"Jada Matthews, this is Aurelio Santos." She made the introductions and noticed that Aurelio was enjoying her discomfort very much.

"Jada, lovely to meet you," he shook hands, laying it on thick. "Caro speaks highly of you."

Son a bitch! Her father used to call her Caroline. Aurelio was the only one who called her Caro. She'd always been Vega at work. She'd also become Vega to herself when she'd been with Soller for those hours and had, had to talk to herself. She'd called herself Vega then. Not Caroline, because Soller kept calling her Sweet Caroline.

"Does she?" Jada batted her eyelashes.

"Find him an office, desk, or meeting room, please," Vega snapped. "And hook him up to the company network as a guest. Thanks."

"Come with me, Aurelio. I'll take care of you," Jada said in her most flirtatious tone.

Joey dropped her laptop and files on Vega's desk when they left and whistled. "Vega, now that's the kind of man I never thought you'd be with."

She frowned. "What kind of man did you think I'd be with?"

"I don't know...someone of the Declan Knight variety. You know? Suit and pretty boy. Not this...what does he do?"

"He runs a farm," Vega muttered.

"Farm boy? Hubba, Hubba, Hubba! He's...I'm sorry for being unprofessional, but he's hot."

But the way Joey said it, it didn't sound like she thought he was hot. In fact, Vega didn't think Joey thought men were hot in general. She'd always suspected her of being bi or gay. But it had a lot to do with how masculine Joey looked and Vega felt like a moron for trying to pigeonhole her because of her appearance.

"Thanks, Joey. Can we get back to the Solarix acquisition? I have to get out of here in an hour."

All humor aside, in an hour, she had to head back to her old life, to the morgue, to talk to the ME. To see a dead body again.

CHAPTER 9

Tuesday, October 3

"Loo, I don't want to involve her further," he told his lieutenant.

"Why?" Nikki demanded. "She was an ADA, which is far better than many of the civilian consultants we use."

Drago sighed. "She's my best friend's brother-in-law's girlfriend."

"That sounds like a *real* close relationship, Drago," Gomez said dryly. "And if this is a copycat, we gonna have bodies dropping in downtown LA. You'll need an expert on the Butterfly Killer."

"For now, we have one body. It could be a coincidence and—"

"Yeah, lots of sweet Carolines in LA to leave that message for," Nikki interrupted. "I don't know what you're worried about. Sure, she freaked out; anyone would. But she pulled it back together. That's a tough broad."

Drago sighed. He wasn't being entirely professional. He'd had an earful from Alejandro in the morning, who'd demanded police protection for Vega, which I'd told him was happening but also suggested he hire someone private. Vega's office was as secure as a maximum security prison during a lockdown. Her apartment was pretty damn close, with it being on the twenty-fourth floor with security cameras and only one way into the building, which was through security. He was happy to put a patrol car on her and Aurelio the rest of the time.

Now that the Santos family knew what had happened to Vega in Dallas; they were becoming protective mother fuckers who looked at Drago like he was the bad guy. If they found out he was asking Vega to look at dead bodies, he'd be a dead body real soon.

Vega didn't seem to care what the Santos family wanted and told her watchdog, Aurelio Santos, to wait at Drago's desk in the bullpen instead of coming to the ME's office with them.

"So, you can see a dead body, but I can't?" he demanded.

"Yes," she replied. "This is an investigation, and you're a fucking civilian."

"So are you, baby," he'd countered.

"Let's take this into my office," Gomez instructed wearily and glared at Drago.

He shrugged. Hey, you want the woman to consult? You gonna get the whole Santos clan up your ass with a flashlight.

Aurelio leaned against the wall, arms crossed. "What the fuck, Drago? She's traumatized and—"

"I'm right here, and I can speak for myself," Vega cut in, her Southern accent sharper when annoyed. "I want to do this. I need to do this. So, let's go see the ME. Do you have an ID on the victim?"

Gomez grinned. He liked Vega. Of course, he did, Drago thought grimly. She was everything he wanted in an ADA. Intelligent, sharp, and with a hot-as-hell body.

"Just came through," Nikki said as she flipped through her phone. "We identified her by going through recent missing person reports. Lorna Wilson, twenty-one, works at Blondie, a diner on Los Angeles Street. She lives on Spring with a boyfriend. Blake Holland has a rap sheet. Shoplifting, a drunk and disorderly, and one assault...looks like a fight gone wrong. He's the one who reported her missing."

"She a server at the diner?" Vega asked for clarification.

"Yeah. But she's, you know, she's *really* a model," Nikki finished. "This is LA; everyone is working on their dream careers."

Vega took a deep breath. "Soller's first victim, Kristy Reed was a server, twenty-two years old. He got her in the parking lot of her apartment complex, which was a shithole in Buckner Terrace. No cameras, no lights, no nothing. We know this because her car was left open. By the time we got to it, there was nothing left, the car was stripped. It's the neighborhood. There was no forensic evidence. But we suspected he had a van that he used to kidnap his victims. It was a delivery van for his outdoor gear business. It was painted black with a small decal referring to Outdoor Living, his retail store. Ultimately, that's how we got him…the first time. Someone remembered seeing the decal."

Aurelio watched her with something like awe and horror. Yeah, Vega was born for this job, Drago thought. She remembered details from a case that was nearly a decade old.

"He waited two weeks before killing Brit Marling, a postal worker," Nikki offered.

"Yeah. He liked to pick up the girls on a Friday. That way, he had the entire weekend with them. He'd tell his wife he was going fishing or hunting." Vega rotated her neck as if to loosen it. Drago wished he could tell her to go home and get better, not think about this creep, but if there was going to be another victim, and he suspected there would be, they needed her.

Vega was going back to a time she'd tried to stay away from, and he respected the hell out of her for doing what she was now. He knew cops who, after a shooting, didn't come back. Hardened cops who walked away after seeing something horrific. Here, she had experienced the horrible, and yet, she could stand up and talk about it clinically.

"He's already started stalking his next victim. As soon as Soller got rid of one body, he started looking for the next. He'd take his time, follow them, and take pictures, times, and dates. His job was flexible, and no one cared whether or not he was in the store—he had employees. His second victim was taken outside a bar where she'd gone on a blind date with someone her aunt had set her up with." Vega slumped slightly in her chair as if she was suddenly exhausted, carrying the weight, and as if sensing that, Aurelio pushed away from the wall and stood behind her, his hands on her shoulders, gently massaging, as if giving his strength to her.

Gomez and Nikki noticed as Drago had that Vega was crumbling a little under the pressure of remembering.

"How about a soda?" Nikki asked cheerfully.

"Yeah, I could go for a Coke," Vega said absently, leaning further into Aurelio.

"Vega," Gomez began, "I'd love to tell you to go home, forget about this. But first, we may have a copycat. Second, the son of a bitch left a message for you."

Vega nodded. "He's on one. I was number five. I have time."

Aurelio flinched at her calm words. Drago felt for the man. If it were his woman going through this, he'd want to tear the world up into little bitty pieces.

They drove together to the Los Angeles County Department of Medical Examiner on Mission Street, which was six minutes away from LAPD HQ.

Aurelio agreed to stay in the ME's waiting room because Vega had been adamant that he not be touched by this. He'd relented because it was obvious that the idea of him seeing the body was upsetting her.

Drago understood. She could've been the dead body at one point, and she didn't want Aurelio to carry that vision in his head. This was the kind of shit people in love did for one another.

Drago offered a small plastic bottle of Vicks VapoRub to Vega and Nikki before they entered the morgue. They each dabbed a bit under their nose, the potent menthol scent of the ointment providing an immediate, albeit temporary, relief. As they stepped into the morgue, the sharp menthol was a welcome barrier against the harsher odors that awaited them. Yet, even the strength of the Vicks struggled to mask the pervasive smell of death, the unmistakable and unsettling aroma of decay that seemed to cling to the air.

They put on gloves and masks that were in a holder by the door with a sign: NO MASK, NO GLOVES, NO DEAD BODY.

In the sterile, clinical atmosphere of the morgue, Dr. Chen stood over the autopsy table, her demeanor composed.

"Dr. Chen, this is Caroline Vega," Drago introduced.

They shook gloved hands, and Dr. Chen regarded Vega with a grave expression. "Lieutenant Gomez informs me that you've been retained as a consultant on this case."

Vega nodded, but her eyes were fixed on the face of the naked dead woman on the table. The sight was severe, a harsh visual reminder of the cruel end the woman had met, that Vega would have met if not for her rescue.

Drago noticed that Vega's expression was a mix of professional detachment and a trace of underlying empathy, a combination probably honed through years of dealing with the aftermath of violence.

Dr. Chen followed her gaze. "As you know, we have identified the victim. Lorna Wilson. Female. Twenty-one years old. The victim shows signs of prolonged torture. There are multiple contusions and abrasions consistent with electric shock," she indicated to the darkened bruises mottling the body.

"He used a cattle prod," Vega's voice was hoarse. "Soller didn't like to leave scars. He kept the voltage low."

Drago, his eyes scanning the report, interjected, "Any indication of the time frame for these injuries?"

"They appear to have been inflicted over several days, from when she was taken, I'd say about forty eight hours or so," Dr. Chen answered, turning a page in her file. "The ligature marks on her wrists and ankles confirm that she was restrained for an extended period."

Drago couldn't see Vega's face under the mask, but her blue eyes were clouded. "Did he use a rope to restrain?"

"Yes," Dr. Chen said. "That's a departure from Soller, who used leather restraints. I've sent the fibers to forensics."

"Friday is day one," Vega spoke clinically. "He takes them at night. After the kids have gone to bed, so to speak. Day two, he focuses on rape and torture. It's a long fucking day. On Sunday, after Church, he goes back and works on the tattoo, after which he uses the trustee garrote to kill his victim. He dumps the body

Sunday night. Do we know how he got the body up that building on Fig?" Vega peered at her ligature marks closely.

"Only one elevator is working. Crime scene has gone through the building. There is no sign of a murder torture room. She was killed elsewhere and brought here," Nikki filled in. "Canvas has brought up nothing. We didn't expect much. The building is abandoned, and the lone security guard was busy getting a blow job from a hooker."

Dr. Chen nodded gravely. "Sexual assault is confirmed. There's evidence of repeated sexual violence. No DNA. He used a condom."

Vega stopped moving. "A condom?"

"He didn't do that before," Nikki said, looking through her notes.

"No, he didn't. But that's how he got caught," Drago supplied. "Looks like the copycat is trying not to make Soller's mistakes."

"May I...," Vega cleared her throat, "see the tattoo?"

"Yes, the dorsal tattoo," Dr. Chen moved the body so she lay on her stomach. Chen gestured to the large, intricately inked butterfly on the victim's back. "It's a fresh application, ink still settling in the dermis. The preliminary report from forensics shows that it's an exact match for Soller's work."

"We never made the tattoos public," Vega sounded like she was on another planet; her strong voice had become frail. "But there was a podcast host who published the pictures. She got them from the family of Annie Bauer, the fourth victim. She was a student at Southern Methodist University."

"So, anyone could copy the tattoo?" Nikki wondered.

Vega shrugged. "The podcast thing happened after I left Dallas. You should talk to Detective Ari Schwartz. He was primary on the case...not *my* case, the initial one. Detective Wyatt Taze led the task force to find me."

Drago put an arm around Vega. "You okay?" he whispered.

"Yeah," she replied unconvincingly and then, as if seeing something moved back to the body. "The message...the script is jerky like the unsub had trouble with it. The whole tattoo lacks the sophistication of Soller's work. *He* was an artist. His sketches were damn good. Our unsub here is probably not. He is emulating. Copying. It's not *his* thing."

"Or maybe this message is more personal than others, and his hand shook?" Nikki wondered.

"Because he was probably excited? Yeah, I can see that," Vega mused. "Soller didn't complete my butterfly...or my transformation to a butterfly as he'd put it. I'm still alive."

Drago folded his arms, his expression hardening. "And you're gonna stay alive."

Nikki's eyes narrowed and she spoke softly as she stared at the body. "It's a chilling personalization, suggesting a different psychological game at play like this is not just about the killing, it's about you."

"Agreed," Vega said.

"We need to dive deep into the victim's background, associates." Drago's mind was already racing with next steps. "We'll coordinate with the cyber unit for any digital footprint to see if we can trace her movements before the abduction."

"What do you need from me?" Vega asked.

"For now, go home. Clear your head," Drago requested. "Go away from LA. Take time off, Vega. Take a break. We're on this."

She nodded but looked unconvinced. "He already knows who he's killing next. He's going to take her next week." Her voice sounded haunted.

Nikki took her arm. "Come on, Vega, let's go find Aurelio."

Drago stayed with Dr. Chen as Nikki took Vega away.

"What the fuck is Gomez thinking bringing that poor woman into this case?" Dr. Chen demanded. "I read the case file. What she went through? Killing her would have been a mercy."

"She wants to be involved. Her life is in danger," Drago said the things he'd been telling himself to make it okay that he'd dragged Vega into this mess.

Dr. Chen's eyebrows furrowed in concern. "Being involved could be cathartic, or it could be catastrophic for her. This case...," she sighed heavily, "...it's going to be like walking into a psychological minefield for her."

Drago rubbed the back of his neck, feeling the weight of responsibility. "I know, but Vega's insight could be invaluable. She understands the mind of someone like this, maybe better than any of us."

The ME shook her head, her expression a mix of frustration and resignation. "Just make sure she doesn't get too close to the edge, Horvat."

Drago nodded, his expression grim. "I'll keep an eye on her. We all will." And even if he didn't, he was sure Aurelio, and the Santos family would.

Chapter 10

Wednesday, October 4

Jorja Levey turned thirty, three weeks ago. She'd never thought she'd be divorced, childless, and single at this point in her life. But her high school sweetheart, whom she'd married at the tender age of twenty-two, had apparently been playing fast and loose with his zipper. So, the second time she got an STD, she decided enough was enough. Her mother said this happened when you married the high school heartthrob and varsity team quarterback. So, two years ago, she divorced Dwayne's sorry ass—which didn't seem to have impacted him much because a few months later, he got engaged to Tiffany, one of the girls he'd been banging on the side. If Tiffany thought she could keep

Dwayne zipped up, well, more power to her because Jorja was done.

She left the small town of Carneros and moved to Downtown Los Angeles.

"Oh, but the crime?" her sister had protested. Jorja had told her to calm the F down. She loved DTLA. She loved her tiny apartment on Fifth Street, even if it was a little too close to Skid Row. She loved living here. She'd dated casually since she moved and loved the rhythm of her work at the downtown LA post office. She loved that she could walk to work; in fact, it was faster to walk than take her car. She could also take the metro and go all the way to Santa Monica Beach and bypass all that hairy traffic.

It was a Tuesday morning, and the usual bustle of the city seemed to funnel into the small, fluorescent-lit space where she sorted mail and attended to customers.

From Jorja's viewpoint behind the counter, the world was a parade of faces—each with a story and a destination. She greeted each customer with a practiced smile that didn't quite reach her eyes but was warm, nonetheless. Her interactions were a dance of courtesy: stamps for Mrs. Hernandez, who always sent care packages to her son in college; a registered package for Mr. Kim, whose rare stamp collection was his pride; cheerful banter with college students mailing out hopeful job applications.

There was a quiet strength about Jorja. The regulars noticed it—the way she handled the constant demands with unflappable calm, and her laughter rang clear even after her shift ended. Yet, there was an undercurrent of something else, a hint of melancholy that she couldn't entirely conceal.

Jorja leaned against the counter during a lull, her gaze drifting to the street outside. The world moved relentlessly, people chasing dreams, running from fears, or simply existing in their routines. She often wondered about her place in that ceaseless flow.

"Hey Jorja, you okay?" asked Sam, her coworker, as he sorted a stack of mail.

She snapped out of her reverie, offering him a half-smile. "Yeah, just thinking."

"You're too good for this place, you know," Sam remarked, half-joking, half-serious.

Jorja shrugged, her smile becoming a bit more genuine. "This place is good for me, Sam. Keeps me grounded."

As the day wore on, Jorja's interaction with each customer added a layer to her story. She was the listener, the sympathizer, the fleeting friend in the transactional moments of life. Yet, in those exchanges, there was a sense of isolation, a wall she had built around herself since her divorce.

Closing time approached, and Jorja tidied her station. She paused, looking at the small world she had become a part of—a world that had given her a semblance of order in her upturned life.

Stepping out into the LA evening, Jorja took a deep breath, the sounds of the city enveloping her. She was one among many, her story untold, her struggles unseen in the vast tapestry of the city. But in her quiet, unassuming way, Jorja Levey was a fighter, a survivor in a world that moved too fast, and tonight, she walked home with the weight of this realization settling in her heart.

The Butterfly Killer, or as they liked to call themselves, the New BTK, was a play on the serial killer Rader's Bind, Torture, Kill. They'd wanted to deviate from Soller's process in small ways, but Jacob had stopped that. He'd been very clear about what he wanted done and how he wanted it done. Maybe once they were finished with Caroline Vega, they could find their own path, different from Jacob Soller's.

As Jorja walked, they followed her, wondering if she could feel them. The New BTK, reveling in the fear and chaos they were orchestrating, watched from a distance. They had studied Jorja just as they had studied their other targets. In her, they saw not just a victim but a symbol, a piece in a larger, twisted game they were playing against the city, against the police, against normalcy itself for Jacob: father, guide, mentor, and tormentor.

While they followed Jorja, they wondered what it would be like to kill a man. Kill Jacob Soller.

Jacob Soller's methods were a blueprint for them, but they craved more. They wanted to carve out a legacy uniquely theirs, to be remembered not just as a copycat but as a new brand of terror. The thought of diverging from Soller's ways was exhilarating, yet Jacob's strict guidelines loomed over them like a shadow.

Their eyes lingered on Jorja, contemplating the thrill and possibilities of the hunt. She represented more than just another victim; she was a step toward their ultimate goal—Caroline Vega. Initially, they had been reluctant; Sweet Caroline was Jacob's prey. But as they learned more about Vega, their desire grew. They yearned to see her capitulate. Oh, how beautiful it would be to make Vega a butterfly!

But first, they needed to transform Jorja, the woman lost in her thoughts, oblivious to the malevolent gaze tracking her.

Chapter 11

Thursday, October 5

Vega and Aurelio had lunch in her office. She'd asked Jada to order sushi because she knew Aurelio had missed it in Golden Valley. Another reason she couldn't imagine living away from the city. She was a city girl, through and through, thriving in the urban jungle of Los Angeles.

Aurelio picked up a piece of sushi with his chopsticks. He was pensive. She could see the strain he was under. "Are you annoyed with me?" she asked.

He looked up at her and smiled. "Not at all, baby. I'm...scared. For the first time in my life, I'm afraid, and I don't know how to protect you."

Vega put her hand on his. "I'm so sorry to drag you into this. Aurelio, go home. It's—"

"Shut up, Caro." He moved his hand away from her. "So, what are you saying? Hey, a serial killer is after me, and it's messy, so now let's end this relationship?"

"Yes," Vega confirmed, "that's exactly what I'm saying. Why do you want to get involved—"

"You think I have a choice in this?" he demanded, pushing his food away. "You think falling in love with you was a fucking choice? Do you think this is a great situation for me? You think I want to be fucking in love with someone who doesn't give a goddamn inch."

"If I'm so difficult to be with, leave. I'm sure you'll get over me."

He pushed back his chair and walked up to Vega and hauled her out of her chair. "Stop fucking with me," he muttered as he roughly pulled her to him.

"Excuse me?" A thrill coursed through her. He was angry, aroused, the kind of alpha male you read about in books. Aurelio was usually laid back and easygoing, but when his buttons were pushed, he let go, and the animal came out.

"You think because I don't push you to admit you fucking love me as much as I love you, you can walk all over me?"

She licked her lips, and his eyes fell on her mouth.

"You think because I'm in love with you, you can lead me around with my pecker?" he demanded.

"What?"

"Asking me to leave? Asking me to end our relationship? Is that what you really want?" He shook her as he spoke. "Is it?"

He pulled her hips against his, ground into her, and god, help her because she was excited. She took a deep breath, and Aurelio's eyes darkened.

"This is what I mean when I say lead with my pecker," he muttered. "You want me, baby?"

"Yes," she whispered, her mouth searching for his.

"Tell me you love me then."

She blinked. "What?"

"Tell me you fucking love me. Give me the words."

She tried to move away from him, but he didn't let go. Instead, he pushed her against a wall and bent to kiss the hollow sensitive area behind her ear.

"Aurelio," she whimpered as his hands moved to unbutton and unzip her slacks, finding her wet, wanting, ready.

"You want to come, querida?"

"Yes." He had this effect on her. No other man had elicited what he had. She'd been as sexual as any person, but after Soller, she'd abandoned that part of her. She had needs; she found a man here and there to meet them, but mostly, she relied on a vibrator. Aurelio was supposed to be a one-night stand; he was supposed to scratch an itch, but he'd wormed his way into her heart.

She closed her eyes as his fingers strummed her clitoris, and then, just like that, he pulled away. He zipped up her slacks, patted her pussy.

"What?" Her body screamed for release.

"You want me to help you come, baby? You need to say the three f☐cking words you refuse to say."

"Why?" she whined, "And why now?"

"Because there's a madman after you, and I don't want to fucking argue with you all day, every day, about my place in your life. So, say the damn words and commit."

"I...." Vega buttoned her slacks and looked at him, pleading to let her off the hook. She'd pushed too hard, she realized. She wanted Alpha Man. Well, here he was, and he was making demands.

Aurelio looked at his watch and made an impatient gesture. "I have a meeting with Alejandro. Oh, and just so we don't argue about this anymore, we're going to Golden Valley tomorrow morning, so you better ask Jada to set your Friday up with Zoom calls."

"Aurelio, I don't want to spend the weekend with—"

"Like I said, it's not up for discussion."

He took his sushi plate, picked up his backpack, and stormed out of her office.

Fuck! He was pissed, and he had every right to be. She'd told him she needed him here, and ever since he'd shown up, she'd been trying to get him to leave. She hated being vulnerable, and that's exactly what she was with Aurelio. With him, she felt exposed, a state that opened her up to potential hurt.

She put Aurelio out of her mind as she got back to work. Her computer beeped with a FaceTime call, which she took, smiling.

"Vega." Agent Thomas Delfino, a profiler, and an old friend from the Behavioral Analysis Unit (BAU), smiled at her.

She'd texted him after she left the morgue to see if he'd have time to catch up. She knew Drago and Nikki would probably go to the FBI through official channels—but she wanted to get some insights about the copycat unsub. In her career, she'd prosecuted only one serial killer, a few serial rapists but never a copycat.

"Delfino," she acknowledged. "Thanks for calling."

"Of course. All well?"

Vega shook her head, feeling her pulse thrum. She missed this. She missed working with experts to prosecute criminals.

"Tell me?" he said softly.

She told him about the copycat, and he patiently listened.

"LAPD has not reached out to us," Delfino said thoughtfully, "because then I'd have heard. I was the profiler on Soller."

"They'll probably reach out *after* the second murder," she said sadly. There would be another. She was sure of it.

"Fucking hell." Delfino ran a hand over his bald head. He was an experienced profiler who'd been with the BAU for over fifteen years. Before that, he'd been with the Dallas PD, working on crimes against persons. "You're right. There will be another. And another, depending on how long it takes for LAPD to find the unsub. Considering the message on your first victim, you're the end game."

"Yeah, I gathered that."

"Copycats are complex. They're driven by a fascination or obsession with the original killer but also want to be seen as superior, which means that you, as the end game, is to one-up Soller."

"Why not start with me?" she wondered.

"I need more details to develop a profile," Delfino said, "but from what you've told me, here is an informed guess. Your unsub is in contact with Soller somehow, which could mean they are following Soller's instructions."

A chill ran up Vega's spine. "Soller is on death row; his communications are monitored."

Delfino shrugged. "You know how it is, Vega. No prison is impenetrable. And Soller is a wily son of a bitch."

"You said the unsub would want to show he's better than Soller. So, do you think the message for me is from Soller or the unsub?"

Delfino leaned in closer, his tone grave. "I can't say. The message is personal and could mean the unsub is not just copying Soller; they're making this their own narrative. And you're a part of it. Or, Soller has communicated that he wants to complete what he started."

Vega felt a chill that made her want to find Aurelio so he could hold her and ward off this deep freeze inside. "What do we watch out for?"

"The key is going to be in the deviations, the changes the unsub makes to the original MO," Delfino advised. "Those will tell us what the unsub wants, what they're trying to prove. And most importantly, it might give us a clue about their next move."

"Okay. Is it okay if I ask Detective Horvat and Wasco to contact you directly?"

"Sure. I'll clear it with the powers to be, and if the LAPD wants to keep it informal, we can do that as well. But, if the unsub is following Soller, they have already found their next victim. Soller killed four women in eight weeks before he was caught. But we always suspected that there were others he'd killed while he perfected his MO."

The weight of Delfino's words settled heavily in the room as Vega processed the implications of their conversation.

"Thanks, Delfino," Vega said, her voice tinged with appreciation and concern. "I'll relay your insights to Detective Horvat and Wasco."

Delfino's expression was earnest. "Anything you need, Vega. I don't need to tell you that this unsub is very dangerous. And you, being the end game, adds a personal dimension that will make it hard to predict their actions."

"I know. It's unsettling. The message was meant for me. It's like I'm being drawn back into a world I thought I'd left behind."

"I know. I'm sorry." Delfino had been someone she'd talked to when she'd decided to resign as ADA and leave Dallas, move to another part of the country, and start fresh.

Delfino leaned forward, his tone insistent. "Stay vigilant, Vega. If this killer is trying to outdo Soller, and you're the target, you must be proactive about your security. Don't fuck with that."

She sighed, fear and resolve mingling within her. "I won't be doing that."

Once the call concluded, Vega sat silently, the enormity of the situation washing over her. After she got a hold of her emotions, she picked up her phone and texted Drago, asking for a quick meeting. She needed to warn them about what Delfino said, to offer whatever help she could. Her expertise might no longer be in the courtroom, but she understood the inner working of Soller's mind and, to some extent, because of it, the copycat's. And right now, that understanding was crucial.

Purposefully, she opened her office door to find Joey standing on the other side.

"Oops. I just wanted to see if you had time to review the due diligence report for Solarix."

Vega waved to her office. "Wait for me. I need a minute."

She walked into the meeting room Jada had secured for Aurelio. He was on the phone, his booted feet atop the table.

"I can take care of it when I'm back on Friday," he said. "Look, I still haven't convinced Vega to come along, so don't tell Mama and get her hopes up."

He turned to face her when he heard her footsteps as she closed the meeting room door behind her. "Alejandro, I've got to go. Say hi to Maria."

He didn't take his boots off the table but put his phone down. "Hey."

"I love you," she blurted out.

Aurelio's expression shifted from casual to startled, his boots came off the table as he sat up straighter. "What did you say?" he asked a mixture of surprise and hope in his eyes.

Vega took a deep breath, feeling a wave of relief mixed with nervousness. "I love you, Aurelio. I've been holding back, trying to keep my distance because... because I was...am...afraid. Afraid of getting hurt, afraid of losing myself in someone else's world. But I realize now that I'm only hurting both of us by holding back. I'm okay hurting myself...but I don't want to hurt you."

Aurelio's face broke into a wide, genuine smile, the kind that reached his eyes and lit up his entire face. "I've been waiting to hear you say that," he whispered, walking over to her.

He took her hands in his, their eyes locking. "I love you too, Caro."

Vega nodded, a tear escaping her eye. "I know."

"You won't lose yourself with me. I won't let that happen."

She leaned her head on his chest. "I know. I've been so focused on protecting myself that I didn't see how much richer my life could be with you fully in it."

Aurelio pulled her into a gentle embrace, a perfect fit. "We'll take this at your pace, Vega. No pressure, no expectations. Just us, learning and growing together."

"And the weekend in Golden Valley?" she asked.

"My family knows what happened to you and...I'll be honest, they're protective, and if you don't come to Golden Valley with me, there's a good chance they'll descend here."

"I don't need anyone's pity." The old feelings resurged.

"How about support then?" he argued. "How about love and affection?"

She nodded. "I'm not used to family."

He kissed her forehead. "I know. Why do you think I've not pushed this earlier?"

He always knew she thought. He just always knew what was bothering her and how to manage her feelings. She touched his heart. "You give me so much...what do I give in return? I don't know why you're with me."

"Why am I with a beautiful, smart, intelligent, and good woman who gives excellent head?" he teased.

She flushed.

"You make me step away from my comfort zone. You give me strength. You make me believe I can be more than I am. You are my friend, my lover, my confidante. You make me happy. I love you, Caro. When I'm with you, fuck, baby, I'm ten feet tall."

She hugged him close then, letting his strength seep into her. "Your family doesn't resent me for not engaging with them?"

He lifted her chin, so she'd look at him. "No. We're not in the business of judgment, and your reasons are yours. All they care about is that I love you, and because I do, they also love you."

She smiled weakly. "I was dating when Soller took me. Jamie and I'd been together for a couple of years, and we were engaged. We were going to get married, live a normal life. But when I was in the hospital, he bailed."

"He left you after what you'd been through? Christ, Caro, you were engaged to an asshole."

"He said he couldn't handle it."

"Fucking coward! His woman was brutalized, and he leaves her."

"What would you have done?" she asked.

"I'd have made you feel safe again so...," he paused, emotion moistening his eyes, "I'd hold you, Caro, and I'd be there all day, every day, physically, emotionally. But you're never going to go through that again."

She twisted a button on his shirt. "I'm afraid, Aurelio."

"Me too."

"I thought I'd left Soller behind—"

"You still have nightmares, querida. You didn't leave him behind."

She nodded. "I better get back to my office. Joey is waiting for me."

He kissed her gently. "Mateo and Raya have invited us for dinner tonight. I told them I'd ask you."

Vega sighed. "Yeah, I got a message from Dec. He and Esme will also be there. I'm assuming everyone knows."

"I don't know. Alejandro and Maria know, and my parents."

"And Isadora?"

Aurelio thought about it and shook his head. "Alejandro wouldn't tell her and neither would I. We still treat her like our baby sister. Pisses her off. But you know she and Drago are good friends, so there's a chance she may know."

"Drago is LAPD; he doesn't gossip."

"Have you met my sister?" Aurelio said, baffled. "She's got mad skills when it comes to extracting information."

"This is the problem with family."

He kissed her nose. "You're looking at it the wrong way. That's the advantage of family."

Chapter 12

Thursday, October 5

Detective Drago Horvat leaned against the edge of his desk in the bustling LAPD bullpen while his boss Gomez sat on his chair. Nikki sat across from Gomez at her desk. The open-plan office was alive with the usual blend of seriousness and light-hearted banter characteristic of long hours and high-stress work.

"Anything new on Lorna Wilson?" Gomez wondered.

"We've made calls and started interviews; we're on our way to Blondie's as soon as we're doing here," Drago filled him in.

Gomez looked up, his expression a mix of interest and concern. "Do we like the boyfriend at all for this?"

Nikki chimed in, "Blake Holland. A rap sheet with shoplifting, drunk and disorderly, and an assault that seems more like a bar brawl than anything premeditated."

From a nearby desk, Detective Martinez called out, half-joking, "So, a model citizen then?"

Drago shot him a wry smile. "Yeah, right up there with you, Martinez."

There was a ripple of laughter around the bullpen. Despite the grim nature of their work, you could be rest assured that detectives would have time to yank each other's chain.

Gomez refocused them. "Any leads from Holland?"

"We're bringing him in for questioning," Drago replied. "But it doesn't feel like he's our guy for the murder. His alibi for the night she went missing checks out."

Detective Lee, poring over some files at her desk, added, "Plus, the MO doesn't fit a crime of passion, or a simple assault gone wrong. This is methodical, planned."

Drago nodded in agreement. "Exactly. We're looking at someone who's calculated and enjoys the theatrics. Like our copycat theory suggests."

Gomez sighed, rubbing his temple. "Alright, keep on it. And Horvat, try not to scare Holland too much."

Drago grinned. "No promises, boss."

As they dispersed, the dynamic in the bullpen shifted back to the controlled chaos of a major investigation. Detectives huddled in small groups, discussing leads and strategies, while others were glued to their computer screens.

Drago and Nikki went to Blondie's where Lorna Wilson worked. The scent of coffee and fried food filled the air. The mood seemed forlorn, it could be because a colleague of theirs was dead or it was how the diner usually was.

They spoke first with the manager, a middle-aged woman named Rita, who seemed genuinely upset about Lorna's disappearance. "Lorna was a good girl, always on time, hardworking," she told them, wiping her hands on her apron. "Can't believe she's mixed up in something like this."

As they moved through the diner, talking to Lorna's colleagues, Drago observed their reactions. Most were shocked, some scared. None seemed to have seen anything unusual or suspicious in Lorna's recent behavior.

They spoke with a server named Marissa, a close friend of Lorna's. She mentioned, somewhat hesitantly, that there were a couple of regulars who might have been a bit too interested in Lorna. "They hit on her a few times. But she always brushed it off," Marissa said, playing with her order pad nervously. "She was all into Blake the Flake."

"Yeah?" Nikki grinned.

Marissa shrugged. "He's a moron. Lorna can do so much better and..." She trailed off, her eyes filling with tears.

Drago exchanged a look with Nikki. "Did she ever mention feeling threatened by these regulars?"

Marissa shook her head. "No, nothing like that. She just laughed it off and said they were harmless. Just some guys looking for some attention."

After collecting descriptions of the men, Drago and Nikki left the diner. But as they followed up on the leads, checking security footage from the diner and talking to other guests, they hit one dead end after another. The men were just that—regulars with no apparent connection to anything sinister. Their interest in Lorna, while perhaps unrequited, seemed innocent enough.

Drago could sense Nikki's frustration mirroring his own. They were back to square one, with no solid leads on who might have targeted Lorna.

As they regrouped in the bullpen, Drago leaned back in his chair, his thoughts racing. The killer was careful, leaving no obvious trail, no easy connections.

Nikki was tapping away at her computer, her brow furrowed. "This is fucking frustrating," she muttered.

Drago nodded, his gaze distant. "Tell me about it," he said.

The day had brought them no closer to understanding Lorna's last days or the identity of her killer. They hoped they'd have better luck with forensics, where the team was led by Dr. Simmons, who had been meticulously analyzing every piece of evidence from Lorna Wilson's case.

Dr. Simmons held up a plastic bag containing fibers. "These fibers," he began, "are from the rope used to restrain Lorna Wilson. They're not just any rope—it's a specialized type commonly used in nautical applications. It's distinct from the leather restraints the original Butterfly Killer used."

By now, everyone working the case had all the necessary information about Jacob Soller and was actively comparing notes wherever possible. This was particularly important since the FBI had informally indicated that finding this unsub would hinge on deviations from the original MO.

"Yeah, Vega mentioned that the rope was a deviation. It could be the unsub is making his own mark or...he didn't have the right equipment. Anything else?"

"We've found small deviations in the tattoos as well."

Nikki stepped forward, her eyes sharp with curiosity. "Such as?"

"The overall design mimics Soller's butterfly, but there are subtle changes. For instance, the wing patterns are slightly altered and less symmetrical. Although the colors are the same, they are used in different combinations. I don't know if this is significant, but we wanted to let you know in light of the BAU's advice on identifying changes from the original MO."

Drago mulled over this information. The copycat was not just imitating; they were adapting and evolving. They wanted to be like Soller but also distinctly themselves.

Nikki was thinking along the same lines. "He's trying to outdo Soller, isn't he? Make his own statement."

"Could be," Dr. Simmons replied.

Drago nodded slowly, his mind racing with the implications. "This means he's not just following a script; he's writing his own. Fucking unguided missile."

"I don't know, Horvat, I don't think this lunatic being guided is a better thing," Dr. Simmons murmured.

"No shit," Drago agreed.

Chapter 13

Thursday, October 5

Aurelio watched as Vega talked to Mateo. Amongst all her colleagues who were friends in LA, she was closest to Mateo, who was like a brother to Aurelio.

Dinner parties were not his scene. He was an introvert and preferred to spend time alone rather than in groups. But he felt Vega needed time with people who cared about her.

"Hey." Raya slipped a hand around his waist and leaned into his shoulder.

Aurelio absently brushed his lips against her forehead. Raya, their surrogate sister, and her husband, Mateo, had seamlessly woven themselves into the fabric of the Santos family.

Raya, standing just a few inches below Aurelio's six-foot-two frame, was effortlessly stylish in her own rugged way. She was a good-looking woman. Sure, she was a sister, but he had eyes. Raya kept her blonde hair short, framing her face in a way that accentuated her sharp features, and she favored jeans and sturdy boots over dresses.

Whenever Aurelio saw her with Mateo, the difference between them was striking. Raya's light, carefree demeanor sharply differed from Mateo's more reserved and meticulously groomed appearance. His dark, carefully styled hair and penchant for crisp, tailored suits made them an unlikely pair to the casual observer. Yet, there was an undeniable harmony in their differences, a balance that seemed to make each of them more vibrant when they were together.

"How are things with you and Mateo?" He took a sip of his beer.

"Good," she chuckled. "Really, really good. How are things with you and Vega?"

"She told me she loved me today," he told her, and she whistled softly. He grinned. "Yeah. Took her a while to get here. But I feel like she felt she had to say this because she's not sure she's going to make it through...." He couldn't say it, not out loud. But he knew a part of Vega wondered if this would be the time she'd not be able to cheat death as she had last time.

She'd told him once, "If someone wants to commit a crime, they'll commit a crime no matter what deterrents we put in place. Some people can't help themselves, and that's why cops and lawyers are in business."

And here was someone who was gunning for her. Fucking hell! Leaving a message on a dead body. Talk about a mind fuck.

"Dec said he spoke to Alejandro, and they're going to up security at her place and the office, and if you're taking her to Golden Valley, which the family prefers, Alejandro already has increased security," Raya told him.

Aurelio hadn't expected any less. Vega wasn't used to having family, but he was, and he knew that as soon as they knew she was in any kind of danger, they'd do everything they could to keep her safe.

Dec came up to Aurelio and Raya. "How's it going?"

"Like shit."

"Yeah, I can imagine," he concurred. "Any news from Drago?"

Aurelio shook his head. "They've got nothing. And by that, I mean nothing with a big N."

"How's Vega handling it?" Dec asked.

"A bit too well," Aurelio supplied. "And I'm not buying it."

"What aren't you buying?" the woman in question asked as she joined their group.

"That you're okay," Aurelio said, looking into her eyes. Oh, she wouldn't like it at all that he was talking about their business. She was a private person and didn't like to share anything with anyone. Well, tough shit, this was family.

Mateo put an arm around his wife and dropped a kiss on her lips. They were something, he thought, opposite in so many ways and yet perfect together. But Aurelio knew theirs was no fairytale marriage. Raya had experienced trauma as a child, as had Mateo, who grew up in the foster care system. Yet, they had worked their way to have a healthy relationship. Once Raya had told him that it was all about love and that gave them the strength to grow beyond their childhood, their past. In fact, it was the non-fairytale parts of their relationship that made them work so well together.

He looked at Vega, who was frowning at him. Of all the women he'd thought he'd ever end up with, he'd never thought it would be a tough city lawyer who had bigger balls than him. But then, love could take many diverse forms. It wasn't about similarities or fitting a conventional mold. Sometimes, it was about the unexpected connections, the differences that challenged and complemented, that made a relationship truly special.

"I'm fine," Vega countered, and she looked around at her friends and sighed, "I am fine."

"No one's saying you're not." Raya quirked an eyebrow at her. "But you doth protest too much."

She flung her arms in the air. "For fuck's sake. I am—"

"Baby, if you're fine that someone tattooed a macabre message for you on the body of a twenty-something innocent young girl, you'd be in need of immediate mental intervention," Aurelio said lazily. "I'm not fine with this. I don't ever want to be fine with something like this. It's ugly. It's dark. And you know what, it's downright fucking scary."

He'd have gone to her, held her close because he could see she was holding it together by a thread, so Aurelio didn't. She wouldn't want comfort right now; she'd snarl at him or, worse, break, and then she'd hate him for it, hate herself for it. She had such strength in her. She'd spent thirty-three hours with Soller and came out a survivor, a fighter.

"If you're all going to look at me like I'm some kind of victim—"

Esme, Declan's wife, put a hand on Vega's shoulder and then drew her into a hug. It was her way, Aurelio had learned. Esme reminded him of his mother, because they both were social workers and had committed their lives to helping battered women and children.

"We know you're the toughest bitch in the room," Esme said as she held Vega close. "But we're not. So, we need a hug to feel safe."

The hug didn't make Vega feel better; he knew because she disliked being the center of attention. He didn't know whether this was how she used to be, or this was how she'd become after what happened to her. She liked to stay in the background. She probably only saw Dec and Mateo amongst all the people at work as friends; everyone else was an acquaintance. She went out for drinks with the girls at times, but it was rare.

"I don't want to go to Golden Valley," she announced when she got into bed with him that night. Aurelio knew it was coming. He'd been waiting for it as he went through emails on his phone.

"I know, baby."

"Then we don't have to go?" she sounded wistful, childlike.

"No, we're going to go. I'm not leaving you alone here for the weekend, and I have a shit ton of work to get through." He didn't look up from his phone because he knew it would irritate her and he preferred if she was angry rather than melancholy.

Lorna Wilson's death was weighing on her. The poor girl had been tortured, raped, and tattooed like Vega. The body on the metal gurney she had seen could have been hers. It also sent a chill down his spine. He hadn't wanted her to enter the medical examiner's autopsy room alone, but he knew she didn't want him to see the woman who had died—a victim of what she had endured, a reflection of how easily she herself could have been the one lying dead.

Cristo! Couldn't she see that this was as hard on him as her? They weren't separate entities. He fucking loved her. Stubborn goddamn woman!

She sat stiffly in bed, her hands clenched, holding the duvet cover nervously. "I don't want to keep talking about Soller. I want to get back to my life."

He put his phone down because she was staring at the painting on the wall across from the bed. It was a nice painting, an original she'd told him of a nude woman in repose.

He pulled her into him. She flinched. He drew her close, and she relented, resting her head on his shoulder. Her arm came around him. "I don't want him to take over my life. This is exactly what he wants."

"You think Soller is in touch with this copycat?"

She stiffened and then nodded.

"Drago think the same?"

"Yeah. They'll look into who Soller is talking to, but he's too smart to be just chatting away with a protegee, giving him guidance on who and how to kill. If he's in contact, he's using alternative means of communication."

He liked it that she was thinking about this tactically, like an ADA instead of a victim. He wondered when she'd realize that she wasn't designed for this tedious corporate job that she'd fallen into because it was safe.

"Are people on death row allowed to use a computer? Get on the Internet?" he wondered.

"Death row inmates in Texas are typically not allowed computer and Internet privileges. TDCJ has—"

"What's TDCJ?"

"The Texas Department of Criminal Justice maintains strict regulations regarding privileges for death row inmates. In general, these inmates have limited access to recreational and communication facilities. They are usually confined to their cells for the majority of the day and have limited contact with other inmates. Their access to the outside world is heavily restricted."

"How do they communicate with their lawyer or family?"

Vega shrugged. "Usually, comms are limited to letters and, in some cases especially with their attorneys, monitored phone calls. Visitation rights are strictly controlled and supervised. The emphasis is on security and the maintenance of a controlled environment."

He nuzzled her hair. "Then maybe he's not in touch with this copycat, and this psychopath is on his own trip."

She took a deep breath and then straightened, and he could see those gears in her mind start to turn. "He could be using coded messages or someone else as a go-between. Prison guards have been known to facilitate contact with the outside world," she speculated, her voice steady as she shifted into a more analytical mindset. "Someone like Soller knows how to play the system *and* manipulate people."

He admired her sharpness, her ability to dissect a situation despite the personal turmoil it caused her. "You think he's got someone on the inside?"

"It's possible," she mused, her gaze distant. "Or maybe he's manipulating another inmate. There are ways to get messages out. I've seen it happen before."

He tightened his hold on her slightly, proud yet worried about how deeply she was delving into this. "You're thinking like the ADA you once were, not just a victim."

She pulled back slightly, looking into his eyes. "Aurelio, I need to be a part of this investigation, even if it's unofficial. I know you disagree and—"

"I absolutely agree," he said and knew he surprised her. He saw the determination in her eyes, the resurgence of her professional identity. "You can't see it, but I can. You're made for this job. I know it's fucking horrible, and you suffered...fuck more than any human should, and yet, you're ready to go right back because you don't want anyone else to get hurt. You're amazing, you know that? You're not meant for a desk job, hidden away. You're a fighter."

Her eyes searched his to see if he was speaking from his heart instead of saying what he thought she wanted to hear. "You won't mind?"

"Not as long as you let me be with you, which means you're going to have to compromise and be with me in Golden Valley for some of the time," he grinned.

She sighed and chuckled. "You're slick, you know that?"

He wanted to crush her into him because he was frightened out of his wits that something would happen to her. He'd asked Alejandro to help with Vega's security. He didn't know how to keep her safe. This was brand new fucking territory for him. This was way out of his experience. How could he keep his woman safe from a goddamn serial killer?

"You talk to your friends in the FBI?" he asked.

"I talked to Tom Delfino; he's a profiler at the BAU."

"What did he say?"

"That copycats want to best the original. This unsub wants to be better than Soller. Wants to show he's smarter than him."

Neither of them said what hovered between them. Killing Vega would be the prize. Finishing that tattoo would make this unsub better than Soller, he'd have one-upped his idol.

Chapter 14

Thursday, October 5

Vega couldn't sleep. She tried and hoped that as Aurelio slid into slumber, his calm heartbeat would take her, but it didn't.

She battled every day to not think about what Soller had done to her. Usually, she succeeded, but right now, it was nearly impossible. Her heart hurt that she'd drawn Aurelio into this. He didn't deserve this. He was a small-town farmer, bless his heart. He wasn't supposed to be here, yeah? He was supposed to be ensconced in Golden Valley with this family. His indulgent mother. Loud and loving father. Perky sister. Seriously, hot brother. Okay, so Alejandro was Aurelio's brother, but she wasn't blind. The man was seriously sizzling. She wasn't surprised that he'd ended up with the elegant Maria Caruso. They made a handsome couple. They fit. He was a CEO. She was a CEO. And here she was with Aurelio. She was damaged goods, and he was the all-American farm boy.

Vega stroked his face. She loved him. Madly. How did it happen that you met someone at a bar and suddenly they became your whole life?

She bent to kiss him on his lips gently. His lips moved. He smiled. And because he did, she kissed him again, softly this time.

His hand snaked up behind her head, and he pulled her to him, slamming her mouth into his. He devoured her. Farm boy had a healthy sex drive. She had to give him that—and that had been the draw at first. This intense mating was unique, theirs.

He pulled her atop him, his hands now running over her back, molding her body to his. "I love how you wake me, baby."

He was hard, just like that. She'd never been with a lover who got aroused as quickly as he did and stayed hard. And as the cliché went, he could keep it up all night long.

She rubbed her mound over his erection. Her pajama shorts the only barrier between them. He slept in the nude. She needed to wear something. It hadn't mattered before, but since Soller...*god*, everything in her life seemed to be before and after those thirty-fucking-three hours.

"Aurelio," she whimpered. "Make me forget. Damn it, I don't want to think about it anymore."

"Oh, Caro. Querida." He rolled her onto her back and kissed her gently.

In the past year, their sex life was varied. They'd done it in restaurants, the car, the woods near his place, and on Dec's airplane when they'd gone to Scotland for his sister's wedding. It was sometimes hard and fast, occasionally sweet, and long, and sometimes mind-blowing and full of love. They knew what each other needed. Right now, they both wanted their senses to take over. They wanted, affection and connection.

He removed her clothes as he slid down her body.

No matter how many ways they made love, she never let him take her from behind, even in the dark. The tattoo burnt on her skin, and Soller had violated her from behind. Hurt her. Brutalized her.

"Stay with me, Caro," he whispered as if he knew where her head was at. "Stay with me, baby. I got you."

He kissed her belly and stroked her pussy. "You're beautiful, you know that? Every time I look at you, I want to be inside you."

He talked dirty with the best of them, but then he also loved so sweetly that he disarmed her.

"I'm sorry," she whispered when he cupped her.

"Why, baby?"

"I'm not wet." She felt ashamed. She wasn't exactly aroused. She just wanted to forget. Aurelio could always take her away from the darkness.

He kissed her pussy lips. "Oh, I wouldn't worry about that. I know how to make you wet. Juicy and delicious."

He spread her thighs, and she felt the first forerunners of desire when she felt his breath against her labia. He kissed her clitoris and then licked her long and patient.

Her breath caught.

He slid a finger inside her, and she was already getting slippery. "I love being in here. And I love to taste you. Do you know that?"

"Yes," she breathed, her hands tangled up in his hair.

He slid two fingers and started to pump, and her body began to dance to the rhythm he set. He suckled her clitoris and got a third finger inside her. Her hips started to buck as she followed his mouth.

"Yeah, like that," he whispered. "You're so wet, Caro. And you taste like...fuck, you taste...like you're mine."

And that's when he suckled her clitoris hard, and she felt a pulse within her hammer. It started deep down at the base of her spine, and she felt the orgasm build and build and build....

"Come for me, baby," he commanded, and she did as he ordered.

"Come inside me," she begged as her thighs shook and her release claimed her. She wanted to be crammed full of him because when he was deep inside her, he was also around her, holding her, keeping her safe, aroused, loved, happy.

He licked her as aftershocks hit her.

"Please, Aurelio," she pleaded.

"I know, baby. But I want to feel you come around my cock, and I want to build you up so you will. Let go, Caro. Just let go. Close your eyes and feel me. Feel how much I love you."

She closed her eyes and gave in. He took her control away, and in the beginning, she wouldn't give it to him, but now she did. It was the easiest thing to do because she trusted him. She loved him more than she'd love anyone, even herself.

When she was on the brink again, he rose above her and eased into her, oh so slowly. Her sensitive tissues clenched around him as he entered.

He kissed her lips, her eyes, her cheeks, her nose as he moved within her. His movements were languid like they had all the time in the world, like their alarms weren't going off in a few hours—so they could beat traffic and head to his home.

His muscular thighs held hers, and she loved the feeling of his roughness against her softness, of his muscles against hers. She loved to see her light skin against his dark hue. Ying and yang.

He surged inside her. "Tell me, Caro."

Usually, she asks him to tell her he loved her. The fact that he was asking her to open her heart was poignant because he was equally as afraid of what could happen to her and wanted her to comfort him. She'd never known love could be like this, where when you gave, it was like receiving a hundredfold. She'd never known it could be this warm, this fulfilling.

"I love you," she said, tears in her eyes, "so fucking much."

"Yeah, baby." He smiled and kissed the tears that rolled down her cheeks. "I love you too, Caro. Immensely. Fuck! You hold me inside you with so much love. I'm gonna come, love. Come with me."

She reached down to stroke her clit, and he put his hand on hers so he could direct her movements. It was erotic, this give and take.

She felt her release ram through her, not gently like before but harder, rawer because he was inside her. His movements became more urgent, and he began to slam into her harder. He threw his head back and grunted his release.

When he crashed, it was in the crook of her neck. "I'm never letting you go," he comforted her as she held him tight.

Chapter 15

Saturday, October 6

Drago had better things to do on a Saturday. A woman he'd been seeing casually had asked him if he was free, and he'd told her he wasn't.

He could have been having sex with a good-looking woman, instead, he was in the near-deserted LA bullpen even though he wasn't on shift because the Lorna Wilson case was gnawing at him. He was even more driven because of the connection to Vega—and he was sickened by the idea that if this was a copycat, Lorna Wilson was the first victim, and there would be four others.

He'd spent all his time the past three days reading everything he could find on Jacob Soller. They called him The Butterfly Killer. Drago hated the practice of giving serial killing assholes catchy names. The sons of bitches didn't deserve it.

The profile of Jacob Soller was written by FBI profiler Dr. Thomas Delfino. Vega had mentioned that she'd reached out to him and that he would be happy to work with the LAPD to put a profile of the copycat unsub together. Gomez was working the channels. So far, Wasco's mother had refused to feed the media piranhas by calling the death of Lorna Wilson as part of a serial killing. As of now, it was a garden-variety murder.

Oh yeah, how many garden fucking variety murders tattooed their victims and left messages for former ADAs?

Fucking politics.

The Butterfly Killer's profile, before Soller was caught, had been accurate. It described the unsub as a sadistic serial killer, a sociopath lacking in empathy and excessively concerned with impression management. Everything fit Soller to a T. Male, likely between 30 and 50 years old. Soller was forty-two.

Married and has a stable job. Soller had a wife, a son, and a daughter. He was the owner of a sporting goods store in Frisco.

He was average-looking, unremarkable, and not easily identifiable. Soller was all that.

The unsub would have an undiagnosed personality disorder and lead a double life, presenting as a family-oriented, respected member of society while harboring a hidden, dark side with a deep-seated psychological need for power and control over women. His selection of victims based on certain physical attributes and occupation suggested a specific psychological gratification.

The butterfly tattoo was a symbol of transformation and rebirth. Soller believed he was facilitating his victims' transition from a mundane life (caterpillar) to a beautiful and transcendent existence (butterfly), possibly driven by a delusional desire to play a god-like role in their lives. The act of tattooing the butterfly could represent Soller's need for control and ownership over his victims, and it also served as a permanent mark, symbolizing his complete dominance and possession of their bodies, even after death. The act of tattooing was connected with gratification beyond the sexual. He raped his victims and tortured them by using a cattle prod. Only his first victim had scars; he seemed to have evolved from that, and his other victims showed trauma but no scars.

The unsub copycat had left scars—probably not as practiced as Soller with a cattle prod. He made a note of that as yet another deviation from the original MO.

The use of the Emily Dickinson's poem From Cocoon Forth a Butterfly was Soller's signature, a deliberate clue, and a way to leave his mark and communicate with investigators to fuel his ego.

He kidnapped his victims in his van, held them captive in a warehouse for approximately three days, and then staged the bodies in abandoned buildings. This indicated careful planning and organization and a high degree of intelligence.

According to Agent Delfino, Soller chose blonde and slender women because, well, everyone has a type. He preferred women with jobs because it was easier to get to them.

Now, a copycat would not have this same profile. The BAU would have to build a new one. Drago rubbed a hand over his tired face.

"Well, look who's also decided to ignore the concept of a weekend," his partner quipped as she walked towards him. "I thought you had some kind of private life."

"Just as much of a private life as you do, apparently," he retorted. He pointed to his computer monitor, "Have you read Soller's BAU profile?"

"Yeah. But the copycat is not going to have this profile." She sat down at her desk across from him. "You pissed with my mom for not letting us reach out to the FBI?"

"I'm pissed at the chief of Ds, not your mom," Drago corrected. "This case haunting you too?"

"Yep," Nikki replied, putting her boots up on the desk and leaning back. "Thought I'd come in and see if I could make any headway without the usual circus."

Their conversation was interrupted by the unexpected appearance of Lieutenant Gomez, who also seemed to have forgone the idea of a weekend off. He strode in, his eyes sharp and focused.

"Don't you two ever take a break?" Gomez asked, though his tone was more amused than exasperated.

"Says the man who practically lives in this place," Drago shot back, earning a chuckle from Nikki.

Gomez leaned his hip against Nikki's desk. "Any new leads on Wilson? This case is turning into a real brain-teaser."

Drago nodded, his expression turning serious. "We're still waiting on the communication logs from Gainesville. Might give us something on Soller's connection to our copycat."

Nikki added, "And I've been going over the witness statements again. Hoping to catch something we missed."

Gomez surveyed the room, the sparse presence of personnel lending a solemn air to their weekend endeavor. "Well, I'm here to dig into the forensics report again. Maybe there's a detail we overlooked."

Drago understood that what was troubling about this case was the timeline: depending on the copycat's approach, he had either already taken a woman or would do so in precisely five days. And they had fuck all.

Drago's cell phone rang with a Dallas area code, and he answered it immediately. The background noise of the bullpen—the clatter of keyboards, the inaudible murmur of voices, the occasional ring of a phone—faded into a distant hum as he focused on the call.

"Horvat," he answered.

"This is Warden Johnson. I got your message, Detective. So, what can I do for ya'll out in sunny California," the Warden's voice, thick with a Texas drawl, came through clearly.

Drago leaned back in his chair, giving Nikki a thumbs-up sign. "Thanks for calling me back on a Saturday, Warden."

"The missus is havin' a book club meetin' at home with her lady friends, so I decided to get some paperwork out of the way."

Drago chuckled. "I wanted to reach out to you about Jacob Soller."

"The Butterfly Cuckoo? Sure."

"We're investigating a murder that bears a striking resemblance to his handiwork. I'm looking to see who's been in contact with him."

The Warden's tone was nonchalant but cautious. "Well, Detective, you know how it is with these high-profile inmates. You've got to go through channels. I can't just hand over information to you."

"And we're working on that," Drago quickly said, "But I wanted to get some insight from you on who comes and goes when it comes to Soller. Warden, a twenty-one-year-old, was murdered, and she had a butterfly tattooed on her back. There was a message tattooed as well, we think, for the ADA who worked the case. The message said, *'Sweet Caroline, are you ready to become a butterfly.'*"

"Fuckin' hell. Like Vega didn't get enough trauma because of that sumbitch," he said in disgust, "I never had the pleasure of meeting her, but from all accounts, Vega was one classy lady and a damn good ADA. I heard she moved to LA and left law enforcement, not that I blame her. After what she went through...fuck...goddamn it all to hell and back."

Drago was not surprised to hear that Vega had fans in Texas as she did in Los Angeles.

"Death row victims are not allowed to communicate without supervision. Soller gets a shit ton of letters like all the fuckin' cuckoos do. We screen 'em all. No one visits Soller, you understand? His wife bolted with the kids. Left the state."

"Any inmates he chats with during yard...recreation time?"

"Soller's a loner type. I see him talk to no one 'cept his lawyer."

Drago rubbed his forehead, his intuition telling him there was more beneath the surface. "Could anything slide through?"

"We run a tight ship here, Detective. His mail's mostly from those morbid curiosity types, and his calls are few and far between. But they're all recorded and monitored."

"Any chance I can get access to—"

"Detective, you want the recordings you got to go through channels," Warden interrupted. "You know the drill."

"Yes, sir, I do. Ah...any guards he talks to?"

There was a long pause. "Well, we got a couple of guards there who have contact with the high falutin inmates; and that includes Soller."

"Could I talk to them?"

"Sure. You want them to call you?"

"Or maybe I can come down to you and we can make sure everything goes through the channels." Drago nodded at Nikki, who was listening to his side of conversation and catching the gist. She grinned and gave him a thumbs-up sign.

He hung up, and Nikki raised her eyebrows. "Well?"

"*Well*, that was the Warden of Cooke County Jail. He can't give me anything unless we go through channels. But I was thinking we can head to Dallas...maybe talk to Soller and the guards." Drago began to type up his call with the Warden.

"You think Gomez has a budget for travel?"

"He's here on a Saturday because he's as stirred up about this case as we are. I think he'll spring."

Chapter 16

Saturday, October 6

The late summer sun cast a warm, golden glow over the rolling fields of Golden Valley as Aurelio and Vega rode side by side on horseback. Aurelio, familiar and at ease with the rhythm of the horse beneath him, glanced over at Vega. He noticed how the gentle sway of her horse and the beauty of his valley had brought a peaceful expression to her face.

They rode in comfortable silence for a while, the only sounds being the soft thudding of hooves on the earth and the distant calls of birds. Aurelio loved these lands, the sprawling expanse of the farm that had been part of his family for years. He felt a sense of pride and responsibility towards it, a feeling he often shared with Vega.

Breaking the silence, Vega turned to him, her eyes reflecting the vast, open sky. "Thank you. I didn't realize I needed a break."

"You don't have to thank me, baby."

"But I have to," she told him. "I didn't even know I needed this."

"That's my job, Caro, to know what you need and deliver."

They rode for a while longer in silence.

"I have a question...or rather a thought," she told him.

"Tell me."

"How would you feel if I...left Knight Tech and went back to law enforcement?"

Aurelio smiled; he knew she'd get there. "You're meant for it, fighting for justice, giving a voice to the voiceless."

She had talked to him about the work she'd done as ADA before Soller. It was like her life was divided into before and after that asshole. Aurelio didn't know her before, but he suspected that some of the walls she'd put up didn't exist prior to her attack. Who had she been like then? Had she laughed more? Had she been more lighthearted? Did she trust more easily?

"May I ask you something?" Aurelio requested.

"Honey, you know you may ask me anything; but I may choose not to answer," she said cheekily.

Aurelio laughed. "Were you always Vega?"

"What do you mean?"

"I mean, were you Caroline or Caro or...were you always Vega?"

She grinned as they stopped at a vista point. She leaned to stroke the neck of the chestnut mare she was riding. "You're a good girl, Dakota," she whispered, and the mare's ears perked. "I was Caroline with friends and family. At work, I was Vega. And when Soller took me he kept calling me Caroline so to keep sane, in my head, I started to call myself Vega. After I moved to LA, I even started to think of myself as Vega. You're the only person who calls me Caro."

He hated that she'd had to forge a new identity because of Soller but he was also in awe of her being able to have done that. She was a fighter and a winner, his Caro.

"I like it. ADA Vega...dun, dun," he made the iconic Law & Order sound. "You liked being an ADA."

"I loved it. It wasn't just about putting the bad guys away; it was about getting justice for someone who died or was raped. It wasn't easy. I saw a lot of rapists walk. Victims didn't want to press charges, or juries would go to the age-old she was asking for it defense," she spoke with passion, yes, but also a calm as if this is what she was born to do. "But then I'd put some asshole away who raped a fifteen-year-old, and she'd tell me that now she could heal, now she could get past it. That made it all worth it. You know, they put me on the Soller case because of the rape element, and as my boss said, you look like his victims; that'll rattle the son of a bitch to have you take him down."

She had that faraway look, one she was getting more frequently these days when she thought about the past.

"Baby?"

She smiled, a hint of the passion he had always admired in her flickering in her gaze. "It's a part of who I am. I miss it, the challenge, the purpose. I mean, I work on fucking mergers and acquisitions and personnel nonsense at Knight Tech. Don't get me wrong, it was what I needed seven years ago when I came to LA. I desperately needed to do something else, anything else—that paid the bills."

"You know, Alejandro is good friends with the Fresno county District Attorney," Aurelio offered.

"You won't mind then?"

"Mind? Baby, whatever you want to do is fine with me. Sure, I'd like it if we could find a way to live together sooner rather than later. I can't live in LA. I can't run a farm from there."

He let it go at that. He knew it would be easier for her to live here in Golden Valley and work in LA. But her problem with moving in with him was not about her job. It was about her reluctance to commit. But he'd gotten her to say the three little words; now he just had to work on the next two little words: I do.

"I know you want me to move in with you," she said quietly.

"I do."

"My work is—"

"Don't cook something up, baby," he interrupted her, "If you wanted to live with me, we'd find a way to make it work like

Gordon has with Isadora; like Maria and Alejandro have. This isn't about your job, baby."

"I'm so sorry, Aurelio. I—"

"Baby, I told you, we'll do this at your pace. I want you to move in. I don't want to force you to move in."

She smiled at him then. "How did I get so lucky with you?"

"I think it's I who is lucky."

Their conversation shifted to more mundane subjects as they reached the crest of a hill, the farm sprawling below them.

Aurelio gestured towards it. "You see this place? It's more than just land and crops. It's a legacy, a responsibility. I've been thinking about the future too, about what it holds for this farm, for us."

Vega followed his gaze, taking in the vast beauty of the land. "It's beautiful, honey. I can see how much it means to you."

He looked at her earnestly. "And I want you to be a part of it, Caro. I know your world is in the courtroom. But maybe there's a space for you here too, in this quiet, in this peace. But I know you need time. And I'm happy to give it to you. Just stop pushing me away. Can you do that?"

Vega reached over, her hand finding his as their horses walked side by side. "I will try."

"Good."

"How come you're all in all of a sudden?" she asked. "I mean...we did the whole yes and no, and yes and no for a long time and then...you stopped saying no."

"Because I'm in love with you, and it's not all of a sudden. We've been together for over a year, Caro."

"I love you too," she said sincerely.

Aurelio felt a surge of happiness at her words. He knew he always would. He'd never taken them for granted.

"You'll have to be patient with me...we need to get through...whatever this is with the whole...." She let her words trail away.

"Okay."

"You sincerely mean that, don't you?" she asked in surprise.

"Yes, I do. Caro, baby, this is what it means to be in love—to give and take; to be there for one another no matter what storm is raging around us." He'd wanted to say *in sickness and in health*, but then she'd take off on Dakota and run all the way back to Los Angeles. She was as skittish as a newborn filly, his Caro was. He'd get her to marry him. Slow and steady.

He made her feel petty. He gave so easily while she struggled to let him in.

But he'd finally gotten her to tell him what was in her heart. And now that she had said it once, she could say it again and again. And she liked how it sounded and how it felt.

For the first time in years, she felt safe. For Vega, it was a gift.

"Baby, can you open a bottle of wine?" Aurelio called out from his porch.

He was cooking or rather grilling.

Vega didn't cook. She could toss a salad, and she could open wine. She opened his wine fridge and looked through it. He was grilling steaks, so she opened a Napa Cab. She tasted it, poured two glasses, and took them outside. It was a beautiful fall day. It had been extremely relaxing to spend it horseback riding, having a picnic in the woods, and now a dinner that her man was cooking.

"You want me to make the salad?" she asked him as she held out his glass of wine.

"Just sit and relax," he instructed, taking the glass. "I got the food."

He didn't say it, but she knew he'd wanted to go to the main house for dinner. But he also knew she wasn't ready to deal with his family one-on-one. Especially right now when she was feeling vulnerable. She felt guilty about that as well. Aurelio was close to his family. She'd not wanted to spend time with his family when she was still doing the on-again, off-again dance. But now that dance was over, and she found that it didn't scare her or make her want to run. Still, she wasn't ready for the full embrace of the Santos clan.

"The grill should be ready, and while the steaks cook, I'll take care of the salad." He kissed her gently.

It was so fucking domestic.

In LA, they ate out or ordered in—once in a while, he cooked, but it somehow didn't feel cozy like this. Here, surrounded by his farm and the mountains, it was charming, and unnerving.

"I can help," she urged.

He kissed her again. "Now, I don't want you to freak out, but my mother is going to show up. My father, as well. But he'll send her first to test the waters and then come by. They're worried about you."

Vega's back automatically straightened. They knew about Soller. Would they look at her as a weak woman who'd been raped and tortured?

"They think you're ridiculously brave, and my father told me you're very beautiful and, that according to Mateo, you are also very smart, which he thinks makes me a very lucky pendejo."

He always knew what to say, and he could read her very well. And she could read him as well. He knew it made her uneasy to deal with his mother, but she'd do it because it was important to him. This was love, wasn't it? Knowing one another and taking care of each other.

On cue, Paloma, a gorgeous petite woman wearing jeans, boots, and a sweater, waved from a distance.

"You don't want to do this; say the word," Aurelio looked at her, watching her reaction, "My mother has thick skin. She won't take offense if I ask her to leave."

Vega shook her head. "No, honey. It's fine. Why don't you go in and fix dinner, and I'll visit with your mother."

"Aurelio," his mother said as soon as she stepped onto the porch. He kissed his mother's cheek.

"Mama, I'll get you a glass of wine."

Paloma smiled at Vega and took a seat across from her. She thanked Aurelio who gave her a glass of wine and told her to behave and treat his Caro nicely before he left them alone.

Paloma was warm, charming, and genuine, like Aurelio and with her bright smile and open demeanor, had an air about her that made people feel instantly at ease.

Growing up, Vega's experience with family warmth had been truncated by her mother's untimely death and her father's subsequent remarriage. She had learned to build walls, to keep people at a distance, especially after Soller.

Paloma leaned and put a hand on Vega's. "I know you don't want to get too close to us, but we're so worried about you."

Speak of feeling petty! She felt like a complete shit. They were worried about her, and she worried about getting too close to avoid getting hurt.

It was hard to stay closed off in the presence of such open affection. "Thank you for being patient with me."

Paloma grinned and sat back, picking up her glass of wine. "You're very beautiful. And very brave. Silvano, my grandson, has a crush on you after he danced with you in Scotland at Isadora's wedding."

Vega laughed. "He's a very impressive young man." Silvano was a gifted child with a high IQ and talked about particle physics and soccer with the same ease. "And if I weren't nearly twice his age, I'd have a crush on him as well."

Paloma's laughter filled the air, light and carefree.

"How are you doing?" she asked, her eyes keen.

Vega shrugged. She found she couldn't lie to Paloma. She was so open that it almost demanded the same from her. "I'm scared."

"Oh, yes. I can't even imagine." Paloma shook her head. "I'm so sorry you had to go through what you did. But we're here for you in every and any way. Alejandro has already gotten more security here. And he has said you'll have someone with you in LA as well."

Vega gaped at her. "Excuse me? Why would Alejandro do that for me?"

"Because you're family."

She felt the first prick of tears in the back of her eyes. Family? She'd been pushing them away, and they thought of her as family. She looked up and saw Aurelio watching her as he leaned cross-armed by the doorstep of the porch.

"Mama, you're making her sad." He pulled away and crouched in front of Vega. "Hey."

Vega nodded, holding back tears.

"What did I do?" Paloma exclaimed. "Arsenio will never forgive me if I upset you. He told me I should leave you alone."

Aurelio kissed her forehead. "It's okay, Caro."

"I'm so sorry," Vega confessed. "You're all being so nice, and I feel like a complete git for keeping my distance."

"Oh, please don't," Paloma immediately said. "We're all a bit too much. Well, not me, you understand, I'm not too much. My husband, now he's just over the top."

"Papa is not over the top," Aurelio muttered, "Like anyone could top you and Isadora."

"And Isadora," Paloma added, "She's a lot too. I'm really very easy to get along with."

"Yeah, just do everything she wants and she's easy as apple pie," he quipped, still watching Vega, waiting for her to catch up with the change in tempo and let the melancholy and guilt go. He had said that his family was not into passing judgment and it looked like they didn't resent her one bit for staying away from them. They were also not going to shy away from approaching her—and if she were to reject them, they'd give her time and try again. She knew what Aurelio would say to that, "Family doesn't give up."

Vega smiled through her emotional outburst. "Are we having apple pie for dessert then?" she asked and broke the tension.

"Of course, we are," Paloma announced. "I'll ask Arsenio to pick a pie up from the Inn. Chef always makes extras."

"See," Aurelio whispered while his mother called his father, "you say you want pie, and the family will get it for you."

"I can see that."

"I love you, Caro."

Her heart felt like it would burst, it was so full. "Yeah and thank god you do."

Arsenio joined after Paloma gave him the all-clear and instructed him to bring apple pie. They had dinner together on Aurelio's porch. A simple meal of steak and a salad and apple pie, of course, with some excellent wine and good company.

Vega found herself drawn into the conversation, the words flowing more easily than she had anticipated. The evening air was balmy, carrying the scent of blooming flowers from the garden, and the soft clink of their wine glasses punctuated their conversation.

"Now, I don't want you to get upset when my Paloma starts up on when you're getting married and having children," Arsenio informed Vega.

She almost choked on her wine. "Excuse me?"

Paloma scoffed. "Now you've upset her."

"Well, you've been going on and on about Aurelio getting married and having children," Arsenio said defensively.

"You both are being greedy," Aurelio teased, "Both Isa and Maria are pregnant. I think you can wait a while for another grandchild."

Vega had never thought about children. She'd never even thought about enough stability to get married. She felt panic climb inside her. She'd just told the man she loved him, and her family wanted them hitched and her knocked up. She'd make a terrible mother. She was certain of it.

Aurelio held her hand and leaned close. "Steady. One day at a time. Okay?"

She took a deep breath and smiled uneasily.

She got more and more comfortable as first one and a second bottle of wine were emptied.

"Now, I've heard a little bit from Raya and Maria about how you and Paloma met, Arsenio. I'd love to hear the story," she requested.

She wasn't a lawyer for nothing. She steadily moved the conversation away from her and to easier topics.

Aurelio held her hand through it all, and she felt safe again, not just with him but with his whole family.

CHAPTER 17

Sunday, October 7

She lay in Aurelio's massive bathtub and let the warm water do its thing. She was exhausted, she realized.

"Hey, baby."

She opened her eyes as a naked and very aroused Aurelio slid into the bathtub. He sat across from her, his feet tangling with hers in the huge bathtub.

"Hey."

"You look supremely relaxed."

"I am. This bathtub is heaven."

"<u>You</u> have a bathtub."

"It doesn't have you in it." She crawled in the water and straddled him. He held his hands on my hips, balancing me atop him. "Aurelio."

"Yes, Caro." He moved her so she felt him between her legs.

She moved her hips so she could stroke her clit over his silky erection. Velvet over steel.

"Are you wet, Caro?" His voice was harsh, which happened when he was aroused.

"Yes," she whimpered.

He stilled her movements, lifted her, and then slowly slid into her. She gasped when he was fully seated.

She tried to move, but he stilled her. "No."

"But—"

"No," he said firmly. He brought one hand between her legs and found her clit. He stroked her, not letting her ride him until she was frustrated, sobbing with a need to release.

"Please," she begged.

"I know, baby," he whispered. "But we're going to go slow tonight. I want slow."

Would sex with him ever become monotonous? Pedestrian? She couldn't imagine a time when she'd be so used to him she wouldn't feel the way she did whenever he was around. Her heart, body, and mind were involved—attracted—impaled by him.

He pinched her clitoris, oh, so gently, and she came hard, falling apart, not able to recognize the cries coming from deep inside her.

"I need more, baby." He helped her out of the bathtub and held her back against his chest.

"Hands against the wall, Caro," he ordered and helped her do the same.

She struggled to turn to face him. She didn't like being taken from behind. "Aurelio..."

"Baby, it's going to be alright," he soothed. "I promise."

She stood stiffly, her legs wobbly after the orgasm. He stroked her back, his fingers touching the unfinished wing of the butterfly.

"Let me take you like this," he urged.

Tears pricked her eyes as she stood still. She wanted to be free of Soller and he knew that. This was just one more way in which he was trying to help set her free of her past. Why was it so hard then to give him what he wanted? What she wanted?

She took a deep breath and then leaned her hands against the wall. He pulled her hips out and stroked her ass to clit.

"You have the sexiest ass is the world, baby." He cupped her ass cheeks and stroked. He leaned so his lips were against her ear, his erection throbbing against her. "Anytime you want me to stop, you say stop."

"Okay."

"Can I take you like this, baby?"

"Yes," she whispered.

"You're so beautiful," he whispered. "I wish you could see what I see."

He adjusted her hips and slid inside her slowly and once in, he soothed again. One hand cupped a breast, played with her nipple, while another strummed her clitoris. When she began to shake, forgetting how he was taking her, he began to pump in and out of her.

It had never been like this, she thought as the world collapsed around her. But it was never the same with him, was it? His hands were punishing against her hips.

"My nipples," she gasped, "please."

"Yeah, you want me to pluck them?"

"Yes."

He cupped both her breasts and rolled her nipples between his fingers.

"Harder," she whimpered.

He plucked at them until she hurt. Pleasure and pain dissolved within each other.

"Aurelio, faster. Harder," she moaned.

He pulled out completely and then slammed inside her, hard. "Fucking hell, Caro. I love being inside you, I love fucking you."

They came together. They laughed that they needed to get clean *again* and this time fooled around in the shower.

That night, when they were nearly asleep, Aurelio murmured, "Never leave me."

"Never," she promised because she knew she'd never be able to walk away from this man and how he made her feel.

CHAPTER 18

Sunday, October 7

They were unsteady. They didn't want to wait another five days. They wanted to go get Jorja now. She worked late on Friday evenings, leaving the post office after it was deserted. They'd identified the best place to pick her up from.

A little prick of a needle to sedate her and tumble her into the van, and they were off to the races.

The unsub was restless in their art studio, tucked away in a desolate corner of Pico Union near Venice Street. The walls were plastered with everything needed to target Jorja – maps detailing her movements, her residence, and the most opportune locations for a blitz attack. The room around them was arranged with chilling precision, mirroring Jacob Soller's murder room warehouse.

Pacing restlessly, they muttered to themselves. "Come on, come on, come on. Give me the go. Give me the go."

The message from Soller on the phone's screen seemed to burn through the dimly lit art studio, casting a shadow over the meticulously arranged tools and plans. The unsub's eyes, alight with a mix of reverence and impatience, scanned the words, a semblance of calm returning to their previously restless demeanor.

Soller: I read the news. Good work.

A slight, satisfied smirk briefly crept onto their face but was quickly replaced by a frown as they typed out a reply, their fingers trembling slightly with a cocktail of eagerness and frustration.

Unsub: Ready for Jorja. Everything's set. Can I proceed?

There was a pause, a stretch of silence that seemed to expand and fill the room with palpable tension. Finally, the phone beeped again.

Soller: Prepare. Plan. Patience. Wait five more days.

He always said that the unsub thought, irritated. Prepare. Plan. Patience.

The unsub's hand clenched around the phone, a flash of anger crossing their face. It was always the same with Soller—he was always controlled, always calculating, never swayed by emotion. They wanted to scream, to argue, to demand why they had to wait, but they knew better. Soller would not bend.

Unsub: Understood.

Even though part of them yearned to rebel, they succumbed to the twisted paternalistic bond they felt with Soller. Despite chafing under his control, they craved his approval and guidance. He was more than a mentor; he was a father figure, shaping their very being.

Soller: How is Sweet Caroline doing?

Here, at least, there was glee. Sweet Caroline would get her due.

Unsub: She's spending a lot of time with the farm boy.

And then a thought struck them.

Unsub: Why don't we kill farm boy?

Soller: Stick to the plan. We'll take care of Sweet Caroline when the time comes. The farm boy is not important.

That was the last message.

In less than sixty seconds, all the messages disappeared from the messaging application they used to communicate. The unsub didn't know how Soller managed to get hold of a phone. But knowing Soller, he'd probably manipulated a guard. He was after all the master of manipulation, of getting his hands on whatever he wanted.

They were aware of being groomed and molded into Soller's image, yet part of them rebelled against this. They longed to prove that they were more than just a copycat, that they had the capability to lead and make their own decisions.

But for now, they would wait. They would follow the plan. They had to. Soller was watching, always watching, even from behind the cold prison walls. The thought both comforted and unnerved them.

As they turned back to the wall, studying the maps and photos of Jorja Levey, a mix of anticipation and resentment simmered within. They were ready to step out of the shadows to be more than just a disciple. But they couldn't deny the pull to continue to be the obedient child, thirsty for the father's approval.

CHAPTER 19

Monday, October 8

"Who leaked this?" Vega spoke calmly, though inside, she felt a rage bubble.

Gomez shook his head and shrugged. "This is LAPD, and cops are worse than a sewing circle. You know that."

"It's out in the media now. Don't you understand what this means? I'm going to have every fucking true crime podcaster and nut job at my doorstep," Vega bit out.

It began almost as soon as she got back to LA from Golden Valley. She'd convinced Aurelio to stay at the farm as Alejandro had put a bodyguard on her.

Roman Woo, an ex-military, or special forces operative of some kind, thankfully didn't dress in the stereotypical black suit of a secret service agent. Instead, he blended in like any other muscular, Chris Hemsworth-esque figure in Los Angeles, with the exception of a sidearm concealed by a specially designed jacket. Woo was not much of a talker but served as both driver and companion. He dropped her off at work, where Knight Tech's security took over, and at home, where building security was in charge.

"Am I allowed to go to a restaurant?" she'd asked him when they met in Golden Valley to go through how he'd protect her.

"Yes, ma'am."

"Vega," she corrected him.

"Yes, ma'am."

"I mean, call me Vega."

"Yes, ma'am."

"Fuck. Fine. Am I allowed to go to a restaurant?"

He didn't even smile. Just calmly, to the amusement of Aurelio, said, "You can do whatever you want to do, but I'll be there with you if you're out in public. If you don't have a problem with me sitting at your table or the one next to you, no problem."

"I guess I can't go running anymore?" Vega liked to close out four out of five work days with a run in the city. She wasn't an idiot. She'd go to the gym in her building until this was resolved, whatever *this* was.

"You can run as long as you're okay with me running next to you."

"And make me feel bad because you probably won't even be winded after three miles, would you?"

"No, ma'am."

Aurelio told her that he liked Woo, and felt better that the bodyguard would be with her at all times. He'd not accompanied her into Gomez's office but was out in the bullpen, looking very much like a cop; she realized, so he didn't seem out of place at all.

She sensed something was amiss when she received an email from Margo Jean, the host of the true crime podcast *Jean On Crime*, demanding an interview. Margo Jean had intermittently featured shows on Soller, maintaining, like some conspiracy theorists, that Soller was innocent. She added fuel to her narrative by claiming that the lack of a second trial for Vega's kidnapping was due to it being a fabricated story. The truth, however, was that Soller had pleaded guilty. But since he was already on death row, no additional sentence was imposed on him.

Granted, the conspiracy theorists were few and far between, but those who believed Soller to be innocent and that his conviction was a frame-up by Vega were loud.

Margo Jean was the loudest.

Vega had researched Margo Jean and watched her podcast on the 'Jean On Crime' YouTube channel. Jean, in her mid-thirties, was born and raised in a Houston suburb. She rose to prominence nearly a decade ago with her first true crime show, which led to the retrial and subsequent acquittal of Joel Gatta, a man serving a life sentence. Personally, Vega thought the ADA who prosecuted Gatta and the police who fixated on him for his girlfriend's murder had done a subpar job, especially considering the evidence available for Gatta's exoneration. To Vega, it was a classic case of an ADA with a god complex and cops with tunnel vision. She knew such scenarios weren't as common as TV shows suggested, but they did exist. Believing in the principle that it's better to free ten guilty men than to wrongly convict one innocent, Vega was actually pleased when Gatta was released.

But then Margo Jean walked off the deep end, zeroing in on one death row inmate after another, doing deep dives that led to nowhere.

Soller was a particular favorite of hers. She'd met Soller and co-wrote the book *The Butterfly Killer Is Still Free* with another conspiracy theory nut, a journalist, who'd been fired from the Dallas Observer for making up stories about crime in Dallas suburbs that could not be substantiated by data.

Armed with Lorna Wilson's crime scene photos (god knows how she got that), Margo had gone on the offensive with social media posts: The Butterfly Killer has moved to Los Angeles and is taunting former ADA Caroline Vega, who framed and prosecuted Jacob Soller.

"I'm so sorry, Vega," Gomez was sincerely apologetic. "But the good news is that Chief Wasco has now agreed to let us contact the FBI."

Vega shook her head. "This is all sorts of fucked up, you know that right?"

"Yeah, I do. But at least now she can't stop the serial killer angle of the story getting out."

There was a knock on the door, and Drago stepped in. He came up and hugged Vega. "I'm so sorry, sweetheart. How are you holding up?"

This hugging thing needed to stop, Vega thought. All of these people hugged. Paloma. Esme. And now Drago.

Vega stepped back and quirked an eyebrow. "I'm not holding up well. And do not tell Aurelio; he has work, and I don't want him dropping everything to be here with me."

"I met Woo outside. He seems top-of-the-line professional," Drago said instead of responding about Aurelio. She he'd tell the Santos family, he'd have to, they were his family too now.

He turned to Gomez. "Agent Delfino is ready to talk to us today. You wanna join us, Loo?"

"Yeah." Gomez sighed, running a hand through his hair. He looked at Vega. "You wanna come along?"

She stared at him, first surprised and then grateful for including her. "Yeah. Agent Delfino is a friend. I talked to him last week, and he said he'd start to look at Soller and see if he can build a profile for the copycat."

Gomez nodded soberly. "Fuckin' hell! We have one murder, and now we're waiting for a woman to go missing. I feel fuckin' helpless."

Just then, Gomez's phone rang. He answered it, listened for a moment, grunted something in the affirmative, and hung up. "Speaking of feeling helpless. That was the Chief. She wants to see us in her office."

Drago groaned. "Of course, she does. Does she want Nikki there? Because she's out interviewing Wilson's mother and sister in Riverside."

"Just you and me," Gomez said and then looked at Vega, "and you."

"Me?"

"Civilian consultant," Gomez said grimly.

They made their way to Chief Wasco's office. She greeted them coolly and motioned for them to sit. Vega and Gomez each took a visitor's chair while Drago stood, leaning against a wall.

"Thanks, Miss Vega, for working with the LAPD on this case," she began. "I didn't want to escalate this case to being a serial when we had just that one body. But now, this case has taken on a life of its own. The mayor just called and ripped me a new one. This Jean woman has them all in a tizzy about a serial killer loose in LA."

"You do have a serial killer on the loose in LA," Vega responded flatly.

Wasco shook her head. "She's creating hysteria over nothing. We don't even know for sure if these murders are connected."

"I have a quarter of a butterfly tattoo on my back, Deputy Chief," Vega kept her voice calm, but she couldn't keep the rage out, "this isn't going to become a non-issue because you don't want it to."

Monique Wasco looked Vega in the eye. "I'm sorry about what you've been through, Miss Vega, but a butterfly—"

"It's the same butterfly, Chief," Drago interrupted softly. It looked like he had a relationship with the deputy chief because she didn't blister his ass for cutting her off. "Whether we like it or not, another body is going to drop, and Vega's life is in danger."

The chief nodded. "We need to get out in front of this, which is why I'm approving the BAU to aid in this investigation. But we'll hold off on any official press statement."

Until there's another dead woman with a tattoo on her back, Vega thought.

"We have time set up with an Agent Thomas Delfino," Drago informed her. "He wrote the Jacob Soller profile. He said he has some theories about the copycat unsub that can help us."

Chief Wasco nodded. "Very well. I still have reservations about claiming we have a serial killer without stronger evidence. But given the sensitivity around your history, Miss Vega, and the media attention, it seems we have little choice."

She turned to Gomez. "Coordinate with the FBI and utilize whatever resources you need. But tread carefully; we don't want hysteria or vigilantes making matters worse."

Gomez shrugged. "It's what it is, Chief and it's gonna be what it is. We'll work the case as we would any other."

Chief Wasco turned to Vega. "I can only imagine how emotionally distressing this is for you. Are you sure you want to work with LAPD on this?"

Vega nodded. "Yeah, I do. Because if this is a copycat, I'm his ultimate trophy. I'd really like for that to not happen."

They met in the conference room to talk to the BAU agent, and Vega had to agree that LAPD had nicer facilities than Dallas PD.

The room was fitted with a big screen through which Dr. Thomas Delfino's face now appeared, larger than life. His eyes seemed to scrutinize each of them in turn, as if he could reach across the digital divide and tap into their thoughts.

"Hey, Vega," he smiled. "And you must be Detective Horvat and Wasco?"

They got the niceties out of the way and got to the profile. With the push of a button, the screen split, one side displaying Delfino's composed visage, the other flashing through slides that profiled The Butterfly Killer's copycat.

"As you can see," Dr. Delfino's voice filled the room, every syllable underscored with the urgency of their mission as the crime scene photos of Lorna Wilson filled the screen, "the attention to detail here is meticulous. There are some deviations. The unsub used rope instead of leather straps to restrain the victim. There are some changes to the butterfly tattoo though I believe that shows the unsub's unfamiliarity with the design and not an act of defiance against the original."

Nikki leaned forward, her gaze fixed on the images that Delfino was dissecting. The crime scenes were a grotesque echo of the past, a chilling homage to the Butterfly Killer's legacy.

"With a copycat, the deviations tell us as much as the similarities to the original murder," Vega interjected.

Delfino nodded, a slight smile cutting through the gravity of his features. "This unsub is not just living out a fantasy. They're communicating through their crimes, and we need to listen closely."

"And what are we hearing, Agent Delfino?" Drago leaned back on his chair.

"Demographics suggest our unsub is likely male, given historical data, but we cannot rule out a female offender. The age range is variable, typically younger than the original perpetrator, fitting the copycat pattern. This individual may have had a longstanding obsession with the Butterfly Killer, possibly idolizing or fixating on the case for some time."

Drago flipped and shuffled through some, which looked like interview statements. "Do you think the unsub is in contact with Soller?"

Drago's question lingered in the air. Dr. Delfino leaned slightly closer to the camera, his expression turning serious.

"There's a strong possibility," Delfino confirmed. "The deviations from Soller's original MO could be a form of evolution or a signature to distinguish themselves. It's not uncommon for copycats to seek some form of validation from the killers they idolize."

Nikki's pen paused over her notepad. "Validation? So, this could be a personal relationship?"

"Could very well be," Delfino continued. "The use of rope instead of leather straps indicates a personal touch, a signature that sets them apart. This unsub is carving out their identity, but they're doing it in the shadow of Soller."

Vega put her elbows on the table. "If the unsub and Soller are communicating, it's on the down fucking low. I know of Warden Johnson, and he runs a tight ship."

"That's what he told me," Drago agreed, tapping a finger against the stack of interview statements. "He said if I wanted to get transcripts of recordings and Soller's letters, I needed to go through channels."

"I can help with that." Delfino wrote something down. "Easier when it comes from the BAU. It becomes less of a jurisdictional pissing contest."

"You think the Feds don't cause jurisdictional...ah...pissing contests?" Nikki quirked an eyebrow.

Delfino grinned. "No, what I meant was that we have the bigger dicks."

"That's what they all say," Drago chuckled. He waved a hand, asking the BAU profiler to continue.

Delfino moved to the next slide. "Psychologically, we're looking at someone motivated by notoriety, control, and a desire to emulate a perceived success. They're not just replicating Soller's methods—they're seeking the same sense of power and recognition."

Nikki's voice broke the brief silence that followed. "So, they want to be seen, to be acknowledged?"

"Exactly," Dr. Delfino confirmed. "Their behavioral patterns will be their biggest tell. The victim selection will be specific, mirroring the original cases closely. Occupation, physical attributes—they'll be looking for a match to recreate the essence of those initial crimes."

"Which means that right now, he's looking for a postal worker?" Drago wondered.

"Maybe," Delfino said, "but the copycat could interpret that as a USPS or FedEx worker. Someone who works for a P.O. box. It could be someone at an Amazon drop-off location."

Drago, ever the skeptic, interjected. "It feels like we're just waiting for them to make a move."

"That unfortunately is how it looks," Dr. Delfino sighed, "In my experience, sometimes the only way to catch these unsubs is for them to kill again and hopefully make a mistake. Eddie Seda was a copycat who wanted to establish himself as a successor to the Zodiac Killer. Like the original Zodiac Killer who famously sent cryptic letters and ciphers to the police and newspapers, taunting authorities and claiming responsibility for his crimes, Sada also communicated with the police and media through letters."

Nikki nodded. "But the letters and style of communication had noticeable differences from the original."

"Seda used less sophisticated cryptograms, and like the Zodiac Killer, his spelling and grammar were atrocious but different. The Zodiac was more sophisticated while Seda was more straightforward in claiming responsibility for the shootings and also included threats of further violence," Delfino explained.

"And he got caught because of those letters. He left his fingerprints; the Zodiac was too smart to do that," Nikki finished. When both Drago and Vega stared at her, she shrugged, "I've been studying up on copycats."

Delfino grinned. "Good work, Detective Wasco. The Zodiac marked his letters with a symbol, and Seda did the same but adapted it to distinguish his own identity as a copycat. The Zodiac was more confident; Seda was seeking attention, riding on the Zodiac's coattails."

Vega read through the profile on the slide of the screen as Delfino spoke.

In essence, this could be a man or woman younger than the original perpetrator with a history of fascination with the original Butterfly Killer case, potentially displaying signs of obsession. Like Seda, this unsub was likely motivated by a desire for notoriety, power, or a twisted attempt to replicate the perceived success of the original Butterfly Killer.

"He's following the same patterns for victim selection," Drago added, "Same physical attributes and so far the same occupation.

"Yes, a copycat offender does this to replicate the essence of the crimes. So far, from the Lorna Wilson murder, it's evident that the unsub is mimicking Soller's MO closely, such as abducting victims, keeping them for the same period, tattooing a butterfly on their backs and using a garrote to kill them. These actions are likely intended to recreate the ritualistic aspect of the original crimes. And as you know, rituals are important for these types of unsubs," Delfino finished.

"And we're certain he's going to kill again?" Drago asked.

"Yes," Delfino said somberly, "In fact, the unsub has already identified their next victim and is right now stalking her."

Vega felt a chill run through her. "Erica Mercuri was Soller's second victim. She was thirty years old, blonde, slender with prominent cheekbones, just like Kristy Reed, his first. DPD identified five other unsolved murders with the same MO, but they could not pin those on Soller, and he didn't confess to them."

There had been no justice for Harriet Walter, Laura Aikman, Stella Stocker, Mary Guelff, and Nancy Wright. Vega and Detective Schwartz had suspected they were Soller's, but they couldn't prove it. Their bodies did not have butterfly tattoos; instead, he'd left dead butterflies near the bodies. There had been two years between these killings and the ones he'd been caught for. They were certain that there would be other unsolved murders that Soller was responsible for but unless he started talking they'd not know.

The BAU had determined that the first stressor that had sent Soller on his first spree had been the death of Soller's mother. At the same time, the second had come about seemingly out of nowhere until they discovered that Soller's wife had been contemplating divorce and had even talked to a divorce lawyer.

As soon as DPD had cleared Soller's wife, she'd taken her children and disappeared, probably changing her and her kids' legal identity to keep the media hounds away.

Vega had met Nora Soller several times while preparing for the trial against Soller, hoping to get more clues into Soller's psychology. She'd learned much from the pretentious woman. Soller was dominating and controlling. He was also charming and funny. She'd always thought herself fortunate to have snagged such a great catch as Jacob Soller until she found out he liked to torture, rape, and kill women in his warehouse. Appearances were important to Nora Soller, and she was more upset that the Soller reputation was ruined rather than the fact she'd been living with a killer.

"Do you think the unsub could be one of Soller's children?" Vega asked.

Delfino considered that for a long moment. "He has a daughter and a son. I'd interview both of them. Do we know where they are?"

Vega shrugged and looked at Drago who shook his head. "They seemed to have disappeared from the face of the earth."

"It's common for the families of serial killers to do that for their own personal safety. But it could also be someone who worked for Soller or knew him in passing, met him in Church or the store," Delfino concluded.

"What's next?" Vega asked the detectives after they ended the call with Agent Delfino,

"We're going to Gainesville. The more information we have, the more we have a chance to save the copycat's victim number two," Drago told her.

Vega considered that for a long moment. "Would you mind if I tagged along?" She couldn't believe she was putting herself on a collision course with Soller.

"Not at all," Nikki said when Drago shook his head in what looked a lot like despair.

"I have a problem with this," Drago muttered.

"It's the right thing to do for the case," Nikki retorted.

"She's a friend, Wasco, and—"

"And we don't have time for friendship," Vega interrupted. "I'll be in Gainesville with you guys. However, I'll be flying there, not adhering to the cop monkey class per diem or diner budget."

"Don't blame you one bit," Drago replied. "Vega, when was the last time you saw Soller?"

This tattoo is going to look so beautiful. And as soon as I get out of here, I'll come back and finish the job. So, get ready, Sweet Caroline, to become a butterfly.

Vega unnecessarily cleared her throat. "I met him in prison before I left Dallas."

"Why?" Drago asked, baffled.

"Because I wanted to prove to myself that I could—and it was cathartic to see him locked up and handcuffed...like I'd been when he had me."

Nikki whistled. "I told you, Horvat, Vega here has some big hairy cojones."

Chapter 20

Monday, October 8

By the time she got to work, she was behind on everything. She was trying to get through it all when her assistant brought her a cup of coffee and sat down across from her.

"What's up?" Vega asked as she looked at the coffee. Jada was her executive assistant and never got her coffee.

"I love true crime," she began, and Vega sighed, leaning back on her chair.

"You listen to Margo Jean?" Vega shook her head. She'd never expected the straitlaced no-nonsense Jada to be into true crime podcasts by conspiracy nutcases.

"That and the fact that Miss Jean has called here three times asking for you gave me a clue."

Vega pressed her fingers against her temples, massaging in small circles in an attempt to soothe the throbbing headache that was blossoming. "I'm assuming it's in the air supply at Knight Tech now?"

Jada shook her head. "Not yet, but it's only a matter of time. The media will pick it up: Dead Woman. Butterfly tattoo. Serial killer."

"And everyone knows I used to be an ADA in Dallas." Vega closed her eyes. She'd promised herself she'd give Aurelio some time to take care of his work. He'd told her he'd be back in LA on Thursday as they'd stand vigil, waiting for the copycat to take his next victim.

"Yes, unfortunately it's not going to take someone to be a rocket scientist to connect the dots." Jada wore a somber expression. "How are you doing, Vega?"

"Like shit," she confessed.

"What do you need?"

"I need to get this Solarix acquisition work done. Get Joey in here."

Jada nodded, understanding the urgency in Vega's voice. She stood up, but before leaving, came up to her boss and placed a comforting hand on Vega's shoulder. "I'll get Joey. Anything else?"

Vega opened her eyes, meeting Jada's gaze. "Let me know if I need to do damage control. And Jada, thank you for the coffee," she added, a hint of gratitude softening her usually stern demeanor.

As Jada left, Vega sipped the coffee, its warmth providing a brief respite from the chaos of her thoughts. Her mind was a whirlwind of legal strategies for the Solarix acquisition and the unnerving developments of the copycat case. She was no longer the hard-charging ADA chasing criminals in Dallas, but the past, it seemed, was not done with her.

Vega dialed Dec's assistant, Baker, her Southern drawl more pronounced under stress. "Hey Baker, can you check where Dec's at? I need to set aside fifteen minutes with him. Oh, and if y'all could, I'd like Mateo there too."

"Done. You okay, Vega?" Baker's concern was palpable through the phone.

She let out a weary sigh. "You know as well, huh?"

Baker's voice was tinged with amusement. "Know what?"

"Oh, for the love of God," Vega groaned, frustration seeping into her voice. "I just got word from Jada that she knew. Is the gossip just floatin' around in the ether here?"

"I know because Dec told me to bump up security at Knight Tech. Ain't no gossip...yet," Baker assured her, his tone soothing. "But the word's gonna spread sooner or later when it hits the local media. Margo Jean's been throwing your full name and where you work out there."

She was once again, fucking doxing her. Bitch! Wasn't it enough that she had been tortured and raped? Wasn't it enough that she still had nightmares? Wasn't it enough that she was still broken? Afraid she was going to drown in self-pity, Vega sat up straighter and took a cleansing breath.

"You okay?" Baker asked.

"Fuckin' A," Vega cursed, her accent thickening with her annoyance.

"You need anything else, you just holler. Okay?"

"Yeah, thanks, Baker."

"And, Vega, between us, Dec's been leaning on the PR team to try to keep your name out of the whole mess."

Vega chuckled humorlessly. "That's like tryin' to plug a hole in the ocean with your thumb."

The door opened again, and Joey entered. She was young, eager, and always ready with a spreadsheet or a legal precedent. "Hi, Vega."

Vega straightened up, pushing aside her worries. "Hey, you got an update for me?"

Joey nodded, pulling out her laptop. "Yes, ma'am."

"Ma'am?" Vega grinned.

She looked at her sheepishly. "Sorry. You know, born and raised in Georgia, sometimes it just slides out."

"I hear you. I sometimes find myself saying bless your heart. Born and raised in Dallas, and when I'm stressed, I'm all get-out Texan."

Joey laughed gruffly. "I had to stop saying bless your heart. I sound like my mother, and that was just creepy."

Vega nodded. There were times when she'd also feel that way, but it didn't creep her out, maybe because her mother was dead—it made her remember her fondly.

Joey's fingers flew on her keyboard. "Okay, back to business. I've already started modeling some scenarios based on their recent financials. But there's a hitch in their patent portfolio that could cause some problems."

Vega listened, focusing on the details. The work was a welcome distraction, a world away from the grim realities of serial killers and media frenzy.

"You look tired," Joey mentioned after they were done and had identified next steps. "Are you okay?"

"It's just a busy time," Vega mumbled.

Joey cleared her throat. "Ah…I know about…you know."

"Know about what?" she snapped and immediately regretted it.

Soller was succeeding in pushing her buttons. He'd made her leave a career she loved, and now he was taking her hard-won composure.

Joey closed her laptop.

Vega sighed and raised her hand to stop Joey from leaving. "I'm sorry. It's just…yeah, it's stressful."

"I can only imagine," Joey drawled sincerely. "I obviously don't have all the details, but what I know is grim."

"What exactly do you know?"

She didn't have the energy or desire to listen to Margo Jean's mouth off on her podcast and go on about how Soller was a frame-up job. The real Butterfly Killer was still out there, and this new murder in Los Angeles was proof of that.

Joey looked uncomfortable, but her eyes glinted. Hell, everyone liked to gossip, and this was juicier than a summer peach.

"Just that there is a murderer in LA that has the same MO as the Butterfly Killer, who you put away in Texas. And...there was mention about how you'd been taken by the killer and...." She trailed off, unable to finish her words.

And were raped, tortured, and nearly murdered.

Vega nodded. "Thanks, Joey. I know this must make you and probably other staff uncomfortable as hell, and I'm—"

"No," she protested and grabbed Vega's hand tightly. "We're worried about you. We care about you. I mean...this is awfully bad stuff, Vega. No one should have to go through somethin' like this."

Everyone would ask questions, Vega realized. Sooner than later, it would be all over the news, and her life would become what it had been right after she'd been rescued. Media hounding. Photographers wanted to take pictures. Detective Wyatt Taze, who'd led the task force to find her, had done what he could to keep it all buttoned down, but the DPD was no better than the LAPD when it came to cops. And they gossiped like fuckin' debutantes at the Cotillion.

What had intrigued everyone was that Soller had been tattooing her when she'd been rescued. Media wanted photographs and thankfully none of those ever made it out of DPD files.

Whenever she thought about it, her back itched in the shape of a butterfly wing.

Soller had been so busy with her transformation, as he called it, that he hadn't noticed what she had, even in her beaten near semi-conscious state. A perimeter of Soller's location had been breached. She'd been sure she'd die as soon as Soller realized that the SWAT team had arrived. And he had tried. He'd grabbed a knife and put it to her throat as the team burst into his new murder room.

Detective Taze had not hesitated or played chicken with Soller; he'd simply drilled a bullet in Soller's shoulder, his knife clattering to the floor. She owed Wyatt Taze more than she could repay. He'd been the one who'd covered her up; he'd been the one who'd removed her restraints, swathed her in a blanket, and carried her out to freedom and light while the rest of his team secured the scene and arrested Soller.

He'd taken her to a private room in a hospital, never leaving her side.

The doctor had insisted on a rape kit, and she'd clearly told them that she had been violated by objects but not Soller.

The doctor didn't believe her when she said that and condescendingly told her that it was okay to not be ashamed.

"He gets off on fear," Vega had told the doctor coolly, "I didn't give him that. Hard to rape, pun intended, when your dick won't cooperate. In any case, do what you have to do. I don't need to convince you of shit."

Before the doctor could speak, Taze had interjected, "I want you out of here."

The doctor, a woman in her late thirties, gasped. "Excuse me."

"You judge," he held his hand up when she was about to say something, "with your attitude and your words. You don't deserve to take care of her. It's a fucking' privilege to care for the woman who brought Jacob Soller down. So, get the fuck out and send someone else in who is better than you."

The doctor left quietly, feeling ashamed, and the new doctor and nurse team that came in were more circumspect. Kinder.

Taze had started his career in Vice, so, he knew all about rape victims and how judged they felt when being questioned by both law enforcement and medical personnel.

After they bandaged her wounds and declared that all her injuries were, in the large scheme of events, minor...at least the physical ones, Taze had said as he held her hand, "You're the bravest fuckin' person I've ever met, and I served in Afghanistan. You do what you need to do: take care of yourself. You owe no one no fuckin' explanation. Got it?"

They'd remained in touch after she left Dallas. She'd texted him earlier in the day to tell him she was going to see Soller and that she was working as a civilian consultant with the LAPD. He'd simply replied: I'll take you to him. Let me know when you're here.

Vega snapped out of the past and saw how Joey's eyes looked at her with pity. Fuck her, she thought unfairly. She'd lived through the worst humanity had to offer, she didn't need someone to look at her like she was some weakling.

"Don't look at me like that," she told her, "I'm not someone to be pitied."

Joey smiled. "I know. You're someone to be admired."

"Querida." Mateo kissed Vega on her cheek as he sat down next to her across from Dec in his office. Dec immediately pulled out a bottle of Macallan 24. He held it up, and both Vega and Mateo nodded.

Yeah! Vega thought it's been a long fuckin' day!

"Salud," they all said and clinked their glasses.

"I have bad news and super bad news," Dec announced.

He was a good-looking man, and since he'd married Esme, he'd, for some reason, gotten better looking, objectively speaking. He used to be severe in many ways. Dressed in serious, expensive suits. Clean shaved, hair coiffed at some expensive salon, and all about making money. Now, he wore jeans to work. He was growing a beard. His hair was longer than it normally was. But most importantly, he was less and less involved with Knight Technologies, handing over the reins to Mateo and others on his leadership team while he worked with his father, Gerald, with the Knight Foundation, focusing on building and funding shelters for vulnerable women, and youth who were aging out of the system.

Mateo had also become less of a corporate asshole since he'd married Raya. He took more vacations and was building a home in Golden Valley on the Santos estate. His plan was to work remotely, but Vega knew him, and she had a feeling he was going to quit Knight Technologies and do something else.

At one point, she'd wondered how much money is enough money for men like Declan who had family money as well as what he'd made with Knight Technologies—and Mateo had done very well himself. Now she knew. These men had fallen in love and now were focused on doing good things rather than just growing the business.

"Start with the bad news," Vega urged.

"Local TV is going to run a story about Soller and the connection to Drago's case."

"Lorna Wilson," Vega mused.

Mateo took a sip of whiskey. "And what's the super bad news?"

"They're going to reveal your connection to Soller and Knight Tech. We couldn't stop it. Their angle is that Jean already outed you on her podcast."

"Fucking hell," Mateo muttered.

"Is my home address out?"

"No," Dec assured her. "We managed to make sure of that. I spoke with your bodyguard, and we've come up with a protocol, which will mean that even if someone follows you, they won't know where you live."

Vega closed her eyes and shook her head. She then opened her eyes and smiled. She knew what she had to do. "Gentlemen," she raised her glass, "I think I have to take a leave of absence, which may have to morph into—"

"Come on, you're not quitting because of this, are you?" Dec was shocked.

Vega shook her head. "Not in the way you're thinking. I think I'm going to go back into law enforcement. Aurelio said the Santos family is good friends with the Fresno County District Attorney."

Mateo put a hand on her shoulder. "Querida, you sure about this?"

"Yeah." She looked at Dec. "I'm not leaving right away. I'll finish the Solarix acquisition."

"I don't give a shit...I mean, I do, but if you need time off, take time off, put your feet up, you've fucking earned it," Dec remarked. "You have your junior counsel, and we'll work with her."

"I'm not taking time off...not like you think. I'm going to Dallas."

"Why?" Mateo asked.

"I'm going to see Soller. I'm going to help the LAPD *and* myself find this copycat unsub."

I'm going to claim my life again, and I'm going to let the past go.

Her announcement left both Mateo and Dec shocked. They were quiet for a long moment and then Mateo broke the silence, "How can we help you?"

She smiled. She'd known that she had friends, people who cared about her, regardless of how many walls she put up. But this was the first time she understood what that really meant. They would stand with her and by her, no questions asked.

"Would you like us to come along with you? Or am I correct to assume Aurelio is probably not going to let you go alone?" Dec mused.

"Aurelio doesn't know...yet," Vega sighed. "He's here on Thursday and I think I might have to have this conversation face-to-face with him."

"When are you planning to go?" Mateo wanted to know.

"As soon as LAPD gets clear from TDCJ... that's the Texas Department of Criminal Justice. Soller is on death row—it takes a minute to get clearance to see him. Drago and his partner will be there as well, so it's not like I'm going alone."

Dec drank some whiskey. "Don't take this the wrong way, Vega. But do you want to put yourself through this because you feel guilty about this woman being killed?" he asked softly.

"Not guilty...responsible in some way to find justice for her. And the sooner we catch this unsub, the fewer victims we will have," Vega said sincerely.

And maybe I'll be able to even save my own life.

She waited for more questions, but Dec changed the conversation by winking at her. "You're a city girl. You sure you'll survive in Central Valley?"

"I've always lived in cities, and I love it...like you." Dec and Esme were absolute city people. "But like you," she turned to

Mateo, "I think I'm ready to see how I'll fare in Golden Valley. This past weekend, it was beautiful. We went horseback riding, and there was something about waking up to wide open spaces."

"Yeah, and those views are something else," Mateo agreed.

"Esme and I are losing all our friends to fucking Golden Valley," Dec scowled.

"We'll come visit," Vega offered, "so keep your guestroom available. I'm going to need a city fix every so often."

CHAPTER 21

Tuesday, October 9

Aurelio told Vega that he was coming earlier than planned when the shit hit the fan and national media picked up the local media story about the sensational Butterfly Killer coming back to life.

The conspiracy theories about how Soller deserved a new trial and that he'd been framed were back on podcasts, chatrooms, and websites.

Vega had told him not to do that because she could handle it. Roman Woo, her bodyguard, had confirmed that Vega was either barricaded in her house or the office. Once in a while, she went to LAPD HQ. When Aurelio had pushed, Woo had admitted that she wasn't doing well and that Vega was holding on so tight she could snap, but he also thought she was doing way better than most people in her situation would.

"It's a clusterfuck," Woo told Aurelio on their daily phone call, "we actually have fuckin' paparazzi waiting for her Knight Tech. We've been using side entrances, so they haven't gotten a money shot, but it's a matter of time before they start sending drones up to get a snap of her. At least, for now, they don't where she lives and we're hoping to keep it that way."

"I'll be there soon," Aurelio announced.

There had been silence on the phone line for a moment, and then Woo said, "And what the fuck do you think you're gonna do?"

Aurelio chuckled. "I'll hold her hand and let her hold mine."

"Right," Woo obviously didn't think that was going to help anyone.

He noticed immediately that she was restless and spent all her time in her office while Aurelio took over her dining table for work.

When Aurelio came into her office, he'd been shocked. He paused at the doorway, taking in the sight of her murder board. It was a meticulous and chilling display of Soller's past crimes, complete with timelines, victim profiles, and crime scene photos. The level of detail was both impressive and haunting. It was clear Vega had immersed herself in the case, perhaps more deeply than was good for her.

He walked over to her, noticing the dark circles under her eyes and the way her hands trembled slightly as she pinned another photo to the board. "Hey," he said softly, placing a gentle hand on her shoulder.

Vega turned to him, her eyes weary yet burning with a fierce determination. "Hi," she replied, attempting a smile that didn't quite reach her eyes.

"You've been at this for hours," Aurelio's voice was laced with concern. "You need to take a break, Caro."

"I can't," she shook her head. "Every minute I spend not working on this is another minute he's out there, planning his next move. I need to find a pattern, something we missed. Anything."

This was how she'd worked cases in Dallas, he thought. This was how she would work in the future. If he wanted to be part of her life, he had to respect that. He still wanted her to take a break, but he knew arguing wouldn't help; Vega was too deep into her investigation mode. Instead, he said, "Let me help, then. Tell me what you're looking for. Walk me through this."

Vega hesitated. "You want to hear about the gory details of a serial killer's repertoire?"

He sat down on an office chair and swiveled to face her murder board. "Two heads better than one and all that." And talking to him, he hoped would reduce the burden on hers to carry all this alone. If she felt she could talk to him about the darkness, then in the future she'd be more open.

"I'm tougher than I look, babe," he teased.

She smiled uneasily. "I know. *But* you don't have to listen to this ugliness."

"Neither do you."

She shook her head. "I do, Aurelio. It may save another life if I do."

"Yeah, and I'm with you so let me help you save that life." *And hopefully yours as well, baby, because all this is fucking scary.*

As if making a decision she stood by the board, facing Aurelio.

"Soller's process for the four victims was he'd go on the offensive on Friday night. He'd take them to his warehouse."

Aurelio leaned back. "They found the first dead body on Figueroa. Are there any warehouses there?"

"Not that part of Fig," Vega stated, she worked her computer to pull up a map of Downtown Los Angeles on her wall screen. "But further down towards fiftieth street or so, sure, it gets pretty shady. Then we have Pico Union with all its warehouses and studios, boarded up buildings. Lots of spaces and places to build a murder room and no one will ever know."

"Anything that could identify which one of these buildings this asshole might be using based on what Soller used to do?"

"Soller soundproofed his warehouse. But this is LA, we have studios everywhere that are soundproofed."

"How did you catch him in the first place?" Aurelio asked.

"Not me. Detective Schwartz did. The profile told him that he was looking for a respected member of society who worked all week. This threw us off because retail is open on the weekends, so he never came up in the electronic searches."

Vega came closer to him and leaned a hip against her desk. "But we caught a break. Someone remembered the van and the logo of a soccer ball. Do you want to know the weird thing? The witness actually saw the van some other time but once Schwartz met Soller, he liked him for it. But he had no probable cause to do a search. He came to me, and we started to look into Soller. I worried that we'd have another victim and that we'd be too late. We didn't have the manpower to watch him twenty-four seven."

She pulled away from the desk and walked back to her wall of photos, her back to Aurelio. "But we got lucky again. We found that he was buying tattoo ink and had recently bought a new tattoo gun. And we got luckier when a judge gave us a warrant to search Soller's house, store, and warehouses. We started with the warehouse because Schwartz and I knew that's where he'd have the space to do what he did. Crime scene found so much evidence that it was a slam dunk. But Soller is a narcissist, so he wanted a trial."

Aurelio walked to her and pulled her back against his chest. "He took the stand?"

"Yes," Vega confirmed. "And after they said he was guilty, he told me I was his type. Once he was sentenced to death, they moved him, and that's when he escaped."

She shuddered.

"He took me on a Friday night from the parking lot of a Seven-Eleven. You read the rest."

Aurelio nuzzled her hair. "I love you."

"Yes, I know." He felt her smile and relax into him. "If this unsub...if he gets me again...I—"

"But he's not. You're prepared this time. You have a bodyguard, and you're hypervigilant. We all are."

"I know he's going to take someone this Friday. I hate that there isn't anything we can do to stop him. I mean...what can we do? Tell the city to stay home?"

"How do you feel about going away for the weekend? We can go to Los Olivos, hit tasting rooms and—"

"I can't," she whispered. "I can't distract myself while a woman is being hurt. It...I just can't."

"Okay."

He heard the pain in her voice, the unspoken trauma that these images and words evoked even though she'd spoken with the detachment of an ADA. But there was also a strength, a resilience that he admired more than he could express.

Her phone rang, and Aurelio saw the call was from Drago. She put him on speaker and told him he was with her.

"TDCJ has given us the go for this Friday."

Vega took a deep breath. "They can't hurry it up? Friday is...well, you know what Friday is."

"Yeah. But Soller is on death row. And his lawyer has been kicking up a fuss. They can't rush it."

"Dec said his plane is at our service," Vega told him.

"Nice. But we can't use his plane for official business," he chuckled. "Why don't you take him up on his offer, and we'll fly commercial. I'll send you details by email."

She looked at Aurelio, a silent question in her eyes after Drago hung up.

"We'll go together," Aurelio assured her. "I'm with you in this every step of the way."

"I don't know, honey, Gainesville is nothing like Los Olivos, not a wine tasting room in sight," Vega tried to joke.

CHAPTER 22

Wednesday, October 10

It had been a long day for Drago. He and Nikki were called in when the partially dismembered remains of a woman were discovered in a trash bin in Los Angeles and Spring. They'd spent the day interviewing their prime suspect, Patrick Gillespie, who, before the end of the day, had been charged with three counts of murder. Gillespie was accused of murdering his wife, Casey Gillespie, and her parents, who were visiting from Minneapolis, John, and Olivia Grant.

Talk about not liking your in-laws!

Usually, he'd dump the paperwork on the junior partner, but Nikki had been flagging, so he sent her to get a drink at Chatterbox Bar on Broadway and completed the Case Closure report. It took him a good hour to get an update on the primary case document that summarized the entire investigation. It included details about the crime, the investigation process, the evidence collected, arrests made, and the final outcome (such as an indictment, conviction, acquittal, or case dismissal).

He slid on a barstool next to Nikki and was concerned because she looked so forlorn.

"Howdy, pardner?" Drago went for a terrible Texan accent.

She looked at him and nodded. "Thanks for taking care of all the paperwork—"

"Don't worry about it. Trust me, you'll be finishing those off on your own soon enough."

Before Nikki could respond, the bartender hollered from the other end of the bar, "The usual, Horvat?"

"Yeah, thanks, man."

It took the bartender a few minutes to slide a cold bottle of beer towards Drago. He caught it and popped the cap off with his keychain and a practiced flick of his wrist. He took a swig, his eyes briefly meeting Nikki's.

She smirked as she sipped her vodka tonic. "What's the word on the street, Detective Horvat?"

"TDCJ gave us the green light to meet Soller on Friday," Drago replied, his gaze lingering on her.

"Damn! Isn't that the day when the unsub's going to take the next victim since we have no way of stopping it?" Her gray eyes were weary. "I read through Soller's victimology, and that man is scum. And now, we have another piece of scum wanting to emulate him."

"Your first case, and it's a serial," Drago murmured. "It's going to fuck with your head." And a very pretty head it was, Drago acknowledged. He liked her. She was way different from his previous partner, who was overweight, balding, and had a Marlboro red pack-a-day habit.

"I'm surprised Gomez hasn't pulled me off it." She downed her drink and waved to the bartender.

"I'm primary," Drago smirked, "And he ain't pulling me. We have Martinez and Lee helping us out. Trust me, if another body drops, we'll have more people up our ass helping with the case, and we need it. But you and I, we'll be the officers on record."

The bartender put a fresh vodka tonic in front of her and took her empty glass away. Nikki absently thanked the bartender for her drink.

"Where do you live, Wasco?"

"Echo Park. Don't worry, I'm gonna take an Uber. I already decided when I came here."

"I'll drive you home," Drago offered. "What's bothering you?"

She shook her head. "I'm excited about meeting Soller. I'm curious about interviewing a serial killer. Does that make me a sick person?"

"No, curiosity makes you a good cop."

"Every time I talk to Vega, I want to ask her five hundred questions," she continued like Drago hadn't spoken. "And she answers, you know, all the shitty stuff that she had to go through. Makes me feel like an insensitive fucking bitch."

"I repeat, curiosity makes you a good cop. You can't worry about being sensitive working a case. You have to get the information you need." He patted her shoulder. "I asked FOD to book our travel to Dallas. We can prep tomorrow with Vega."

The money hawks at FOD, the Fiscal Operations Division, which was part of the department's Administrative Services Bureau and was responsible for managing travel bookings and handling associated expenses. They were also the ones who were up your ass if they saw any violations of departmental travel policies and guidelines. You expense more than your per diem by five cents and FOD would nail your ass to the wall.

Nikki traced the edge of her glass with a forefinger. "You know, my friends, some are still on patrol; they're all so jealous that I have this high-profile case. And I don't see it like that. I see Lorna Wilson, who was raped and tortured, and I...."

She looked so sad that he wanted to give her a hug. He wasn't into damsels in distress. He liked his woman to be smart, sharp, and confident. Nikki was all those things, but then there was this pesky vulnerability, which should make her less appealing, but it made her more attractive. Fuck! He was turning into a cliché. Give a cop a good-looking partner and he wanted to get in her pants.

"Let's not talk shop," he suggested. "How's life outside the badge for Deputy Chief Wasco's daughter?"

Nikki rolled her eyes. "Really?"

"Yeah," he urged. "I like Chief Wasco."

"You've worked with her?"

Drago nodded. "Yeah, when she headed Vice. She's tough but fair. And she has a good sense of humor and has good taste in scotch."

"So, you're a smoky whiskey fan?"

"Yeah." She was smiling, he thought, which pleased him. "Working with her is one thing, how was it growing up with her?"

"Life was...*is* interesting. My father is an entertainment lawyer, but he used to be a Public Defender, that's how they met, she was on patrol, and he was trying to get scum back on the street. Then he decided he wanted to make some money and left law enforcement. I had a great childhood. My father was pretty pissed off when I said I wanted to be a cop. But my brother redeemed himself. He's studying law at UC Berkley, though once he tells Dad that he wants to work for the ACLU and make no money, I don't know how great he'll feel. How about you?"

Drago took a pull of his beer. "I was born in Prague, and we moved here in the nineties when Czechoslovakia became two countries. I was nine, and my younger brother was five. My father is a physicist, and he teaches at Purdue. My mother was an analyst for an insurance company. She's retired. I don't think he ever will."

"How did you end up in LA?"

"I got into UCLA, and then I never left," Drago explained.

"What's your brother doing?"

"He's doing his PhD in psychology."

"Talk about an accomplished family," Nikki mused, "You the black sheep?"

Drago grinned. "Yeah, but I'm Mama's favorite son. So, Jozef can go stick his doctorate degree where the sun doesn't shine."

"Why are you her favorite?"

"Because I buy her flowers on Mother's Day and gift her trips to Paris, her favorite city. He forgets and I don't help him remember," Drago chuckled.

She smiled and nodded. "My mom is great, but I feel like I have to keep trying to step out of her shadow and create my own path, you know?"

"Why? You're here on your own merit; trust me, I checked up on you, so I know. You have a great record, and I know your instincts are sharp. Plus, you're curious as hell."

"Yeah?" Nikki hesitated, her expression softening. "You know you have a reputation?"

Drago quirked an eyebrow.

"That you're no-nonsense, damn good at what you do...and a bit of a lady's man."

"I think the term that I've heard used is man whore."

"I'd never slut shame you for...ah...."

"Sleeping around?"

She raised a hand, flushed, suddenly aware she'd led them into a more intimate conversation than she'd intended. But she was probably on her third drink, and her tongue was loosened. "It's none of my business. Hey, I get the whole dodging relationship business."

A hint of a smile played on his lips. "Who says I'm dodging?"

"Oh, please." Nikki grimaced. "Next thing you're going to say is that you just haven't met the right woman."

"That's actually true."

"And I heard that you don't date cops," she blurted out, and he saw the surprise on her face that she'd said what she had.

"Cops are a poor bet." He was only half joking. Cops *were* a lousy bet. They kept shitty hours, got paid peanuts and they were in harm's way every day. "Also, you sleep with someone in the bullpen, you got to tell Loo and then the nosey fuckers in Personnel. You date any cops?"

She shrugged. "It happens. When you work the hours we do, where else would we meet people?"

"But you're single now?" Shut up, he told himself. Stop talking about dating with this woman.

"Yeah." She licked her lips. "Ah...I should go home."

Drago downed his drink. "I'll give you a ride."

She bit her bottom lip, and he almost groaned. Fucking hell, was she doing it on purpose? "Maybe I should take an Uber."

All playfulness left him, and his demeanor shifted to serious. "Nikki, we're partners, and that's how it's going to be."

"What does that mean?" "I'm not going to fuck you. I'm just going to give you a ride home."

She blushed, and he was charmed. Why did she have to be his partner? Gomez should've given her to Martinez...no, Lee.

Martinez was too fucking handsome, and he slept with cops. Lee was in his late forties and happily married.

"I feel foolish."

"Don't," he immediately said. "I've been down that road as well. And it's not that I don't want to..."

"Fuck me?" she whispered and the blood in his brain vacated and went down south. She smiled then and he realized she was teasing him.

But two could play this game. "Yeah. I do want to fuck you. But it's not gonna happen between us. The partnership, though, I think, is going to be one for the history books. Now, let me give you a ride home."

CHAPTER 23

Wednesday, October 10

The unsub reveled in glee at the sight of Sweet Caroline accompanied by a bodyguard, finding immense satisfaction in seeing her squirm under pressure. When Soller had instructed the unsub to head to Los Angeles and make contact with Caroline, they had felt a pang of jealousy. Soller's obsession with Caroline stirred feelings of anger and unease in them. They had devoted their life to Soller, yet his fixation was on that detestable woman. Dressed in her prim suits and known by the masculine name 'Vega,' they despised her. Their resentment deepened because Soller hadn't killed her, and even more so because he continued to think about her every day.

He loves her more than he loves me!

The rage the unsub felt was taking over their life. They'd wanted to shove Caroline in front of ongoing traffic. There had been one time when she was running that they could have, so easily, and boom, it would be over. They could all move on, right? But no, Soller wanted, no needed to finish her metamorphosis.

Oh, fuck that, the unsub thought as they watched Jorja walk out of the Golden Gopher on 8th Street. It wasn't her usual haunt, but a colleague had dragged her there. She had enjoyed herself, the unsub noted, and they were graciously allowing it. Everyone should have fun on the last night of their lives.

The unsub had decided to not follow Soller's rule of picking up the caterpillar on a Friday night. Geez! The man was such a stickler for ritual, and the unsub wanted their own ritual, their own signature.

They'd parked their van on an alley off of Wall Street. Quiet, desolate...so fucking desolate that even the homeless didn't go there. They waited for Jorja as she walked in her high heels, stupid cunt, wearing heels in the city, wanting to show off her legs. This was the problem with divorced women: they only wanted to get laid—they didn't realize that their man left them in the first place because they were not good enough, they weren't right enough, and they were not transformed.

Well, no worries, Jorja, I have a song for you, sweet and clear...la, la, la...moonlight through the pines, the unsub hummed beneath their breath.

I have Jorja on my mind!

The unsub's mind churned with a toxic blend of jealousy, rage, and warped excitement as they watched Jorja's unsuspecting form navigate the streets. Her cheer and lightness of the evening contrasted sharply with the darkness waiting in the wings. The unsub smiled, a chilling grin devoid of any genuine joy. They loved the idea of their prey enjoying her last moments of freedom, unaware of the fate that awaited her.

Their plan deviated from Soller's meticulously crafted ritual. They craved their own identity, their unique mark on this twisted game. The idea of injecting Jorja with a paralytic agent thrilled them. It was innovative, a personal touch that Soller hadn't thought of. He still used chloroform. Talk about being old fashioned.

In their mind, it was a stroke of genius, an improvement on the old ways. And wasn't that what the new generation was supposed to do? Bring innovative ideas to the table. And that's what they were doing.

As she passed the alley, the unsub sprang into action, moving with a predator's grace. In one swift, practiced move, they injected Jorja with a paralytic agent. She barely had time to register shock before her body succumbed to the drug's effects. Her ability to move or scream was stripped away, leaving her conscious but utterly powerless.

The unsub dragged her limp body to the van, a sense of triumph coursing through their veins. They were about to embark on their own unique brand of transformation, one that would make their mark on this city and send a clear, terrifying message to Caroline Vega. And to Soller that they had come into their own.

As they drove away, the streets of Los Angeles continued their nightly rhythm, oblivious. The unsub hummed their tune, a lullaby to the chaos they were about to unleash, their thoughts fixated on the transformation of Jorja Levey and the ultimate prize that awaited them, Caroline Vega.

CHAPTER 24

Thursday, October 11

Drago called Thursday morning.

They were supposed to leave that night for Dallas, where they'd stay the night, and drive to Gainesville on Friday morning, bright and early, to meet one of the most vicious serial killers in the history of Texas.

"We caught a case, Vega, so we won't be joining you in Gainesville. I talked to Gomez, and he's fine with you going alone with DPD, obviously."

Vega's heart hammered. "What happened?"

"We have a body."

"What? Already?"

"We think it's the same offender. It's a US postal worker. Jorja Levey. Thirty. Divorced."

Vega went through the notes in her mind. "Erica Mercuri was thirty. Divorced."

Should she have talked to the media and told all women who were in their thirties, divorced, and working for any kind of postal service to be more careful. Yeah, that wouldn't create a city-wide panic, she thought dryly.

"There was no rape. Some signs of torture, similar to what we saw on Lorna Wilson," he continued. "The ME is looking at her, and we're still waiting for the tox screen results."

"Drago, when was she taken? How long did the unsub have—"

"We believe she was taken last night."

"That's not enough time. And Soller would not take someone on a Wednesday night."

She heard his long sigh. "It could be a copycat of the copycat. We don't know. She does have a tattoo."

"But that's not enough time to go through the whole ritual, and Soller was strict about his procedure." Vega mouthed a thank you to Aurelio, who handed her a cup of coffee.

"The tattoo is not of a butterfly. Only a message."

"Sweet Caroline, are you ready to become a butterfly?" She took a sip of her coffee and looked out of her tall windows in downtown LA and beyond.

"Yeah."

"You've got to talk to Agent Delfino."

"Yeah, I already booked time with him for later today. The ME believes that Levey was given some kind of paralytic agent, and she had an adverse reaction to it. And Dr. Chen hates fucking surmising, so we have to wait until she has more data. We just don't have anything definitive. Nikki and I need to work this case. There's an ex-husband and a bad divorce. He might've decided to off her."

Thanks to the fact that everyone knew about the message on Lorna Wilson's body, there was no way of clearly knowing if this was the original unsub or someone else.

"Fuck Margo Jean for letting the world know about that message." Vega felt like she was choking. Like Soller's hands were around her throat as he drove to her unconsciousness before bringing her back to consciousness by using ammonium carbonate, colloquially smelling salts.

"Yeah. And thanks to that we don't know whether this is our unsub or someone else trying to pin this on the unsub. I'm sorry, Vega."

"That's okay," she managed to say and then chuckled, "now I regret booking commercial."

"ME is doing a rush, it's all hands on deck, and we're talking to Delfino at two in the afternoon, Pacific Time. You're welcome to come down to HQ."

Vega looked at her watch and sighed. She had a whole day planned, packed with meetings. She had to work on finalizing the Solarix contract with Joey and then present it to Mateo and Dec. Now, Joey would have to make the presentation on her own, which Vega didn't think she was ready for. No one else on her team knew about the Solarix project, so she couldn't send someone with Joey.

"When are you meeting Chen?" Vega asked, making her decision. Solarix was money; her unpaid consulting gig with the LAPD was people's lives.

"She said she'd have something by eleven."

"Where did you find the body?"

"That's the other deviation. It was in an alley off of Venice by a trash can."

"Soller always posed his victims, the back showcased on rooftops of abandoned buildings."

"Yeah."

"So, you can probably get some CCTV footage, right?"

"The guys are looking at it," Drago seemed like he was in a hurry, "I got to go, Vega; they just brought one of the victim's colleagues in. I'll see you around eleven, yeah?"

Vega hung up and looked at Aurelio, who was patiently waiting for her to finish her call and tell him what had happened. She liked this about him. If it was her, she'd be interrupting the call to know what was going on. She didn't have his kind of patience.

"They found another body," she told him, feeling a little sick. If this was a copycat of the fucking copycat, it didn't change the fact that her name was on yet another dead person.

Aurelio nodded; having picked up that much already, she mused from listening to her side of the conversation with Drago. She quickly gave him all the information he had.

"What do you think?" he asked.

She gnawed on her lower lip. "I don't know what to think. It could be a cruel joke on me to have some asshole think he can kill someone and try to pawn it off on Soller's copycat. Or the unsub is devolving, taking chances, changing rituals, so we can't predict his movements."

"I noticed something. When Drago talks about this copycat, he says unsub, and they; you say he."

Vega blinked. "I...yeah, I think it's a man. Eighty-five percent of all serial killers are, after all, male. And Soller was male. Why?"

Aurelio shrugged. "All I know about any of this stuff is from watching episodes of Law & Order or Criminal Minds, and considering how much television I don't watch, that's very little information for me to go by. In all honesty, saying things like unsub feels fucking surreal."

He took her coffee cup and set it on the kitchen counter. And pulled her into a hug. She rested her head against his chest. "I'm so sorry, baby."

"Me too," she whispered and then looked up at him, "for dragging you into this ugliness."

He kissed her forehead. "You're not dragging me; the unsub is. We're a team, baby, and I'm with you all the way."

Jamie, her ex-fiancé, had been young, her age when it had happened. She'd been twenty-six years old when Soller took her. Up and coming, brass balls ADA Vega.

Aurelio was thirty-eight years old. He was a grown-up. He was self-aware, sincere, and doing what he wanted to do, not what was expected of him. She had to learn to trust him. When he said he was with her, she had to believe him and not let the fears of a boy from a previous life cloud this relationship.

"I know, honey," she replied. "And I'm so grateful."

"No gratitude needed. Not between family."

Her eyes filled with tears.

"Baby." He kissed her nose. "No crying."

"I'm just so fuckin' emotional. I don't know what's wrong with me." She rested her forehead on his chest. "I hate this. I hate that Soller is still controlling my life. It's like he's still got me strapped to that fuckin' metal gurney of his."

He hugged her harder.

He didn't offer stupid platitudes like "it's going to be okay" because that didn't matter. How she felt now had nothing to do with how this would turn out in the future. He understood that she had to, after all, live through today to get to tomorrow.

She dropped by the office and could do nothing about Aurelio coming with her and sitting at her office with his laptop. The other meeting rooms were fully booked, so she'd agreed to let him work from her conference table.

She realized she didn't mind having him here. She liked it, in fact. There was a coziness to it, which obviously meant she was losing her ever lovin' mind. She was Caroline Vega; she didn't do fuckin' cozy. The man had completely unraveled her.

Joey looked perplexed when she came into her office to find Aurelio at the far end of the conference table. They usually would meet at the conference table so they could view documents on the wall monitor.

"Let's just take it at my desk," Vega told Joey, who flushed when Aurelio waved to her. He had that effect, Vega agreed, making every nubile woman around him aware of him.

He looked good in his chambray shirt and worn jeans, and she didn't blame Joey for eye fucking him. She had to restrain herself from saying, "Honey, you should see him with his clothes off, and then you'll really cream your panties."

Vega explained to Joey that she would need to take the lead and present at the meeting later in the day to Mateo and Dec.

"Alone?" she asked flustered, Aurelio obviously completely forgotten as panic set in.

"Yes."

"But...ah...I thought you were taking tomorrow off and not today? Maybe we can move the meeting to next week and—" Her voice was hoarser than usual, making her sound more masculine.

"It's going to be fine, Joey," Vega cut in. "You know this project inside out. And I'll be a phone call away. Just text me or pull me into the meeting if needed, though I don't think it will be."

"Are you going to the farm?" She whispered, looking at Aurelio wistfully.

"No," Vega grinned. Aurelio would be mortified that a twenty-five-year-old was looking at him like she'd like to really know what was underneath his clothes. "I'm going to Dallas."

Joey's eyes flashed with surprise. "On vacation?"

Vega laughed. "No one goes to Dallas on vacation. No, I'm meeting some people. Let's go through everything now so you're ready for the meeting, okay?"

Chapter 25

Thursday, October 11

After Vega prepped Joey; Aurelio, Roman and she drove to the medical examiner's office on Mission Street.

Roman and Aurelio remained in the front office while Vega accompanied Drago and Nikki into the cold, sterile room of the LA County Department of Medical Examiner. The air was heavy with the scent of antiseptics, underscored by an unmistakable hint of death, underscoring the grim purpose of their visit. Dr. Chen welcomed them with a professional nod, her expression grave.

"Detectives, Ms. Vega," Dr. Chen acknowledged, gesturing towards the metal autopsy table where the body of Jorja Levey lay, her back exposed.

Vega's eyes briefly met Drago's, sharing a silent understanding of the gruesome task ahead. She steeled herself, the prosecutor within her surfacing, ready to dissect the facts of the case clinically despite the emotional undercurrents.

"The tattoo is, as you can see, completely off." Dr. Chen stretched the skin on the back. "This either points to a different individual or a significant deviation in the unsub's method."

Vega moved close to the body. The back didn't have the telltale butterfly tattoo, just a message: Sweet Caroline, are you reay to becme a buterfly.

"This is not Soller," Vega whispered, "He didn't make spelling mistakes. Soller took pride in his work."

There was also a lot of hesitation inking across the back, like the unsub wanted to tattoo a butterfly but couldn't; and then gave up.

Drago nodded. "Could be the unsub was in a hurry, feeling the pressure, or this is a whole new unsub who doesn't have Soller or the unsub's skill."

"Either way, it's a deviation," Nikki surmised.

Drago pursed his lip. "Yeah. The unsub went off-script. What other deviations do we have, doc?"

Dr. Chen began, her voice steady. "The victim presented with an atypical tox screen. There was a significant presence of a paralytic agent, which is not consistent with any of Soller's previous victims."

Nikki leaned in, her brow furrowed. "Do we know what kind of paralytic?"

"Something similar to succinylcholine," Dr. Chen replied, referring to a powerful muscle relaxant often used in medical settings. "However, there's an anomaly. The victim had an underlying condition—myasthenia gravis—which exacerbated the effects of the agent."

Vega interjected, "Could the unsub have known about her condition?"

"It's unlikely," Dr. Chen said. "Myasthenia gravis is not typically visible or easily detectable without specific medical tests."

Drago's voice was tense. "So, the unsub unknowingly administered a lethal dose?"

"Correct," Dr. Chen confirmed. "The paralytic, combined with her condition, led to respiratory failure."

"She died before the unsub could complete their intended ritual," Vega concluded.

Nikki continued to make notes on her phone; her focus was sharp. She looked up from the screen, directing her next set of questions to Dr. Chen, seeking more specific details that could aid their investigation.

"What do you have on fluids? Anything under the fingernails?" Nikki asked, her tone reflecting the urgency of gathering as much evidence as possible.

"We got the body this morning, Wasco. You're already getting VIP plus treatment," Dr. Chen rolled her eyes. "I've sent all samples to trace analysis, and they're still working on it."

"Any signs of defensive wounds, or does it look like she was incapacitated quickly?" Drago wondered. "Vega, with Soller, were there defensive wounds?"

"He used chloroform," Vega shook her head. "Fast and quick, and not very long-lasting. I wonder why the unsub used a paralytic agent this time?

"It could be because they wanted the victim to be aware of what was happening," Dr. Chen suggested. "This chemical paralyses you but leaves you aware of what's going on. Poor woman. She didn't have a chance; at least she didn't suffer. She died within a half hour of the administration of the paralytic agent."

"Was she aware of what was happening in those thirty minutes?" Nikki asked, and Vega saw the pity in her eyes.

"Only for a few minutes...long few minutes," Dr. Chen said softly.

Nikki tapped on her phone, her expression thoughtful. "What about hair and fiber? Did you get anything that might have been transferred from the unsub or the location where she was held?"

"We've collected several fibers and hair samples. They're also with trace," Dr. Chen replied, amused.

"She's new, give her a break, doc," Drago teased.

"I remember when you were an over-eager detective, Horvat," Dr. Chen chuckled.

"She was last seen at the Golden Gopher...so we need to look at the security cameras from there to her home." Nikki was still focused on the case in front of her.

Ah, yes, over-eager for sure, Vega thought, remembering how she'd been as a young ADA prosecuting her first big case: The Butterfly Killer.

"TID is looking at security cameras?" Dr. Chen asked.

Drago nodded. The Technical Investigation Division (TID) at the LAPD was responsible for analyzing any and all electronic data pertaining to a case. They were backed up like all such departments were, Vega knew. But she'd bet the farm that this case would be prioritized, mainly because the mayor and the chief of Ds would want to prove this was a random killing, not a copycat.

"How many security cameras do we have in DTLA?" Vega wondered.

Drago shrugged. "Give or take a few thousand, but...some are up, and some are not, you know how it is. The majority of the cameras are in the Historic Core, and others are in the Fashion District and Skid Row. So, we could get lucky."

"And the condition of the clothing? Was there anything left that could give us clues about the location or method of abduction?" Vega interjected, her analytical mind working through the possibilities.

"The victim was naked," Dr. Chen stressed, "I'll forward everything I have, full tox screen and pathology report, to your emails, detectives, and to Agent Thomas Delfino in Quantico as requested. And now, if you'll excuse me, it's been a busy Wednesday night in Los Angeles. We have an asshole shooting homeless people."

Drago sighed. "Another serial case."

"Two serial killers operating at the same time in one city...no wonder people think crime is going up," Vega mocked.

"Actually, according to a recent report, violent crime across the country is down by three to five percentage points, except in Washington DC and Memphis," Nikki supplied, "Perception between data and reality is because of the news and social media according to the study. Basically, we're safer than we've ever been, but the news makes us feel like we're not."

"Sounds like someone's stump speech," Dr. Chen guffawed. "Now, get out all of you so I can get back to the business of the dead."

As they walked out of the morgue, Vega wondered, "Can you look into any recent purchases or thefts of the paralytic agent? It's not something you find just lying around."

Nikki nodded in agreement. "I'll put in a request to have TID pull up purchases and theft reports. Might give us a lead."

Chapter 26

Thursday, October 11

"How is she holding up?" Drago asked Aurelio, who refused to leave even after a brief argument with Vega, who told him what the fuck do you think will happen in the LAPD HQ to me.

"By a thread." Aurelio ran a hand through his hair.

And so are you, Drago thought. "Go to her place. I got her."

Aurelio shook his head. "I have a call to make and some documents to go through." He pointed to the area in the LAPD HQ lobby with tables and chairs. "I'll sit there and work through it. Woo is waiting in the car. He'll be here when we're ready to leave."

Drago had a fondness for the Santos family. His best friend, Maria, had married into the family, and they had sort of adopted him. Paloma, the matriarch, mothered him as much as, if not more than, his own mother. When he sprained his ankle over Christmas, they banished him to the Golden Valley resort. There, he ended up uncovering two dead bodies, with Aurelio's sister, Isadora, playing the role of Hercule Poirot.

They treated him like family, which was why he felt compelled to protect Vega, though let's face it, she'd fuck him up if he told her that. Vega could take care of herself.

Leaving Aurelio in the lobby, Drago walked into the bullpen and the conference room where they would be talking to Agent Delfino.

He settled into a chair flanked by Vega and Nikki, facing a large wall monitor.

Since meeting Dr. Chen, he and Nikki had hit a few dead ends in their investigation into the murder of Jorja Levey.

The ex-husband, the prime suspect, wasn't anywhere near Jorja or even in the United States. He was in a hotel in Costa Rica with his *new* girlfriend, Tiffany. Nikki had the dubious pleasure of speaking with the hotel manager, who confirmed that Kelvin Levey was indeed on the hotel's clothing-optional beach for the past three days. Additionally, United Airlines corroborated that a man matching Kelvin's description and carrying Kelvin's passport had passed through passport control and customs into Costa Rica.

Jorja's sister, Julie, who was en route from Oxnard to identify the body—a journey that would take at least three hours in the current traffic—had assured Drago that Jorja wasn't dating anyone new, not even casually.

"She was not ready, detective. Kelvin did a real number on her."

"Do you think Kelvin could hurt your sister?"

Julie had snorted at that. "He could try; but she'd rip him a new one. Have you seen what Kelvin looks like?"

Drago hadn't, in fact, seen Kelvin's driver's license photo only, so as he spoke to Julie, he pulled up his victim's ex-husband's social media profile. "Right, I see your point." Kelvin Levey was a skinny dude and not a very attractive one. How he was getting so much side action that his wife divorced him was beyond Drago's understanding.

Jorja's mother was in a home suffering from Alzheimer's, so she didn't even register the passing of her daughter. Jorja's colleagues all agreed she was easy-going, if a little reticent. Her going to the Golden Gopher the previous night with them was a bit of an anomaly.

Keisha, her colleague whom she spent all day with as they sat side by side, manning the counter at USPS on Flower Street, had cried a lot when she came into LAPD HQ to talk to them.

"I can't believe it, I just can't. I shouldn't have taken her to the Golden Gopher. She was so quiet, I only wanted her to let her hair down and have some fun. Do you think I got her killed?" she wailed, wiping her face with tissues pulled from a pink Kleenex box she had brought along.

After comforting her that it wasn't her fault, Nikki and Drago took a stroll down the historic core of DTLA. They walked from the Golden Gopher to where Jorja lived on Fifth Street, a mile away.

"So many places here to park a van," Nikki lamented.

"Yeah, got to ask the TID geeks to comb through every security camera from the Golden Gopher to her place and see if anything pops up," Drago agreed. A white van would not stand out here, but maybe they'd get lucky as they'd done in the Soller case, and someone would have seen something.

They regrouped in LAPD HQ to meet with Agent Delfino, who'd told them by email that he wasn't ready to offer a complete profile but had some thoughts about who they might be looking for; and if Jorja Levey's murder was perpetrated by a murderous asshole or a genuine serial killer wannabe.

"I'd like to also get you coached on how to deal with Soller," Drago told Vega prior to the call with Delfino, "I can brief Detective Taze on that as well."

She nodded.

"You worried about seeing him again?" Nikki wanted to know.

"It's not a courtesy call, Wasco, just doing the job," Vega said tightly.

Nikki flashed a look at Drago, who shook his head. Of course, Vega was stressed the hell out to see Soller again; anyone would be. But she was not going to show vulnerability, which was probably a good thing. Soller fed off fear and weakness.

As the call connected, Drago noticed Vega's posture stiffen slightly, a subtle sign of her bracing for the insights they were about to receive. Nikki, ever the diligent detective, had her phone ready, finger poised to tap down every detail.

"Hey, Delfino," Vega said, "How's it going?"

"It's a good thing I don't have any hair; otherwise, they'd all be gray," he stated, stroking his bald head. "Thanks for getting the report to me, Detectives. I've only had a preliminary look, so my profile is incomplete at best."

"But you're certain this is the same unsub?" Drago asked.

"Yes, I am. The copycat offender has deviated, and as I said, they do this to be better than the original. Based on this new information, I do have an updated partial profile. I'm now confident in stating that your unsub is in direct contact with Soller."

"Why?" Nikki wanted to know.

"Because of the way they handled this victim. They made a mistake, and you can see the panic. The tattoo was inaccurate, and they could've just let the body go and found a new victim, but they panicked and left the message that they knew Soller wanted them to. Your unsub is afraid, and the only reason for this is that they know that Soller will be pissed about their failure," Delfino explained. "Now we have a vulnerable and weak unsub, and it can go one of two ways. One, they reach out to Soller and beg for forgiveness. The second, they run from Soller and do their own thing."

"Which one is more likely?" Drago asked.

"The first. This unsub is deeply connected with Soller and desperate for his approval. I'd also like to update the profile and say that your unsub is in their mid to late twenties. Almost like a child to Soller's parent. And I can't say this for sure, but based on the calligraphy on this victim because here the unsub is not copying Soller but letting their own psyche and style come through, I suspect your unsub is female."

They all fell silent.

"Using succinylcholine makes sense; it indicates a need for a different kind of dominance...watch what I'm doing to you," Vega mused, tapping her finger on the desk as she slipped back into her former ADA mindset. Although she wasn't as sharp as she would have been had she continued her career, the muscle memory was still there. She was effectively flexing those old muscles, drawing on her experience and insights. "There's a female nuance to it. We know that women killers often resort to poison."

Drago looked through his notes. "Soller had two children, a son and a daughter. We still don't know where they are."

"They disappeared even before the trial," Delfino replied. "I spoke with Soller's wife; she was traumatized, yes, but because of what this meant to their standing in society. The Soller's marriage had a lot to do with keeping up appearances. The children, I didn't have access to. They were teenagers. Did you talk to them, Vega?"

"No," she murmured, "No reason to; we didn't need the family, though I know Schwartz interviewed them to see how much they knew, and it was determined that Mrs. Soller and the children knew nothing about what their daddy was doing."

Nikki nodded when Drago threw her a glance. "I'll ask TID to track them down."

"They've probably changed their names, created whole new identities," Vega cautioned, "Soller had money, they had resources, and they probably used them to live in another part of the country or world."

Drago leaned forward. "In what way do you see the unsub trying to outdo Soller, so we're prepared for what's to come?"

"The introduction of the paralytic agent suggests a level of experimentation," Delfino expounded. "It's as if the unsub is testing their boundaries, seeing how far they can go beyond Soller's original MO."

Vega interjected, her voice steady despite the gravity of the topic. "And this is why you believe Soller has direct control over this unsub."

"Yes, like I said, there's a high likelihood of indirect influence, possibly through correspondence or a third party," Delfino posited. "But what's going to become an issue is if Soller's control weakens further. Then we have a loose cannon. Your next victim will tell you that."

Nikki tapped her pen against her notebook, a frown creasing her forehead. "We have to wait for someone to die so we can do our jobs?"

"Yes, I'm afraid right now there is no way to tell if the unsub has broken away from being a copycat," Delfino confirmed apologetically, "The unsub has already stepped out of line with Soller's known methods. We may see them take an even more divergent path soon, potentially escalating in violence and unpredictability."

Drago's mind raced with the implications. A serial killer evolving under the shadow of another, more infamous one was a dangerous prospect. "I feel like you're saying we have absolutely nothing to go by right now."

"Yes, you do," Delfino said softly, watching Vega, "You have *her* talking to Soller. She's not just an attorney or a victim anymore; she's a key player in his psychological game. He sees her as both his greatest failure and his ultimate challenge."

Vega nodded, taking in every word. Her hands were clasped tightly on the desk in front of her, betraying her nerves.

"Your presence will unbalance him," Delfino continued. "Soller's ego is his weakness. He's proud of his work, his butterflies. You'll need to walk the fine line between curiosity and admiration."

"Admiration?" Nikki scoffed. "Seriously?"

"As serious as a heart attack, I'm afraid, Detective Wasco," Delfino smiled weakly. "Vega, you'll have to make him feel like he still has power over you, or better yet, that he can regain it. This might prompt him to boast or slip up. But stay on guard. He's manipulative and will try to get under your skin."

Vega's brow furrowed in concentration. "How direct should I be about the new killings?"

"Very," Delfino replied. "But frame it carefully. Imply that you think the new killer is inferior to him, that they're tarnishing his legacy. Soller will either agree, giving us insight into his connection with the copycat, or he'll defend them, which could be even more revealing."

"And if he refuses to talk about the new killings?" Drago asked.

"Then shift the focus to your shared history. Remind him of your previous encounter, how you were the one who got away, the one he couldn't transform. It's a risky move, but it might provoke him into revealing something about his current mindset or plans."

After the call, they sat in the conference room, discussing if they should roleplay Vega's meeting with Soller. Drago could see Vega wasn't keen on it, so he didn't push.

"You have to play the victim and adversary, a challenge to Soller's ego and a reminder of his past failures," Drago weighed his words as carefully as he knew Agent Delfino just had.

Vega took a deep breath and released it slowly.

Drago put his hand on her shoulder. "You're stronger than he is. You've survived and thrived despite him. Use that. Let him see that strength, but make him believe he can break you. That's your leverage."

"I hate that you have to do this," Nikki said, "But you're our best shot. He's not going to talk to us; give us what he will give you."

Vega's lips twitched into a small smile. "Ain't that the truth!"

CHAPTER 27

Thursday, October 11

Aurelio reflected on how she had a whole life in Dallas, one he knew nothing about. She had friends and relationships that were a mystery to him. It was as if a part of her life was being revealed to him for the first time.

Detectives Ari Schwartz and Wyatt Taze, two of Dallas PD's finest, each with years of experience, joined them for dinner at the Mansion, a restaurant part of the Rosewood Mansion on Turtle Creek. This was where he and Vega were staying. Vega had made the travel plans, and he had simply come along; after all, this was her world.

Vega and Detective Schwartz had worked on the original Butterfly Killer case, but it was Detective Taze who'd saved her from Soller.

Schwartz still worked in the Sex Offender Apprehension Program (SOAP) squad of the Dallas Police Department. A seasoned Homicide detective, he had a lean, wiry frame and sharp, perceptive eyes that missed nothing. His demeanor was relaxed, but there was an underlying intensity to him, a keen intelligence that came from years on the job. He greeted Vega with a familiarity that spoke of shared trials and deep professional respect.

Detective Taze, on the other hand, was a more prominent, more imposing figure. His presence was almost tangible, a solid, reassuring force. His face, lined with the years and the stress of police work, broke into a genuine smile as he saw Vega. He now headed DPD's Field Services division, which he informed Aurelio included the fugitive and parole squad, SWAT, and security planning.

Taze had a protective air about him, and it was clear from his interactions with Vega that their bond went beyond the professional, which was not a surprise. He had been her rescuer, her savior during the darkest time of her life.

Aurelio watched as Vega interacted with them. She was a different person with them, as confident and assertive as always, but now he saw she was law enforcement through and through.

As Vega sat across from Schwartz, her eyes sparkled with the familiar fire of legal debate and professional camaraderie. "Schwartz, have you finally managed to clean up the chain of custody issues in evidence handling?" she asked, a playful edge to her voice.

Schwartz rolled his eyes, a grin tugging at his lips, setting a glass of wine on the table. "Vega, you know as well as I do that's a never-ending battle. But yeah, we've tightened up the process. No more of the lost in transit fuck ups for any perp."

"Thank fucking god," Taze remarked as he cut into his steak.

Vega laughed. "Good to hear. Remember the Miller case? That fiasco almost let a double homicide perp walk because someone mixed up the evidence bags."

"Yeah, a rookie mistake that nearly cost us," Schwartz acknowledged, shaking his head. "But hey, we learned from it. Now there's a double-check system in place."

Vega took a sip of her wine and leaned forward, her expression turning more serious. "And what about MO tracking? I always thought if we had a more robust system, we could've linked a few of those unsolved cases sooner."

Aurelio could understand parts of the conversation, but his education on these matters came from television. MO, he guessed, meant modus operandi. He'd watch a few episodes of Criminal Minds as well, so he knew they were talking repeat killers.

Taze chimed in then, setting his knife and fork down. "We've got a new database system. Cross-references MOs connect dots we used to miss. It's not perfect, but it's a step up."

Vega nodded, clearly impressed. "Sounds like you guys are finally entering the twenty-first century. Took you long enough."

Aurelio noticed that while she bantered with the guys, Vega wasn't eating and was already on her second glass of wine. He knew she was usually cautious with her alcohol intake, but he also understood that when nervous, she couldn't eat, and the alcohol didn't affect her as much. The woman could certainly hold her liquor!

She discussed old cases and the nuances of police work with a familiarity that came from her time as an ADA.

With Taze, her demeanor softened slightly, but there was still a strength to her. They spoke about the Soller case, and Aurelio could see the unspoken communication between them, a shared experience that had left its mark on both.

"I can tag along," Schwartz offered.

Taze waved it away. "You're in court tomorrow."

Schwartz grinned. "Yeah, that's why I'd like to tag along. You know April Napier? She's the defense attorney, and every time I'm on the stand with her, I feel like my asshole expands by a few centimeters. She knows how to give a reaming and not in a good way."

"TMI, Schwartz," Vega grimaced with humor.

Taze looked at Aurelio. "Are you okay if we talk shop for a bit?"

"Isn't that what you were already doing?" Humor danced in Aurelio's eyes.

Taze shrugged. "You know what I mean."

Aurelio nodded somberly. "Yeah. You can talk about Soller. I've read the case file."

Taze looked at Vega in surprise as if saying, you told him?

The one thing that seemed to have not changed about her was that she used to be a private person, and she still was.

Vega told them what she'd learnt from Agent Delfino, the BAU profiler who LAPD was working with, the same profiler who'd worked the original Butterfly Killer case.

"I don't think it's the kids," Schwartz declared. "I met them. Nora, the wife, she was a piece of work, I got to say. She was on about what people would think. The kids were sweethearts. Kaylea was twelve then, so she's about nineteen now. The son, Kaleb, was seventeen-eighteen and he was really devastated. Had a tough relationship with his old man."

Vega's ears perked. "Why did he have a tough relationship with Soller?" Schwartz let out some air. "The kid was skinny and according to Soller, pardon my language, a bit of a sissy boy. Soller kept telling him he needed to man up. He looked up to him, but he also resented him—like teenagers do. Fact is those kids were broken up. They loved their father and struggled with finding out that he's a sadistic serial killer."

"Do you know where they are?" Vega asked.

Schwartz shook his head.

"I agree with Schwartz, and you know how much I hate agreeing with the sumbitch," Taze joked. "Those kids were traumatized. And Nora up and left right after sentencing. When he...ah...took you, I tracked them down. They were still in the Dallas area, hiding out in some motel under false names. And—"

"Do you remember those names?" Vega demanded.

Something flickered in Taze's eyes. "I probably have it in a file."

"How did you find them?"

"ATM usage," Taze informed her. He paused when the server came to clear their table, and once he left, he continued, "You're barking up the wrong tree."

"Probably but we've got to look at all close associations to Soller. Anyone else you can think of who was close to Soller?" Vega asked Schwartz.

"There was that office assistant...receptionist, whatever," Schwartz pondered. "She was a student who worked at his sporting goods store. She was like seventeen or something. I thought he was fucking her but no evidence of that. She idolized him. Never believed he was the Butterfly Killer. Said it was a set up."

"Yeah, I remember her," Taze recollected, "we talked to her when we were tracking down Soller after he escaped." He closed his eyes and then opened them, smiling, "Pippa White."

Schwartz exclaimed, "Bingo! Pippa White. Sweet girl but confused as fuck."

"She was obsessed with him and convinced that you'd framed him." Taze looked at his phone when it buzzed and then put it face down.

"Can you track her down?"

"Sure," Schwartz said. "I'll ask the guys at DEU to look it up." When he saw the blank look on Aurelio's face, he explained, "DEU is the Digital Evidence Unit; they do the I.T. grunt work for all of us."

As the evening winded down, they'd talked so much about handling the interview with Soller that even Aurelio felt prepared to do so if the occasion arose.

"Do you know that Vega's prosecution rate is still the envy of the department?" Schwartz told Aurelio.

"Undoubtedly." Aurelio put a hand on her thigh under the table because he wasn't sure how she'd feel about PDA in front of two hard-boiled cops.

Taze chuckled. "We all knew when Vega was on a case, the bad guys were going down. No two ways about it."

When Vega excused herself, Taze turned to Aurelio, his gaze appraising, "You're taking good care of her, right?"

Aurelio nodded, charmed that Taze wanted to give him the once over because he was protective of Vega. "I'm doing my best. But you know her; she doesn't make it easy."

"Well, our Vega was and is a badass," Schwartz grinned. "Fuckin' hell, you remember how she'd walk into court, and you could see the judge sigh because he knew she was a bulldozer. Relentless, as they'd say in the movies, in her pursuit of the truth."

"Maybe not the truth," Taze leaned back, continuing to watch Aurelio as though he'd stopped trying to intimidate him.

"But justice," Aurelio offered knowingly.

"Yeah," Taze agreed, and then, as if deciding Aurelio was all right, he offered his fist out for a bump that Aurelio responded to. "She's tougher than she looks. But even the toughest need someone to have their back."

"I got her back, Detective, all day, every day. And I ain't going nowhere," Aurelio confirmed.

CHAPTER 28

Friday, October 12

The unsub's fingers trembled over their phone.

Did Soller already know how they'd fucked up? How would he know? It wasn't in the news yet. But it would be. And then?

They hadn't wanted to leave the studio after they'd gotten rid of Jorja Levey, but they had had to. They had a job and bills to pay and all that shit. They couldn't just sit in a studio and sulk. It had been so hard to keep a straight face, look calm like they hadn't made the biggest mistake of their lives. But they'd persevered because that was the kind of person they were.

You had to adapt, you had to evolve. And they had, hadn't they?

It had been a shock when the stupid bitch died. She *just* died! And ruined their plans. They'd wanted to slash her face, but they restrained themselves. Soller always said: Prepare. Plan. Patience. They'd prepared, they'd planned...but they hadn't been patient. But what difference would a day here and there have made?

They heard a beep from their phone, and their heart raced with a mix of fear and anticipation as they opened the secure messaging app, their last link to Jacob Soller. Nothing. The beep was a text message from work like they gave a fuck. They wanted to reply, I don't fucking care, you cunt. Instead, they controlled themselves and didn't respond at all. It was early on a Friday morning, and it was okay if they didn't get back right away. They wished they could call in sick, but they wouldn't. They'd go to work and behave like nothing had happened. They would fucking persevere!

Maybe Soller would never find out, they decided. And what he didn't know would not hurt them. They had to find a new caterpillar and fast so they could get to them the next night. Yeah, that's what they'd do. And then no harm, no foul. Soller would never know.

They regretted what had happened. Oh, not her dying; that was just bad luck; who knew she was so fainthearted that she died of fear. Their lips curved at that thought. Oh, yes, they'd use the succinylcholine again. The thrill of being paralyzed but aware...that aroused them unbearably.

They'd struck gold with their source for the nerve agent. A friend of theirs worked as a nurse in the OR. They'd hung out with her at work a few times, and that insider access made swiping a vial of the stuff, usually in the hands of anesthesiologists, a piece of cake. As for keeping their helpful friend from spilling the beans? Well, they made sure she wouldn't be doing much talking.

They grabbed some edibles that they chewed on like candy to keep themselves stable. Thank god their workplace didn't insist on drug tests!

They walked up to their computer with a clearer head. Time to find the second victim. They'd just forget Jorja ever happened. They wished they'd not panicked and tattooed her; that had been a mistake. But they'd been rattled, afraid that Soller would be so angry to know their caterpillar had died without transforming into a butterfly.

As they prowled social media to find their next caterpillar, the grip around their heart loosened. They'd be fine. All this would work out.

Their fingers danced over the keyboard, flicking between social media profiles with a practiced ease. The studio, bathed in the cold glow of the computer screen, became their hunting ground. They sifted through countless faces, searching for the one that would be their next caterpillar. The thrill of the hunt began to overtake the anxiety and fear that had gripped them earlier.

The world outside was just waking up, but in the studio, time seemed to stand still. They had to find someone perfect, someone who would fit the narrative they wanted to create.

They needed to regain control, to prove to Soller, and more importantly to themselves, that they were a worthy apprentice.

Their eyes finally settled on a profile. A smile spread across their lips. Perfect. The new caterpillar would fit the pattern they needed. They would be cautious this time, more methodical. They would not rush. They would honor Soller's teachings and make this one count.

With renewed purpose, they started planning. They mapped out routes, studied schedules, and prepared their tools. The nerve agent, their newfound method of control, sat like a promise of power. They felt a surge of excitement, a dark anticipation for the night's work.

But deep down, a nagging doubt remained. What if Soller found out about Jorja? What if he disapproved of their deviation from his methods? The thought sent a shiver down their spine. Soller's approval meant everything; his validation was their lifeline.

They shook off the doubt and focused on the task ahead. This time, they would be perfect. This time, they would create a masterpiece that Soller couldn't ignore. They would be the artist and the city of Los Angeles, their canvas.

As the sun began to rise, casting a pale light into the studio, the unsub's resolve hardened. They would step out of Soller's shadow and prove their worth. Tonight, they would make another butterfly, and nothing would stand in their way.

CHAPTER 29

Friday, October 12

It had taken some doing, but Vega had finally fallen asleep, and now, as the skies turned molten, Aurelio held the woman he loved. Thanks to the time zone difference, they had to wake up at the butt crack of dawn to head to the Cooke County Jail in Gainesville, where Soller was on death row.

She wore a pair of pajama shorts and a tank top. Her blonde hair was spread over his arm and the white hotel sheets. She'd tossed and turned all night and had finally ended up with her head on his shoulder and his arm around her waist. He inhaled her perfume, magnolia blossoms. Almost a cliché for a Southern

Belle, but she was from Texas...were they still called Southern Belles if they were from Texas?

He felt lucky to be with Vega. He hadn't been in many relationships, especially after the botched engagement. *In* hindsight, that had been seriously boneheaded.

He used to not like sleeping with someone. He always felt crowded, and that's why he preferred to sleep at her place so he could come back to his pristine sheets. But with Vega, he knew he was in trouble when he not only liked sleeping with her, but loved waking up with her.

He slept better with her. And that was the god's fucking honest truth. When they were apart, he woke up not as well rested as he did with her, even though the hours he slept were fewer. Both Vega and he had a healthy sex drive, and they made love nearly every night and morning they were together. He couldn't resist her and thank god she felt the same about him.

He stroked her back with his hand, sliding under her tank top and then going down past the elastic of her pajama bottoms to cup her ass.

She nuzzled him and gently bit his chest. "Hmm," she purred, opening her blue-blue eyes. She smiled. "Hey."

"Hey." He stroked her ass, dipped his fingers in between her legs. He loved holding her like this, being inside her, surrounding her. The ease of Vega, the pleasure, the rightness, it was all intoxicating.

"What are you doing, honey?" she chuckled.

"If you have to ask, baby, I'm obviously not doing this right." He moved and flipped her, so she was beneath him. He kissed her softly at first, then languidly filled himself with her taste and scent. God, he loved this woman. He'd never get enough of her.

Her hands encouraged as they stroked his back and held him. Unlike Vega, he slept hot, so he slept raw, there was just the thin fabric of her pajama shorts between him and heaven. His erection nudged the notch between her legs, and she moved her hips, and he felt her warmth and wetness caress him.

"I want you," Aurelio groaned as he pulled down the straps of her tank top. He loved her pink-tipped breasts. They were firm and beautiful. Perfect. "Have I told you that you have the best tits in the world?"

She giggled, and his heart danced at the sound. Caroline Vega giggling! Who'd have thought? It was a lovely sound that he did his damnedest to elicit from her whenever he could. She was so serious, so self-contained, that he wanted to help her have fun.

"Please, Aurelio," she whimpered. "Suckle me." Her blue eyes were ablaze with arousal.

May no one ever say Aurelio doesn't please his woman. He pushed a hand between her legs, dipped inside her and brought that hand up to her nipples. He anointed the first one and then the other with her juices.

She watched him with glazed eyes and moaned when he took her turgid flesh into his mouth. He suckled slowly, gently, licking, tasting. He knew she wanted hard, but he liked to take his time in bed with her, and he wasn't going to let her arousing moans and whispers push him.

After he suckled, driving her into a writhing mass of desperation, he kissed one nipple and then the other. By the time he took her tank top off of her and slid her pajama bottoms out of the way, she was panting.

Her pussy was bare, just the way he liked it, with a landing strip that took him straight to the promised land.

She waited as he draped her thighs over his shoulders, and then when she felt his mouth against her, she closed her eyes. As soon as she did, he lifted his head away.

"What?" she murmured.

"Look at me, baby. I want to see you come."

As she watched, he licked her from ass to pussy, tasting her, smelling her, inhaling her. This warrior woman of his! He couldn't love her more if he tried. She'd taken him over completely and irrevocably.

"Make me come." Her fingers were tangled in his hair, pushing, demanding.

"I will, baby. You know I will." He put two fingers inside her as he suckled her clit, oh so gently. He pumped in and out of her slowly, and as he did, he licked her clitoris.

"Aurelio, please," she cried out. She was thrashing now as she did when he withheld her pleasure, kept her on the edge.

He put three fingers inside her, filling her, and grazed his teeth over her clit. She came like a fountain—warm, delicious, intense. He slid up her body and kissed her.

"How do you taste, baby?" he demanded.

"Like you," she whispered. "You taste like me, and I taste like you."

"Fuck yeah," Aurelio agreed as he entered her. Bliss! Heaven! Whatever you wanted to call it, he thought, this was it, this perfumed ecstasy that he could only find with her, only with her pussy.

"I feel so full." She looked into his eyes.

"You're very tight, baby." She clenched around him, and he groaned. "You want to pull the cum out of me?"

"Yes, honey. I do." She rocked against him, chasing her release as she squeezed him harder and tighter inside.

And just as he felt his orgasm ready to coat her insides with cum, he slid a hand between them and pinched her clit. Her orgasm was instantaneous and hard; wonderful, so absolutely fabulous that when she came for the second time, she took him with her.

Chapter 30

Friday, October 12

As an ADA, Vega had walked in and out of plenty of prisons. And regardless of how experienced she was, every time she went inside and heard those metal doors clang shut behind her, she felt a frisson of fear race up her spine.

What if they left her in here and never opened the door again?

The fear took root in her psyche following a harrowing experience a colleague had at Dawson State Jail. During a visit to see an inmate, the prison went into lockdown, trapping her in an interrogation room with a gang member responsible for five killings, and a newly minted security guard who appeared even more terrified than she was. Though she emerged physically unharmed, the incident left deep psychological scars. Afterward, she resigned from her job and moved out of state.

Vega had reacted similarly after Taze found her with Soller. Sometimes, moving forward just isn't possible—and she felt this acutely now. A familiar tightness gripped her chest as she and Detective Wyatt Taze neared the imposing structure of Cooke County Jail.

The gray prison building loomed above, its bleak walls unyielding. This monument of finality consumed hope, oppressive in its purpose.

As they entered, the heavy metal doors clanged shut behind them, the sound echoing through the sterile corridors. The air was thick with a sense of despair, a palpable weight that seemed to press down on Vega's shoulders. She could hear the distant, muffled sounds of inmates, reminders of the lives trapped within these walls.

Warden Johnson, a relaxed-looking man with a weathered face and a friendly demeanor, greeted them.

"ADA Vega heard so much about you, and it's a privilege to be meetin' you." He shook hands with her and then did some fist bump ritual with Taze, who he seemed to know well. "How're y'all doin'? Spoke with that Detective Horvat of y'all's again, just to let him know we're all set up and ready as can be for your visit here."

They walked down a long hallway, their footsteps echoing off the concrete floors. The warden detailed the protocols for meeting a death row inmate, his voice steady and factual.

"You'll be meetin' in an interview room. Got a table set up in there. He'll be on the other side, both in leg irons and handcuffed to the table. No physical contact permitted under any circumstances, y'hear?"

Vega nodded, absorbing his words absently. She felt a chill run down her spine at the thought of seeing Soller again. "Yes, Warden Johnson."

"Now Taze here knows the drill, don't you, Detective?"

"I sure do, Warden."

Warden Johnson continued, "All interactions are monitored and recorded. Remember now, Soller is manipulative. Don't y'all let him control the conversation."

"Are there any guards he's...well, for the lack of a better word, close to?" Vega asked.

Warden Johnson grinned. "Your Detective Horvat already put that request in. You'll be speakin' with Nat Gluck; he's an experienced guard, been here over ten years. That's why he has the high-profile inmates. And you'll meet Beau Heber, he's new, just eleven months in. Very promising, y'know."

They arrived at a security checkpoint where they had to pass through a metal detector and were patted down by guards. Vega felt a sense of intrusion, uncomfortably aware that in a place like this, privacy was a luxury.

Beyond the checkpoint, the corridor narrowed, leading them into the heart of death row. The area was heavily guarded, the air filled with a tense silence. The cells they passed were small, the barred windows offering just a glimpse of the occupants. Vega could feel the eyes on her, the weight of gazes filled with curiosity, desperation, or blank resignation.

Finally, they arrived at the interview room. It was a bare space with a plain table and two chairs. One on the side of the handcuff rings one on the other. They'd decided that there be only one visitor's chair, for Vega. Taze would stand at the other end of the room, allowing Soller to feel that he had privacy with Vega.

Vega took a deep breath, trying to steady her nerves. She could hear her heart pounding in her ears.

Warden Johnson gave her a brief, sympathetic look. "You'll have thirty minutes. We'll be right outside. Signal us if you need to end the meetin' early, y'hear?"

As the warden left, Vega took a seat, her eyes fixed on the door through which Soller would soon enter.

"You okay?" Taze asked.

"Never been better," she replied from in between gritted teeth.

They waited in heavy silence. The door on the opposite side of the room creaked open, revealing Jacob Soller, accompanied by a guard. Time had aged him, his face etched with deeper lines, but his eyes retained their chilling, unyielding intensity, casting a dark shadow over the room.

Vega's gaze fixed on Soller, the face that terrorized her sleep. His words, his voice, were carved into her being as permanently as the incomplete butterfly wings on her back. "*You're going to make such a beautiful butterfly,*" he had said, a phrase echoing endlessly, a sinister soundtrack to her darkest fears.

The guard seated him and went through the process of securing Soller to the floor and the table. The guard looked at Taze, who nodded, silently saying, yeah, this is good.

Once the guard departed, Soller turned his gaze towards Vega, a slow, twisted smile spreading across his face. His eyes burned with a terrifying satisfaction. Vega felt a cold realization settle in; he had orchestrated this moment, she knew. He had always intended for her to end up here, in this chilling confrontation.

"Hello, Sweet Caroline," he whispered, his smile was all teeth.

CHAPTER 31

Friday, October 12

Drago rubbed his temples, exhausted after hours of fruitless security footage. It was like the perp knew where the cameras were.

He dialed his tech crimes contact, Detective Bishop.

"Bishop here. What's shakin' bacon?"

Drago grinned despite himself. "I've got a question for you. Who has access to the city's security camera layouts? Anyone savvy enough to find the blind spots?"

Bishop paused. "Our tech guys at TID, obviously. And city maintenance for the hardware access, but they can't see the feeds."

"Can you get me a list of those folks?" Drago asked.

"What's this about?"

"The Butterfly Killer. I think he's got inside info, the way he avoids cameras."

Bishop whistled. "You think it's an inside job? That's a bold claim, Horvat."

"Not claiming nothing. Just eliminating possibilities. This guy's too slick."

"Alright, I'll see what I can scrape up. But it'll take some time."

"Thanks, Bishop. And keep it on the down low."

"My lips are sealed, Horvat."

After ending the call, Drago sat motionless, gazing at the blank wall, his mind racing. He sensed a vital piece of the puzzle was eluding them, something glaringly obvious yet hidden. With a renewed focus, he leaned into his desk and began meticulously reviewing the footage again. His eyes darted across the screen, searching for any anomaly, any detail that could provide a breakthrough in this challenging and elusive case.

Nikki came up behind him and rested her hip against his desk. "Heard from Vega; she and Taze are on their way to see Soller."

Drago sighed. "Anything on the succinylcholine?"

Nikki scrolled through her phone, her brows knitting together as she read. "The drug's restricted to hospitals, used by anesthesiologists. Getting it requires either hospital access or a person on the inside. They keep tight controls on it, so casually stealing some would be difficult."

Drago rubbed his chin thoughtfully. "So, our suspect likely has medical connections or knowledge. That narrows the field, but not much."

Nikki leaned in, eyes intense. "There's more. Succinylcholine requires training to use correctly. This isn't an amateur's drug of choice."

Drago's mind raced, piecing it together. "Someone savvy enough to use it, with medical experience, and ties to Soller."

"Or someone stupid enough to use it. He did inadvertently kill Jorja Levey with it. I'm checking hospitals for missing vials or unauthorized access," Nikki said. "Could be our access point."

Drago nodded. "I just spoke to Bishop at TID about security camera layouts. Maybe our suspect has an inside connection there too."

Nikki cracked a wry smile. "Look at you, thinking like a detective."

Drago chuckled. "Well, I learned from the best."

"But you know that's a long shot, baby." Nikki tapped a quick entry on her phone.

He liked how she called him baby. *What the fuck, Horvat? No, you don't like it when she calls you baby. In fact, you should tell her to not use endearments in the workplace.*

"Baby?" he quirked an eyebrow.

She flushed. "I'm sorry. It slipped out." She lowered her eyes as if something important was on her phone and continued, "You think the unsub is planning to deviate further from Soller's MO?"

Drago nodded slowly, his expression grim. "Yeah, I do. They've already shown they're willing to break his pattern. Who knows what they'll do next."

Nikki's phone pinged, and she glanced at the screen. "Horvat, I just got a hit on the succinylcholine. A nurse at the Gynecologic Oncology Surgery at the Pavilion reported one missing vial of succinylcholine this morning."

Drago took his jacket that draped on his chair and put it on. "Let's go talk to her."

Nikki navigated traffic expertly, scanning the road while processing information. "The nurse's name is Linda Martinez. She's worked at the hospital over five years, no issues."

"Could be an inside job, or someone knew what to look for," Drago mused, tracking the city blur outside.

They pulled up at Cedars-Sinai Medical Center, its imposing sign looming overhead. People came and went, absorbed in their own worlds.

They made their way through hospital corridors, badges cutting red tape. They found Linda Martinez in a small office, worried and confused.

"Detectives Horvat and Wasco, LAPD," Drago introduced, flashing his badge. "We need to ask you about the missing succinylcholine."

Linda, middle-aged with a kind, weary face, nodded for them to sit. "Yes, I reported it this morning. It was gone during inventory."

Nikki leaned forward, gentle yet firm. "Can you think of anyone who may have accessed the drugs?"

Linda sighed, running a hand through her hair. "Honestly, it could be anyone. The OR is always busy, with people coming and going. But we closely monitor inventory, and this has never happened before."

Drago scrutinized her, gauging sincerity. "Any staff acting unusual? Suspects?"

She hesitated, then shook her head. "No one I can think of. Everyone here is dedicated."

Nikki's voice softened. "We understand this is difficult, but any information could be crucial. The drug was used to murder someone, who died from the nerve agent."

Linda's eyes widened with realization. "Oh my God."

Drago and Nikki exchanged a glance, understanding the implications. Whoever took it knew what they were doing, under the radar.

"Any strangers around the OR, or the nurses' station recently?" Nikki asked.

Linda thought about it and shrugged. "Maybe. I don't know."

A young male nurse knocked on the open door. "Linda, the doctor wants new labs on bed five."

Linda nodded. "Yeah...this is Zach, detectives."

Zach Haim shook hands. "What's this about?"

Linda explained about the missing nerve agent. Zach nodded gravely. "Can't see anyone here doing that."

"Anybody not belong, hanging around?"

"Ah, there was Giselle's friend last month. Remember?" Zach looked at Linda for confirmation.

Linda frowned. "The one with the weird voice?"

"Yeah," Zach grimaced, "Giselle...Giselle Maura. She was going out clubbing or something and her friend came over to wait until she was done with her shift. She's been here a couple of times."

"What about the weird voice?" Drago asked.

He shrugged. "The friend was a little on the masculine side. I thought they were trans."

"This friend have a name?" Drago asked.

"Jaci or Jackie, something?" Zach mused.

Was that Jaci or Jackie for Jacob? "Can we speak to Giselle?" Drago questioned.

"Afraid not," Linda said. "She quit last week."

"Know where she went?" Nikki thought along the same lines as Drago.

Linda and Zach shook their heads.

"Have an address for her?" Drago asked.

Linda looked through files, hesitating. "I don't know if I'm allowed to give you that."

"No, let's wait for another death," Nikki muttered.

Drago shot her a warning look. "We really need your help."

"I don't know—," Linda began.

Zach interrupted. "Giselle lives in Sherman Oaks, Viking Apartments on Dicken Street."

"Zach!" Linda protested.

"What? You know how dangerous that drug is. And her quitting was odd. One day working, the next she was gone."

Linda sighed. "Sorry. Yes, that's her address. Apartment 314."

"Thank you, Linda and Zach," Drago said as they stood. "We may be back with more questions. Please keep this discussion confidential for now." Drago didn't want Giselle tipped off. The warning was unnecessary.

Drago and Nikki wasted no time, making their way to Sherman Oaks. The Viking Apartments on Dicken Street was a modest building nestled between a café and a dry cleaner. They ascended to the third floor, to Giselle's apartment.

When Giselle didn't open the door after repeated doorbell rings and knocks. Nikki found the security guard who manned the lobby. A stocky man in his late thirties, he had a receding hairline and smelled of weed.

"Is this legal?" he asked as he inserted the key into the door.

"Yeah," Drago muttered.

Both he and Nikki pulled out their weapons and nodded to one another once the door was unlocked. Nikki pushed the door open, and Drago stepped in, and as soon as he did, the smell hit him.

"Call it in," he told Nikki, "And you," he looked at the guard, "make sure the door is open for the police that's going to be coming through."

The security guard craned his neck when Nikki ushered him away from the apartment. Drago went through the apartment, gun in hand. It was a small one-bedroom apartment, and he cleared it in no time.

Giselle was dead in her bathtub. Her wrists were sliced open. The blood had long dried. She'd been, his guess, dead for over forty-eight hours.

"This unsub is crazy if he thinks we're going to buy suicide for the one person who's connected to the missing drug used by a killer?" Nikki shook her head.

"The unsub is crazy," Drago remarked dryly.

He crouched beside her. Nikki scanned the bathroom, her eyes sharp and searching. "No signs of a struggle," she murmured.

"Wanna bet we'll see she was injected with the same drug she helped steal."

"Nah, I like my money." Nikki opened drawers in the bathroom and checked the small wastebasket by the toilet. "No syringe, no vial. Whoever did this cleaned up."

They both knew what this meant. The killer was not only familiar with the drug but also cautious and calculated in its use. This wasn't a random act of violence; it was a targeted hit.

Drago stood, his jaw set. "Fuck me! A third body."

Nikki's phone buzzed, and she stepped out of the bathroom to take the call.

Drago took one last look at Giselle, and his heart clenched. She was twenty-six. A nurse. Such a fucking waste.

"Odpočívaj v pokoji," he whispered in Slovak. Rest in peace.

Chapter 32

Friday, October 12

The interview room in Cooke County Jail was a cavern of desolation, its air thick with the stench of despair. Vega, despite her numerous encounters with inmates, felt a cold shiver run down her spine as she faced Soller. He was a specter of his former self, his appearance now gaunt, with stringy hair and skin sallow, mottled with age spots, a testament to his seven harrowing years in prison.

When they'd first profiled the Butterfly Killer, Agent Delfino had postulated that when he was caught, they'd find the unsub was an average-looking man, someone who blends into a crowd, more wallpaper than center stage. And the profile was right on the money.

His eyes, recognizing Taze, glinted with a predatory malice. "Brought your guardian, Caroline? Still afraid, I see."

Vega smiled, pushing fear and insecurity away. This man was not going to intimidate her, past trauma be damned. "Oh, come on, Soller, it's just you and me here, and we know that I was never afraid."

He'd not been able to get an erection with her because she taunted him and didn't show fear, which was what he got off on. And suddenly, she could feel the cold metal table under her back in that warehouse, feel the pain of the cattle prod he used to hurt her with.

"We don't want scars on that beautiful skin, now do we? From Cocoon Forth a Butterfly. As Lady from her Door. Emerged—a Summer Afternoon—Repairing Everywhere—"

She'd screamed each time the cattle prod touched her skin. And he kept reciting the poem as he continued his ritual of pain.

"Now, it's not like I don't mind being let out of the cell they keep me locked up in, especially when I get to meet my Sweet Caroline...but why are you here?"

She'd known Soller would not dwell on his failure to rape her and the reason for it. She was his failure in more ways than one. He directed his gaze at the detective, who Vega knew was leaning lazily on the wall, arms folded, expressionless. She didn't have to turn around to verify that. She knew Taze, and they'd talked through how they'd manage the room with Soller.

"Someone left me a message from you," Vega told him.

He grinned, and for another instant, Vega was back in the warehouse, his hands touching her skin. "We're going to roll you over now, Sweet Caroline. Don't make it harder than it needs to be. You're going to make a beautiful butterfly."

"Did they now?" he drawled. "What did the message say?"

"You know what it said." If she hadn't let him see her fear while he had her bound and naked, there was no fucking way she was going to let him see it now while he was bound, chained, and incarcerated.

"Do I?" he asked in a made-up innocent voice.

"It's just me here, and I can't send you to death row twice," Vega soothed.

"And you're not even an ADA anymore. I hear you're lawyering in Los Angeles. How is it to work at Knight Technologies, Sweet Caroline?"

Even though she was prepared that he'd know details about her life, it was disconcerting how much he'd gathered when his communication with the outside world was minimal.

"It pays better," she said conversationally and heard Delfino's voice in her ear; keep it easy, like you're two old friends meeting. And stroke his ego. "Now, I know that you know what's going on, Soller. You were always smart about that."

His smile chilled her to the bone. "I did enjoy our time together, Sweet Caroline. Do you still remember those hours?"

This was the thing with narcissistic sociopaths; they were always looking for a weakness. And no matter how strong she was, remembering those hours with him was a wound so big that bile rose inside her. Every fiber of Vega's being screamed to react, but she held steady, her voice even. "I remember every second, Jacob. But what I remember most," she leaned closer to him, "is putting you here, your legs chained to the floor, your hands on the table. It's almost like that metal gurney in your warehouse, isn't it? At least you had leather restraints; TDCJ has sharp, cold metal. Budget cuts. You know."

Something churned inside him. She could see it. He thought he'd manipulate her, make her fear him, feed the beast inside him. But he was finding it difficult to do that. He'd forgotten that she didn't play for a fuck's worth.

His laughter was bitter, devoid of humor. "But I have you here again, in front of me, begging me to give you something. Tell me, Sweet Caroline, are you ready to become a butterfly?"

Vega shrugged. "Like I said, you know that I know that you know what's going on in Los Angeles."

"What can I say, Sweet Caroline? My legacy lives on."

Legacy? The word ran up her spine and lodged itself in her brain. He thought of the new killings as an inheritance he'd left behind.

"I don't know. It's such sloppy work. Don't you think?"

Soller's eyes flickered, a brief moment of genuine interest. "The butterfly was beautiful. Those beautiful wings, each scale, and hair painted on her skin with such precision. You think I don't know? You think I haven't seen?"

He had access to a smartphone; Vega was certain of it now. They had to talk to the guards and figure out who'd been manipulated into giving Soller a line to the outside world.

"Yes, but the second one...man, what a botched job." She oversaw him, noting every micro-expression.

Soller's face hardened. "Second? There has been no second. You fucking with me, Caroline?"

Vega sensed an opening. "Oh, yes, there has been. They lack your... finesse."

He snarled, and Vega wanted to run to Taze and hide behind him. He'd looked exactly like this when he couldn't rape her, so he found a—.

"Your protégé... let's call him that," she said softly and saw nothing to indicate that he found the substantiation of the unsub's gender as male disturbing. "He picked up a postal worker, so he got that right. But then he bungled it. Decided to use a nerve agent instead of your tried and true chloroform."

"You're lying." His agitation was now palpable. Vega's pulse hammered with anxiety and excitement.

"No, sir, I'm not. She had a condition called Myasthenia Gravis, so combined with the nerve agent...she died before he could make her a butterfly."

"No. It's Friday today. It's happening today." He leaned back, convinced Vega was putting him on.

From the breast pocket of her suit jacket, Vega pulled out the printed photograph of the crime scene with the misspelled message for her on Jorja Levey's back and set it in front of Soller.

"You made that up," he snapped.

She shrugged. "Fine. Think what you want. But even the profiler, do you remember Agent Delfino from the BAU? He spent hours talking to you."

Soller had enjoyed his conversations with Delfino, according to the BAU agent. He'd enjoyed talking about his process and victimology; about the power he had over another and the high he got when he transformed a caterpillar into a butterfly.

"Even Delfino thinks that the copycat is substandard," she chuckled. "He thinks it might be a woman. Can you believe that?"

Soller's pathology was intertwined with his need to dominate women—and help them become better. Like most male serial killers, Soller hated women and thought them weak and useless until he made them better.

"Shut your mouth," he whispered.

She couldn't believe she'd done it, Vega thought, shocked. She'd rattled Soller. Again.

"Right now, your legacy is right there next to that poor woman's body." Vega pointed to the dumpster.

His jaw tightened. "No."

Vega leaned back and smiled warmly. "Your children just don't have their Daddy's magic touch, now do they?"

A flicker of something passed through Soller's eyes. Was it pride? Embarrassment? Possessiveness? Vega couldn't be sure, but she pressed on. "I told LAPD it's probably your daughter since Delfino is convinced that this is the work of a woman." She looked at the photo as if critically assessing it, "But maybe it's that son of yours...you know the one who isn't man enough. Because I have to say I expect a woman to do better than this. You know?"

Soller leaned back as well, a slow, chilling smile spreading across his face. He was on to her, she realized, and she'd known it would only be a matter of time before he would. He was smart and psychologically savvy.

"Whatever you came here to get, you won't."

She picked up the photo and then set it down. "I'll let you keep this so you can live the good old days. I hear that your lawyer has exhausted every appeal out there, and the new execution date is probably going to hold. Is that why you sent your...ah...apprentice over to find me?"

"We're finished here," Soller said hoarsely.

"You're right." She rose and winked at Soller. "We are certainly finished."

Chapter 33

Friday, October 12

Beau Heber was in his early twenties and was more than a little nervous about speaking with Vega and Taze. He was a nice-looking kid, Vega thought, and wondered how he ended up with this job and what his story was.

They met in Warden Johnson's office so the security guards didn't feel like they were suspects, which was important to the Warden. He'd kept it casual, saying, "I'm going to go get a cup of joe. Y'all be nice to one another."

"What's Soller like?" Taze asked Heber. They'd decided that Taze would take point with the security guards. A civilian interrogating them would be seen as a sign of disrespect.

"Ah...like?"

"Yeah, what do you think about him?"

"He's...quiet. He keeps to himself. Likes poetry." The young guard smiled, and then, because he realized he did, he pursed his lips.

"What kind of poetry?" Vega asked.

"Ah... them old ones, ma'am. Y'know, like them poets from way back in the eighteenth century. Byron, Blake... that's 'bout all I can recollect." Heber's nervousness seemed to dissipate slightly as he delved into the topic of Soller's literary preferences. "They'd chew the fat over them poems now and then. Nate, he knows a heap 'bout all that old-timey stuff. Him and Soller, they'd get to havin' some mighty long talks."

Vega noticed the subtle shift in Heber's demeanor as he mentioned Nate. "Did you ever join in these discussions?" she inquired, her voice gentle yet probing.

Heber shook his head. ""No, ma'am. I ain't much for poetry myself. I just kinda listened in now and again. Soller's pretty smart, ya know? He talks about these poets like he knew them."

Taze leaned forward, his expression thoughtful. "Did you ever notice anything unusual during these interactions? Anything out of the ordinary?"

Heber thought for a moment, then shrugged. "I don't know, it sure was odd, seein' someone like Soller, what with his history and all, chattin' about poetry. It's like he turned into a whole' nother person in them moments."

Vega exchanged a glance with Taze. It was a familiar pattern with individuals like Soller, who used charm and intellect as a facade to mask their darker nature.

When Warden Johnson returned, Vega and Taze thanked Heber for his time.

"See, I told ya, Beau is a good kid."

Taze took a deep breath and let it out. It was never easy to tell someone that an individual under their command was dirty. "We believe Soller has access to a smart phone. And one of your security guards is helping him."

"Come on, Taze, you just met Beau and—"

"It's going to be Nate Gluck, Warden," Vega interjected.

"Nate Gluck, here is a veteran."

"Then he should have no problem handing over his phone for us to examine," Taze said firmly. "Let's talk to him, and why don't you stay for the conversation?"

"You bet I will."

While Warden went to get Security Guard Gluck, Taze called an ADA he worked with to see if they could get a warrant for Gluck's phone. After he hung up, he grinned at Vega. "Apparently, it shouldn't be a problem."

They needn't have bothered, Vega thought, because Nate Gluck folded like wet cardboard.

Gluck was a ten-year veteran in the prison system, entrusted with the most dangerous inmates. He was calm, collected, and more than a little cocky. His answers initially were concise and professional, but Vega noticed the slight hesitations and the occasional avoidance of eye contact.

"Soller is a monster, and you talk poetry with him?" Taze asked.

"He's treatin' an inmate like a human bein'," Warden Johnson protested.

It took a while to get Gluck to open up because the Warden refused to see what was clear, but ultimately, Gluck confessed, with a mix of shame and disbelief, that he had provided Soller with a contraband cell phone. "I don't know how he did it," Gluck admitted his voice a mixture of frustration and regret. "And once I did that...then...he had me, you understand?"

"Why didn't you come to me?" Warden Johnson cried out. "Damn it, Nate."

"I'm sorry...I... what's going to happen now?"

"Now, you're going to get reprimanded," Warden bellowed.

"Before you do that," Vega held up her hand, "Tell us everything you know about this phone."

CHAPTER 34

Friday, October 12

Aurelio paced the sterile lobby of the prison. Every minute Vega spent with Soller felt like an eternity to him. The thought of her facing that monster was unbearable, no matter how tough she was.

The prison lobby, with its cold, impersonal atmosphere, was giving him the creeps. The faces around him were of families and friends of inmates, each told a story of sadness and complex human emotion. He felt out of place, his own reactions mirroring the heavy air of despair that hung over the room.

When Vega finally emerged, Aurelio immediately noticed the change in her. Her usual composed demeanor was fractured; the mask she wore so well in her professional role had slipped. Her eyes, normally so sharp and focused, were clouded with a turmoil of emotions.

"Not now," she whispered.

He nodded; she needed to keep it together.

Taze opened the back door of his Ford Explorer, not saying anything, giving Vega and Aurelio the privacy, they needed, away from prying eyes.

It was only when the SUV door slammed shut and they were alone that Vega's facade completely crumbled. Aurelio watched, heart aching, as years of pent-up emotion poured out of her.

Aurelio instinctively wrapped his arms around her, offering his silent strength and support. Words felt unnecessary and inadequate in the face of such raw emotion. He held her, a steady presence as she allowed herself this rare moment of vulnerability.

She sobbed, each tear a release of the immense pressure she'd been under. Her body shook with the weight of her experiences, the confrontations with evil that used to be part and parcel of her line of work but not for the past seven years.

He understood then, more clearly than ever, the heavy burden Vega carried. Her encounters with criminals like Soller didn't just end when the case closed. They lingered, haunting shadows in her mind that she battled daily.

As her sobs subsided, Vega leaned back, looking up at Aurelio with a mix of gratitude and apology in her eyes. But he shook his head gently, silencing her unspoken words as he wiped her tears.

"I love you," he told her. "And I think you're the bravest fucking woman in the world."

She went back to resting her head on his chest. They remained there for a while, the silence between them comfortable and understanding, everything she never thought she could have.

CHAPTER 35

Saturday, October 12

That bitch Margo Jean ruined everything.

They had identified the next caterpillar, but before they could put their plan into motion, it went to hell.

Soller had sent a simple message: *You fucked up.*

That was hours ago. Since then, there had been radio silence.

"You need to talk to me," they typed, the words appearing almost desperate on the screen. There was no response, adding to the growing sense of panic and isolation enveloping them.

Minutes stretched into agonizing hours, each ticking second feeding their mounting frustration and fear. The walls of the studio seemed to close in, the shadows darker, more menacing.

They were alone, disconnected from the one person who had given the purpose and direction of their actions.

Finally, a notification chimed. A message from Soller. Their heart leaped, but the relief was short-lived. Soller's words were cold, dismissive: *You're deviating from the plan. You're getting reckless. You're a fuck up.*

The unsub's hands shook as they read and reread the message. Reckless? A fuck up?

They had dedicated everything to this, to him, only to be cast aside so easily? Anger bubbled inside them, a hot, seething rage that threatened to consume their rationality.

They typed, their fingers stabbing at the keys: *I did what you asked. I'm keeping your legacy alive!*

But Soller was unyielding, his next message was a sharp rebuke: *This isn't about theatrics. It's about precision. You're losing control, you're showing how pathetic you are.*

Losing control? Pathetic?

They slammed the phone down, the impact echoing in the quiet room. The unsub paced, their breaths coming in short, ragged gasps. They were not losing control. They were not pathetic. They were evolving. Soller was supposed to guide them, not chastise them like a child.

He played the podcast again. Margo Fucking Jean. Her voice, usually a source of insight, now sounded mocking and patronizing.

"The recent murder of the unnamed postal worker is clearly the work of an amateur, a juvenile attempt by a copycat. The message to Caroline Vega was tattooed like it was done by an illiterate buffoon who doesn't know how to spell," Margo Jean's voice declared confidently through the speakers. "The real Butterfly Killer is in Los Angeles. We have seen proof of that. Jacob Soller was framed by ADA Caroline Vega. The Butterfly Killer has a reason to zone his attention on the woman who gave credit for his work away."

Each word was a strike against their ego, a denial of their efforts. The unsub's fists clenched, nails digging into palms. They wanted to scream, to tear the studio apart. They weren't an amateur. They were Soller's chosen one, his apprentice. How could Margo Jean not see the brilliance in their work?

But deep down, a small, insidious voice whispered doubts. What if Soller was right and they were a pathetic fuck up? The thought was unbearable, igniting a frenzy of self-doubt and anger.

"I'm better than this," they muttered to themselves, their voice gaining an edge of hysteria. "I'll show them. I'll show them all."

They glanced at the array of tools and instruments around the studio, each a part of their grand design. But now, they seemed inadequate, mocking reminders of their failure to live up to Soller's legacy.

The unsub's gaze settled on a photo of Caroline Vega. "Sweet Caroline," they whispered, the name a caress and a curse. Vega was the key. Soller's obsession, their ultimate prize. They needed to prove themselves, to step out of Soller's shadow and claim their own place in this twisted pantheon.

But how? The rage and confusion swirled inside them, a maelstrom of emotions that left them feeling adrift and unmoored. They were Soller's apprentice, but now, they needed to become more. They needed to surpass him.

The podcast continued in the background, Margo Jean's voice a constant, grating reminder of their perceived inadequacy.

They smiled then. Oh, Sweet Margo. Oh, yes!

They typed a message into a burner phone. Long time listener and fan. Thank you for what you're doing for my father. I'm in Los Angeles. Would like to meet you. Kaleb Soller.

CHAPTER 36

Saturday, October 13

"Horvat, Wasco, in my office," Gomez called out.

"Fucking hell! Loo needs to stop working weekends," Drago muttered.

"He's getting divorced, so he doesn't want to be home!"

They came into his office. "Loo, we got a lead into—" Horvat began, but Gomez cut him off with a wave of his hand, his expression grim.

"Margo Jean has gone missing," Gomez stated, his words heavy with both anger and concern.

Drago's brows furrowed, and he leaned forward slightly, his detective instincts kicking in. "Margo Jean, the podcaster? The one covering the Soller case?"

"That's the one," Gomez confirmed, shuffling papers on his desk, a clear sign of his agitation. "She's been vocal about the case, stirring up a lot of attention. Now she's gone, just like that."

Drago's mind raced. Margo Jean's disappearance wasn't just a high-profile case; it was a potential escalation. "How? Where?"

Gomez quickly gave them a rundown on the case. "According to her staff, she was supposed to be at work bright as a button, and she never showed. Last they saw her was when she left work the night before."

"How do we know she's not just blowing off steam somewhere?" Drago demanded.

Gomez turned his monitor to face them and pressed his keyboard. The security camera footage was grainy at best. It was of a parking lot. Margo Jean walked to her car, a white Tesla. As she was opening the door, a silhouette moved behind her, and it was someone in a hoodie, face and body averted.

The son of a bitch knew where the cameras were, Drago thought again.

The two talked, and it looked pretty copacetic. Then, the hooded person got into the passenger seat, and they drove away.

"The Tesla was found this morning in Echo Park. No security camera footage to tell us much of anything. TID is searching, but it's not looking good. We don't know what happened to her after she left the parking lot."

"Crime scene already processing the car?" Drago asked.

Gomez snarled. "Yeah...but this is Los Angeles, we're backed up. So much crime, so few fucking resources. I told them to put a rush on it. They know this is the NBK case."

Drago frowned. "NBK?"

"Yeah, someone in the media called the guy the New Butterfly Killer, and now we're all calling him the New Fucking Butterfly Killer."

Drago ran through his hair. "I don't know why we have to name these assholes."

"You know, from the footage, it looks like she met someone she knew and went with them willingly." Nikki leaned against the wall, her arms crossed.

"Yeah." Gomez picked up his cup of coffee and grimaced at the smell, but too a sip anyway. "Go talk to her colleagues and find this one before someone tattoos her fucking back."

Drago's phone rang as they were walking out. It was Vega. They'd talked the previous evening, and the decision had been made to leave the smart phone with Soller; just clone to it see who he contacts and what he uses it for. DPD had offered resources to help out with the cloning while TID in LA would monitor activity. But the way the resources were spread out, the cloning would not happen until Monday. In the meantime, their unsub was once again back to the business of killing.

"I have an update on Pippa White," Vega told him.

"She's the receptionist who had a big crush on Soller?" Drago threw the car keys at Nikki, who caught them with ease.

He slid into the passenger seat and put Vega on speaker. "You're on speaker. Wasco is here as well."

"Hey, Nikki. Pippa White lives in New York."

"She traveling back and forth to LA by any chance?" Drago really, really wanted a lead on the case; any fucking thing would do.

"We don't think so. She's eight months pregnant and at risk of eclampsia, so she's actually on bed rest. She's not going anywhere," Vega told him.

"We have a problem. Margo Jean was taken by the unsub last night. She didn't show up at work this morning, and they started to worry."

"We sure she's missing and not just out taking a weekend in Vegas?"

"She does a live show every Saturday at eleven. She's never missed except for today," Nikki filled in.

"The unsub took her," Vega whispered.

"Yeah, looks like it."

"This would be the third murder in a couple of weeks, Drago," she sounded horrified, and he didn't blame her; it was pretty horrific.

"Fourth actually," he corrected her.

"What?"

Nikki filled her in about Giselle Maura and her untimely demise.

"Any update from looking at security cameras at the hospital?" Vega asked.

"Hard to do. We don't even have a proper time frame. TID has received the files, and they're going to pore through them," Nikki informed her. "When are you back in LA?"

"I'm hoping to track down Soller's wife and kids," she said.

"You think it could be his daughter? She's what, nineteen now?"

"The profile is not conclusive about it being a man or a woman—there is still uncertainty around that, and when I connected with Delfino, he mentioned that how the unsub is changing behavior and becoming erratic makes it even harder to profile them."

"Yeah, he sent me an email about that," Drago grimaced. "How do you plan to find the wife and kids?"

There was a pause on Vega's end, a long one. "Ah...can you take me off speaker?"

"No. Say what you need to." Drago didn't want to make Nikki feel like they were not partners, that he was hiding things from her. From his experience, not getting along with your partner and lacking mutual trust was a recipe for disaster. And when you're a cop, walking through all kinds of doorways, unsure about who's waiting on the other side, taking such a risk could get either or both of them killed.

"I asked Mateo to help," she said.

Nikki raised her eyebrow, and Drago mouthed, I'll tell you later.

"Nothing wrong with that. If you get something, let us know."

After they hung up, Nikki asked him who Mateo was

"Mateo is the CTO of Knight Technologies, and we can never prove this, but he has a way of getting into systems he's not allowed to, which means he can probably find out where Soller's wife and kids are faster than TID can."

Nikki seemed to think about that for a moment and shrugged, "She's a civilian, and she can ask a friend for help. How he helps her is his business as long as he doesn't trip some digital alarm and get his ass arrested."

Drago grinned. Damn but he liked his new partner, more every day.

Drago and Nikki entered the bustling studio in West Hollywood, the hub of Margo Jean's popular podcast. They were immediately greeted by Robin Marino, her show's producer, a woman with an air of efficiency about her. Beside her stood Thad Thomas, one of the writers for the show, who looked nervous as hell.

"We appreciate you coming in," Robin started, extending her hand to Drago, who shook it firmly. "Can I get you something?" she asked.

"Just as much information as possible about Margo Jean's recent activities, especially any unusual contacts or threats," Nikki said softly, ready to take notes on her phone.

Robin nodded, leading them into a quieter space, a small office crammed with audio equipment and colorful posters. "Last night, she got a text message, and she shared it with us."

Thad interjected, pulling out his phone to show them the message. "It came from an unknown number, claiming to be Soller's son. Said his name was Kaleb and that he wanted to meet with her."

Nikki leaned in, scrutinizing the text on Thad's screen. "Did she believe it was genuine?"

Robin shrugged. "She was skeptical but intrigued. We thought it could be a lead or at least a new angle for the show. She agreed to meet him at the office. He was supposed to come here today before her show, and she was hoping that she could convince him to take part in the live show."

Vega was on the money! Drago was impressed. She was convinced the unsub was somehow connected to Soller's children, and it looked like she was right. Or the unsub was using Soller's kid's name to lure Margo Jean.

Drago's mind was working overtime, piecing together the events. "You think she would've taken a meeting with Kaleb, say, if he accosted her in your parking lot?"

Thad looked pained. "Yeah. Yeah, she would. She was excited to meet Soller's kid and spin the story about how his false arrest and conviction impacted the family. We've been trying to track the wife and kids, but no cigar. They changed their identities and whatever new identity they came up with his airtight.

"We'll need to access Margo Jean's work emails, phone records, anything that can give us more context to this message," Drago said, his tone leaving no room for argument.

Robin nodded. "Of course, whatever helps. We just want to find her, safe and sound."

Drago called the crime scene guys and told them to get to Margo Jean's studio to process it immediately. In the meantime, Drago and Nikki moved methodically through Margo Jean's office, their eyes scanning every inch of the space. The room was a chaotic blend of creativity and disorder, with sticky notes in various colors plastered all over the walls, computer monitor, and even the edges of her desk. Each note seemed to be a fragment of Margo Jean's thoughts and investigations: cryptic messages, names, dates, and questions.

Nikki carefully examined each sticky note, looking for any clue that might indicate Margo Jean's plans or thoughts prior to her disappearance. "She really liked her sticky notes," Nikki remarked, her voice tinged with a mix of admiration and frustration at the sheer volume of notes.

"Yeah, but there's a method to this madness," Drago replied, his gaze intense as he tried to decipher the pattern in the chaos. He began to group the notes by color and theme, trying to construct a timeline or a narrative from the scattered pieces of information.

Among the sea of yellow, pink, and blue notes, one in particular caught Nikki's eye. It was a bright orange note stuck to the underside of the desktop, almost hidden from view. "Drago, look at this," she called out, pointing to the note.

Drago leaned in to read the hastily scrawled message: "Plan questions for Kaleb. Verify ID."

"Well, hell, now she can ask him questions up close and personal," Drago said, his voice low.

"You think she was even aware of the risk she was taking?"

"God knows," Drago said in frustration.

"She took her laptop and phone, probably for the meeting. She might have left a digital trail we can follow."

Just then, the crime scene technicians arrived, bustling into the room with their equipment. Drago briefed them quickly, emphasizing the need to preserve the layout of the sticky notes for further analysis.

As the techs got to work, Drago and Nikki stepped outside the office. They needed to track Margo Jean's digital footprint, starting with her laptop and phone. The mention of Kaleb was now their most solid lead, and they had to act fast.

But first things first, he called Vega.

"If you find Soller's kids, you don't go there alone," he ordered and then told her about Margo Jean and her communication with Soller's son.

"If I find him, I'll take Taze along with me. Good enough?"

"Yeah. You have a piece, Vega?"

"Not on me," she immediately replied. "But I have one at home in a locked safe."

"Bring it out of the safe once you're back home. I don't care if you have a bodyguard, you wear your weapon, keep it close and if this motherfucker comes for you, cap his ass. Got it?"

"Aye, aye, sir," she attempted a joke, which Drago thought fell seriously flat on its face.

Nikki got a text message as Drago ended his call with Vega. "Crime scene has her car. Preliminary report...oh, god, Drago, she pissed herself in the car."

"You think that was a reaction to the drug or knowing she'd just made pally-pally with a serial killer?" Drago muttered, annoyed as hell that this son of a bitch seemed to be one step ahead of them at all times.

Nikki shook her head. "They're going to look through everything, but analysis won't be back for days."

"Margo Jean will be dead by then."

CHAPTER 37

Saturday, October 13

She begged.

They all begged.

Kaleb never understood why. Like what they say would change anything.

"You called me a buffoon," he said, trailing a cattle prod over Margo's tear-stained right cheek.

"I'm so...sorry," she gasped for air, having a panic attack.

She'd already emptied her bladder and bowels out of fear, but that was in her car when she realized who he was. Just remembering the look on her face filled him with glee. He left her soiled clothes in a trash can outside his studio. He would not contaminate his pristine studio with her filth.

"I'm not a buffoon, you bitch. I'm not an amateur. I'm Jacob Soller's seed. I'm his legacy. And you ruined it. He won't even talk to me anymore."

It bothered Kaleb that Soller had frozen him out. One stupid mistake and that's it; Daddy had cut him off. Son of a bitch. One day, he wanted Soller on a gurney like this. Well, they'd put him in a chair and strap him up real soon and fill his body with poison. And he'd go and watch. Yes, he would, and he hoped that his was the face his father would see before he died. The thought made him hard.

Maybe he should fuck this one, he thought. The others he'd not been allowed to fuck. His father had been clear. They were *his* butterflies, so Kaleb had to use a dildo.

But this one was his, wasn't she?

Thinking about how Soller would soon be dead and how he'd become the only Butterfly Killer in the world, he got to work on making Margo Jean the very best butterfly they could.

CHAPTER 38

Saturday, October 13

Mateo found Soller's ex-wife in two hours. Vega didn't ask him how he did it. She knew if she ever had to testify under oath about this she'd perjure herself with impunity.

Nora Soller, now Nora Hoying, lived in Shreveport, a two-and-a-half-hour drive from Dallas. She had remarried a widower, Ralph Hoying, who owned three surf and turf restaurants in Louisiana.

When Aurelio, Taze, and she parked in front of Nora and Ralph Hoying's mansion, Taze whistled. "Holy mother of god, she landed nicely on her feet."

"I'll wait in the Explorer," Aurelio said.

Vega knew he was aware of his status as the civilian consultant's over protective boyfriend meant that he needed to make himself scarce. She'd tried to convince him to go home, but he'd told her that wasn't going to happen.

"I'm protected."

"I'm not here to protect you, though god knows I would if it came to that, and I'd die trying, baby. I'm here to hold you after you slay your dragons. So, let me."

He always had the right words, she thought, now only half annoyed with him.

"You won't mind?" Vega turned to face him, wanting confirmation. She had driven shotgun while Aurelio had been on two conference calls in the back, one with his farm manager and the other with his brother.

He held up his laptop. "I got paperwork up my ass for the FDA. Go, do your thing; I'll be right here."

As Taze and Vega walked up to Mrs. Hoying's doorstep, he said, "That guy is fucking amazing. You know that, right?"

"Yeah."

"He's a farmer?"

Vega grinned. "Well, his family owns one of the biggest organic farms in all of California...maybe the country. If y'all have eaten organic artichokes recently, they probably came from Golden Valley."

Taze nodded appreciatively. "So, he's a rich fucking farmer."

"Oh, yes."

"Nice work, Vega."

"Yeah?"

"He's stand up, I ain't swingin' that way, but he doesn't hurt the eyes, and he's got money coming out of his ass; I think that is what they call a hat trick in the datin' business."

Nora looked better than she had seven years ago. Now, in her late forties, she greeted them with a polite, somewhat strained smile. Her demeanor was more of a hostess than someone whose husband had brought infamy to the family name. Vega sensed a disconnect in Nora, a concern more about appearances and social judgments than the grim reality of her husband's actions.

The living room was adorned with family photos that seemed to have skipped the very existence of Jacob Soller. Vega doubted Nora's new husband even knew about Jacob Soller and who he was, and Nora would not be the one telling him.

"I told you on the phone, Detective Taze, I have only fifteen minutes for you, no more. I don't understand why we couldn't have this conversation over the phone."

Because then we wouldn't be able to tell when you lie to us, Vega thought.

They sat in her living room, the informal one, her on a sofa and them on matching armchairs across from her. In between was a Louis XVI coffee table, which probably put back Mr. Hoying at least thirty-five grand. Vega knew because she had a passion for antiques and had started buying some pieces since her income had caught up with her tastes in the corporate world.

"This is really important, Mrs. Hoying," Taze continued politely but firmly.

She pursed her lips and crossed her feet, embodying a picture of refined elegance. She was dressed in cigarette pants and an olive-colored silk blouse that showed off her arms. Girlfriend had a personal trainer because arms like that did not come for free. Her blonde hair, styled with care, fell gracefully over her shoulders. A strand of pearls, likely worth a small fortune, adorned her neck, paired with high-heeled Stuart Weitzman pumps. Vega, familiar with the customs of the South, knew that such meticulous dressing at home, especially when expecting company, was a common practice in this region.

"We have a copycat killer in Los Angeles," Taze began, "And we—"

"I know. I've read the news, Detective. I'm aware that they suspect a copycat of the Butterfly Killer. But I think it's the real Butterfly Killer. And you know it too, because you framed Jacob," she spit the words out with venom at Vega.

Fool's paradise must be one crowded place, Vega thought, with so many morons taking up residence there.

"Nora, where are your children?" Vega asked, losing patience.

"You stay away from my children," she snarled. "They don't need this in their lives."

"We tracked you down, we'll track them down," Taze said ominously.

She sat up straighter. "Kaylea is...well, she's taking a gap year, after which she will start premed at NYU. Kaleb got his law degree from LSU and is now working at a very prestigious firm in

Atlanta. He wants to work to find people justice when corrupt lawyers like you, Miss Vega, ruin the lives of families."

"Which firm in Atlanta?" Taze asked.

She shrugged. "I don't know."

"Where is Kaylea?"

"I'm here," a voice from behind them spoke. They turned to see a mini version of Nora. Vega's chest tightened. Soller had a type. Blonde with chiseled cheekbones. All three women in this room were his type.

"Kaylea, I told you to—"

"Mama, why don't you leave already for your DAR meeting at Mrs. Picken's, and I'll speak with the detectives."

The part of Nora that understood there was something perverse about a mother leaving her nineteen-year-old daughter to handle a veritable interrogation about her father, who was a serial killer on death row, was minuscule. So, with a warning about being nice to her daughter, she flounced out.

Kaylea sat where her mother had been sitting. "I read about the killings in Los Angeles, and it makes me sick to think that someone is following in my father's footsteps."

"You don't think your father was framed?" Taze wanted to know.

She shook her head. "I listened to his entire trial. Do you know they have recordings of all the trials that take place in state court? I knew in my heart, but after, I knew in my head."

Kaylea, in utter contrast to her mother, seemed less guarded and more open. She also appeared smarter.

"Can you tell us where you've been for the past two weeks?" Taze continued.

She nodded. "I've been volunteering at The Providence House, it's a homeless shelter on Cotton Street. I work seven to four there every day. My goal for my gap year is to volunteer and learn more about myself and...empathy."

Vega had always wondered what happened to the family of serial killers. How did they cope? What did they do?

"And how about your brother?" Taze went on.

She folded her arms as if holding herself and took a deep breath. "Mama doesn't know, but Kaleb got fired. He's not in Atlanta any longer."

"When was this?"

"Four months ago." Her eyes flickered at Vega, who was silent, listening, observing. "You think he's doing this, don't you?"

"Why would you say that?" Vega finally spoke.

Her eyes filled with tears. "Because, like Mama, he keeps on and on and on about how you, Miss Vega, framed *him*. But unlike Mama, he knows that our father did the things he was accused of doing."

"How does he know?"

Kaylea shook her head. "It feels like a betrayal. I... don't think it's him. Kaleb is a lot of things, but he's not a killer."

"Miss Hoying," Taze urged, "what did you mean when you said he knew?"

She cleared her throat. "Kaleb told me this a year or so ago. He's told no one. He saw my father dump a body. It was...ah...the journalist."

"Sandra Blanc?" Vega's eyes widened. That had been Soller's third victim.

She nodded. "Mama had been upset with dad...Soller...for working all weekend, so she told him he had to pick up Kaleb from soccer practice. He picked him up in his van, and...ah, on the way, he stopped and said he had to make a delivery. Kaleb followed him out of curiosity. See, he was eighteen then and I don't know why he didn't come clean with Detective Schwartz when he talked to us."

"*You* think he's doing these killings, don't you?" Vega whispered.

Her eyes filled with tears, and they rolled down her cheeks. "No. I don't." It was a lie and Vega's heart broke for the woman. Sins of the father and now the brother. The universe was being extremely unfair to Kaylea.

"Kaylea?" Vega pleaded.

She sniffled. "He and my father never got along, not really. Dad always thought that Kaleb was not man enough. He'd call him a sissy. Kaleb was not into football...he was into theatre and for our father that was just another sign that his son was not growing up to be a man. Kaleb had it real tough at home."

What she didn't say hovered in the room, that Kaleb wanted to prove to his father that he was as much of a man as Jacob Soller. How far would he go to do that?

"Do you have his phone number? Any contact information?"

Kaylea shook her head. "Since the news broke about what's happened in Los Angeles, I've called him, and it says that phone number is disconnected. His email bounces back to the wrong address. He's cut off all ties."

"Why didn't you call anyone?" Vega demanded. "Three women are dead, and one is right now on a slab somewhere, waiting to die at the hands of your brother."

She began to cry in earnest. "Because how am I supposed to accept that both my father and my brother are monsters? I'm so sorry."

Taze glared at Vega, asking her silently to tone it down. She immediately regretted her harsh words. This was not Kaylea's fault; she was as much of a victim as anyone.

"You have nothing to be sorry about," Vega told her. "I'm the one who—"

"I know what he did to you," Kaylea interrupted. "I know and I also know you left Dallas and law enforcement. How are you involved in this case?"

"I'm a civilian consultant working with the LAPD."

"Why?"

"Because I'm a Butterfly Killer expert."

Kaylea winced. "That's such a horrible thing to be an expert on."

"Yeah, tell me about it," I agreed.

CHAPTER 39

Sunday, October 14

"Detective, we had a female in distress on Pico and Menlo Avenue. We have a bus transporting her to USC Medical, but we have a flag saying this would be a case you'd be interested in."

"Why?"

"She said her name is Margo Jean."

Drago's heart skipped a beat. "Margo Jean?"

"Yeah," the dispatcher confirmed, her voice steady despite the gravity of the information. "She's pretty shaken up, kept saying she escaped from the Butterfly Killer."

Nikki, overhearing the conversation, turned sharply towards Drago, her eyes wide with a mix of shock and realization.

"We're on our way; in the meantime, I want at least two patrolmen to be with Margo Jean at every step," Drago said quickly, ending the call. He turned to Nikki, his expression resolute. "Margo Jean is in USC Medical. If she's escaped from him, he may come after her."

Nikki needed no further prompting. They bolted from the bullpen to their car; sirens wailing, they sliced through the dense traffic with urgent precision.

Upon arriving at USC Medical, they were immediately engulfed in a vortex of frenetic activity. Nurses and doctors, faces taut with concentration, darted through the corridors like specters, their focus solely on the sea of patients. Drago and Nikki, with a sense of foreboding, flashed their badges to the receptionist, their voices terse as they stated their purpose.

They were requested to wait in the lobby, a place humming with low, anxious murmurs. Drago's impatience simmered, barely contained, as he prepared to interrogate the receptionist.

His phone beeped and everyone in the lobby eyed him with disdain. One nurse pointed to a sign saying: *No phones*. He walked out of the lobby and took the call from Gomez.

"She okay?" he asked.

"Don't know. Waiting for the doctor. Once we do that we'll go talk to the paramedics who brought her in."

Nikki peeked out of the lobby door. "The doctor is here, Horvat."

"Loo, I'll call you later and fill you in."

Drago found a weary looking surgeon standing in front of the sea of sterile doors into the lobby.

"Hi, I'm Dr. Huynh," he said and nodded at Drago and Nikki as he removed his surgical cap. "Detectives, I'm afraid there's been a change in her condition. Margo Jean has slipped into a coma."

Drago's heart sank at the news, a mix of frustration and concern etching his features. "Do we know what caused it?" he asked, his voice strained.

"We think that she was given a high dosage of a nerve agent of some kind that—"

"Succinylcholine," Drago informed him. "Her attacker has been using it to subdue his victims. We already have one dead due to its administration as she had Myasthenia Gravis, and reacted adversely to it."

Dr. Huynh sighed, shaking his head. "We believe she reacted to a high dosage of this nerve agent that was contraindicated with electric shocks. She has electric burns all over her body."

Nikki cleared her throat. "The...ah...attacker likes to use a cattle prod to torture his victims."

"This is the Butterfly Killer that we've been hearing so much about?" Dr. Huynh asked, and when they nodded, he continued, "I'm not a forensic expert, but this is what I can tell you. She's been raped multiple times."

"Any fluids?"

"Yes, we're doing a rape kit," he continued. "But...look, I'm not a forensic; I save lives, so I—"

"Spit it out, doc," Drago demanded, flustered.

"I think he also used a dildo to rape her," he concluded. "Based on the tears and trauma, a human penis didn't do this to her."

Nikki stepped closer to the doctor. "Did she say anything at all before she went into her coma?"

"No, but you should talk to the paramedics who brought her here. She was more lucid with them."

"Will she wake up?" Drago asked.

"One can never say. Look, I don't know how she escaped, but that woman is one hell of a fighter, so if I had to put odds, I'd put them in her favor. Now, I have to go back. Someone will make sure you're kept updated. Just leave your contact information with our receptionist here."

"Doc, I want two patrolmen outside her door."

"Yes," the doctor didn't argue.

"You understand why?"

"He didn't finish the job, and you're worried he may come in here to do it. Not a problem. I'll also ask hospital security to beef up their presence. Anything else?"

"Thanks, doc."

They found the paramedics next, who were in the hospital cafeteria, drinking coffee. Timothy LaForce was a tall, sharp-looking man, and his partner Natasha Lambo looked like someone had dimmed the light in her face; she looked so forlorn.

"We were just going off night shift when the dispatcher called," LaForce began, probably because it looked like Lambo was in three different kinds of hell right now.

"Do we know who made the call?"

"In that part of DTLA? Hell, we're lucky someone called." LaForce ran a hand over his face. "We get there before the cops, and she's...well, she's bleeding and swaying."

"Bleeding?"

"She had cuts all over her stomach like someone was trying to slash her with a scalpel, but slowly so it'd hurt," Lambo said softly, speaking for the first time.

"Was there any kind of tattoo on her back?" Nikki asked.

They both shook their heads.

"Did she say anything?" Drago wanted to know.

"Very little," LaForce replied. "She was disoriented and in shock. When we got to her first, she was a little lucid. She spoke to us, I don't know with what strength. She said, I'm Margo Jean. I escaped from the Butterfly Killer. Please help me. After that, she wasn't coherent...she was given some kind of anesthetic because she was going into paralytic shock."

"He probably injected her with Succinylcholine," Nikki informed them.

"Son of a bitch! I don't know how she managed to run away with that drug in her system," Lambo choked out. "That's one brave woman."

"Any personal effects," Drago wondered, though he already knew the answer.

The paramedics shook their heads. "She didn't have any clothes on, Detective."

CHAPTER 40

Sunday, October 14

They got on a conference call: Vega from an airport in Shreveport waiting for a chartered plane to bring her and Aurelio back to Los Angeles, Drago and Nikki at LAPD HQ, and Agent Thomas Delfino in Quantico.

"I'm still surprised that this unsub is male, but sometimes there are mistakes made in profiles," Agent Delfino admitted, "From what you've found out recently, yes, I do believe that Kaleb Soller has devolved. The fact that he saw his father leave a body and said nothing is indicative. He wasn't a child; he was eighteen, a grown-up by all accounts, which tells us that he's always had a propensity for violence, and seeing his father do it gave him the green light to pursue the kills."

"You think he's done this before," Vega surmised as she held Aurelio's hand. They were sitting on comfortable leather chairs in a private airport. They'd decided to forego commercial, and as Aurelio had put it, he'd only do something this extravagant if there was an emergency. Right now, he couldn't think of a more urgent one.

Vega had told him she was glad he had the money because there was no way she could afford chartered flights.

"I'd ask Atlanta PD to look for unsolved murders, probably done with a knife and frenzied," Agent Delfino agreed with Vega. "Kaleb didn't just start with Lorna Wilson. He has been practicing for years, and once he felt he could live up to his father, he approached him. You'll also find that Kaleb has been training under a tattoo artist. He's spent the last seven years becoming someone who can take his father's place as the man of the house. But now that he has failed to follow in his father's footsteps, his behavior is unpredictable."

"Is he going to come for Vega?" Drago asked.

"Yes."

"We have his identity, so we have something," Nikki soothed, "We don't have any recent photos of Kaleb Soller. His digital history is wiped clean. We have an old driver's license. TID is looking through his digital footprint and we have someone doing that aging software thing to give us a facial rendition of what he looks like today."

"What last name was he going by?" Vega asked.

"Marshall. Nora changed her and Kaylea's last name after she remarried. Kaleb had already left home by then," Drago informed her.

After the call, they boarded the plane and Vega didn't care that it was only noon and ordered a whiskey and gave a thumbs up to the flight attendant when he told her he had Woodford's Reserve. Fuck it, she needed a drink. Actually, she needed a few drinks.

Aurelio stuck with coffee probably because he wanted one of them to not be drunk as a skunk by the time they landed in three and a half hours in LA.

Vega settled in her seat and called Mateo after she had her first pull of liquor.

"Querida, how are you?"

"I need your help again."

"Tell me."

"Find out where Kaleb Marshall is." She gave him the information she had about him going to school at LSU and working for a law firm in Atlanta.

"I'll have something for you shortly," he said with a confidence that bordered on arrogance.

She licked her lips. "I have something else. I don't know if I succeeded because I didn't want Detective Taze to know."

Aurelio looked at her curiously.

"I...ah...cloned Soller's phone. The one that a security guard slipped him. To avoid Soller from getting caught with the phone, the guard gave him the phone at only certain times of the day; the rest of the time, he kept it in his locker. We were allowed to examine it and...I cloned it."

"Whoa!" Mateo said, "*You* cloned his phone? Do you know how?"

"Yeah," she said, offended, "I work for a tech company. I used a cloning app...but I don't know if I did it correctly. If I give you my phone, can you find out how Soller is communicating with his son?"

"Absolutely. Bring the phone over as soon as you land. Anything else you want to confess to that you did is illegal in the state of Texas?" he joked.

Vega chuckled. "Thanks, Mateo. I owe you."

"I'll see you soon, Vega. Stay safe."

Aurelio was smiling from ear to ear as the plane took off. "You cloned Soller's phone?"

"I know. I hoped we'd get lucky and find his smartphone. So, I asked someone in IT at Knight Tech to show me how to clone a phone. It was a long shot."

"And now you have his phone on your phone?"

"See, that's the part I don't know how to do unravel," she confessed. "Now I can have Mateo commit a crime along with me."

"Is it a crime to clone a phone?"

"It's tampering with evidence," Vega pointed out. She thanked the flight attendant, who brought a refill for both of them, coffee for him, and whiskey for her.

She closed her eyes. "I'm exhausted, but I can't sleep...my mind is running five hundred miles a minute."

Aurelio sat down next to her and pulled her into his lap. He kissed her forehead and held her like she were a child. "Go to sleep, baby."

"On your lap?"

"Yeah, what? You say you're not comfortable?"

"I'm going to get super heavy and—"

"Are you saying I'm not man enough to hold my woman?"

Vega sighed and kissed his nose. "That's not what I'm saying."

He put her head on his shoulder. "Sleep, baby. Just for a minute. It's going to be a shitshow once we get to LA."

It was a shitshow because while they'd been flying, news had leaked that Margo Jean had been attacked by the Butterfly Killer. She'd escaped and was now in a coma.

"There's a mob outside your apartment and Knight Tech; sorry, we couldn't keep your home address concealed," Roman Woo told her when he came to pick them up at LAX.

"By mob, you mean media?" Aurelio asked.

"Yes. But I changed vehicles, so they won't know it's you I'm driving in and out of the buildings. Where can I take you first?"

"Knight Tech," both Aurelio and Vega said in unison, as they both wanted to get Soller's clone to Mateo ASAP.

By the time they got back to Vega's apartment, they were both beat. It had been a long day, and they'd achieved quite a bit.

Mateo had been able to extract Soller's clone and had set it up as a separate phone so Vega could see what he was up to. He'd also determined the messaging app he was using to communicate with someone whose screen name was NBK_2023. She didn't tell Drago about the phone and how she cloned it. He might be family, but he'd have her head if he thought she had jeopardized their case by going rogue and doing something illegal.

"I just want to crash," Vega told Aurelio.

Once they were in bed, they held each other close. Since she'd first met him, Aurelio had been there for her. And even now, when the going was getting tough, he'd not left.

She cupped him, wanting to feel close to him.

"You're so beautiful, baby." He nuzzled her as she lay her head on his shoulder, her naked body entangled with his.

"I'm glad you think I'm beautiful," she whispered as his hand slipped to caress her ass, dipping his fingers between her legs, finding her warm, wet, wanting.

"I thought you were tired," he teased as he slid a finger inside her. "God, you're so snug, baby."

She arched against him, so he'd finger her deeper as she pumped him.

"Do you know I can't get enough of you?" he whispered as he became harder, her need fueling his.

She undressed hurriedly and rolled over him. She kissed him gently on his lips. "Good. Because neither can I."

He held her hips over him, and she trembled.

"Caro." He lifted his hips as she sheathed him. "Ride me, baby."

As she did, he whimpered. "No woman I've been inside has been this perfect. Sex with you, baby, is flawless. No pussy takes my cock as well you do."

He cupped her breasts as she rose and fell over him, with him inside her.

"Aurelio, please," she whimpered as she always did when he pinched her nipples, suckled her, and made her wetter.

Had sex ever been this volatile? This fulfilling? This comforting? No. It had been raunchy, reckless, and fun at times—but never this visceral, this all-consuming.

"You're mine, aren't you, baby?" He lifted her hips and let fall slowly, teasing both of them.

"Yes," she whispered.

"No one else's." His demand came from deep within him. He wanted her to be only his. Only, only, only his.

"Yes." She bucked as she came, her head thrown back. She looked like a pagan goddess with her blonde, lush hair all around her face. Her body bowed, sweat making her breasts shine and her lips...god, those lips that gave the best blowjobs he'd ever had, parted, just the way he liked to see them.

Whenever they made love, it was like she slipped into the best part of the world. With it came the certainty that this was where she was supposed to be. Her heart had never felt this strong, this content.

"Honey, I'm too sensitive," she protested when his fingers strummed against her clitoris. The pleasure was almost painful.

"I know, baby, but you can take it; you're made for this and me."

He made her come just like that. She clenched around him, and he gritted his teeth as if holding back. "One more, Caro, my Caro, you need to come for me again. I want to feel you around me." It was the urgency in his voice that drove Vega over the edge, and this time, she took him along with her.

The chemistry between Aurelio and her was potent. Every time they'd tried to break up and end the relationship, they'd ended up together in bed. It seemed inevitable. And once he'd said those three little words, it had become clear that this relationship was here to stay. Scary, scary thought!

Sex with Aurelio was the best she'd ever had. He was inventive, fun, and a fucking boss with his hands and tongue.

She lay draped on him as he stroked her back, calming them both down. "Stay inside me as I fall asleep," she said. "Don't let go."

"I won't," he whispered.

"Promise?"

"Yes."

"I love you, Aurelio."

"I know, baby. I love you, too. More than you can imagine, more than I thought possible."

CHAPTER 41

Sunday, October 14

Kaleb was tired, scared, and tweaked up on methamphetamines.

If he were honest, he'd know that his lack of discipline, which his father always told him would be his downfall, had led him to be lax with Margo Jean, and he'd lost her.

He was embarrassed, ashamed that he'd not even started her transformation. He'd been busy fucking her and loving it; and that's when he'd slipped.

Already, the news was out about it.

Margo Jean escapes copycat butterfly killer.

In the dim confines of his cramped, unkempt studio apartment, he paced frenetically. His mind was a whirlwind of chaos and desperation. Margo Jean's escape was a blunder he hadn't anticipated, a failure that gnawed at him with the ferocity of a caged beast.

He'd worked so hard at this. Since he'd first started to communicate with his father six months ago, he'd meticulously planned every step.

He left Atlanta. Came to LA. Got close to Sweet Caroline. Stayed away from drugs.

He'd succeeded at everything except that last one.

The room felt suffocating, the walls echoing back his ragged breaths and the frantic beat of his heart. In a frenzied state, he'd rummaged through a drawer, hands trembling, and retrieved a small bag containing methamphetamine. The drugs had become a crutch, a means to dull the sharp edges of reality and amplify his resolve. With a swift, almost ritualistic motion, he inhaled deeply, letting the drugs flood his system, a temporary balm to his unraveling psyche.

In his drug-induced haze, he fixated on Caroline Vega. She'd become the epitome of his twisted redemption, a key to earning the elusive approval of his father. And as the drugs coursed through him, a searing clarity pierced the fog of his mind.

I'm not Jacob Soller. I'm Kaleb Soller. I'm my own person.

He no longer wanted to be a mere extension of his father's legacy. The time had come to forge his own path. But before he could do that, he needed to finish his father's work. He owed him that much, didn't he?

So, what if he lost Margo Jean? He'd get Caroline Vega for his father. And that's the last thing he'd do for that son of a bitch.

He grabbed his burner phone, the lifeline to his father, and looked at it with a mix of contempt and liberation. This device had been his connection to Soller, a beacon of his approval and guidance. But now, it represented chains, shackles binding him to a past he yearned to escape.

He sent his last message to his father.

Dad, I know you're disappointed, but I'm going to finish your work. I'm going to make Sweet Caroline a butterfly. Goodbye.

After he pressed send, with a decisive motion, he smashed the phone against the wall, watching as it shattered into pieces, each fragment a symbol of his emancipation. The act was cathartic, a physical manifestation of his internal rebellion.

As the remnants of the phone lay scattered, a new determination took root within Kaleb. He'd do Caroline on his terms, a demonstration of his capabilities, free from the constraints of Soller's influence. Unlike his father, who couldn't get it up with her, he would, and he'd do her.

Soller had been clear that Kaleb never penetrated the caterpillars; after all, they belonged to Soller. Selfish asshole. He'd bought a dildo to imitate Soller. Not this time. This time, he'd do what he had to do.

He planned how he'd take Caroline and what he'd do with her. All these rituals his father had put in place were bullshit, a waste of time. This time it would be his way, and while he was at it, he'd get rid of that fucking farm boy, always hovering around her.

Did he really think he could protect her? Against Kaleb Soller? Well, think again, pretty boy. His time was up. Her time was up.

Kaleb Soller's time had just begun.

CHAPTER 42

Monday, October 15

"No," Aurelio said firmly yet again when Vega insisted that she had to go to work.

"What the fuck, Aurelio? Tone down the alpha male, will you?" Even though it gave her a small...tiny...*minuscule* thrill when he ordered her around, there was no way she'd let him run her life.

"This isn't alpha male, this is just your regular garden-variety male."

"Look, we're this close to getting this Solarix and Knight Tech merger through. Joey and I—"

"Joey can come here." Aurelio waved around her apartment. "You can work in your home office."

Vega sighed. "I'll be protected. Roman will be—"

"Can we please not take a chance with your life until Kaleb Soller is in custody?" Aurelio pleaded.

"I know what you're doing," she accused.

"Doing what?" he asked.

"Going from asshole alpha male to understanding boyfriend...*and* it's working."

He kissed her mouth. "I have a meeting, which I will take from the living room. You tell Joey to come here to work with you, and we're all good."

Vega went into her office. The good thing about not going to work was that she could spend her day in jeans and a T-shirt. She looked out from her expansive windows onto the city and felt better than she had in a long time. Someone was still trying to kill her, but the past weeks had shown her who she really was, and that had made some of the past trauma fall away. She had no idea why being an ADA again made her feel better about what had happened with Soller, not worse. When she quit law enforcement, it was out of sheer desperation, plain old survival instinct. Now, she had distance. Now, she had Aurelio.

Vega wasn't one of those women who walked around thinking she needed a man to complete her. Hell no! Vega was complete, and she wanted a man to complement her. And Aurelio did that. She was more with him than she was on her own.

She called Roman Woo and let him know that she'd be staying in her apartment for the day.

"You want me to hang in the apartment with you? Or I can be outside."

"Take the day off, Roman," Vega chirped, "We're home, and no one is coming up without security checking them through."

"You sure?"

"Yeah, I am sure."

Vega wasn't stupid. She was making sure she was protected because she knew what happened when you weren't, and she'd do anything not to go through that hell again.

She'd taken Drago's advice and pulled her gun out of the safe. She'd cleaned it and loaded it. She put the gun in the top desk drawer of her office. Very Noir Private Detective, she thought sourly.

She got to work and decided for a short while to ignore fucking serial killers for the normalcy of corporate narcissists and sociopaths. She sent a message to Joey, requesting her to come to her apartment in the afternoon for their meeting. She apologized for the inconvenience, and Joey said not to worry.

She then called Jada to tell her she was working from home.

"Everything okay? You sick or something?" Jada deadpanned.

"Very funny," Vega muttered, "Just want to work from home for a day or...maybe two. Nothin' wrong with that. Everyone works from home these days."

"Yeah, everyone ain't you," she teased. "You want to keep your meeting with Dec over Zoom or change it for tomorrow...that is if you're coming in tomorrow."

"Just leave it on the calendar. I need to catch him up on the Solarix stuff anyway after Joey and I meet."

"You want me to come along with Joey to your place?" Jada asked.

"No, I think we should be fine. It's the last fine tune of the agreement. She's raised some yellow flags, and I want to go through them."

"She did fine presenting to Mateo and Dec on her own," Jada said, and Vega heard the pride in her voice. It was always a pleasure to help a junior associate grow and develop. Joey had a long way to go, but she was a fine lawyer, and one day, she'd be able to take over as General Counsel for a company just like Vega had.

"I got a text from Dec congratulating me on a good hire," Vega stated, "Joey's a good egg."

After hanging up, Vega dropped a quick message for Mateo, asking him if he'd uncovered anything from Soller's phone and then went right back to contracts that needed her eagle eye and attention.

She checked in with Drago on Margo Jean and felt unsettled about the woman, who was apparently still in a coma.

Since Joey would be visiting, Vega covered her unofficial NBK, New Butterfly Killer murder board, with a sheet of white paper, securing it over the wall with cellophane tape.

Now they knew who the killer was. And now that they knew, she felt an easing of the heart. She trusted Drago and his team to find Kaleb Soller. She had to believe that they would because anything else was untenable.

As she worked, she heard Aurelio over the phone and felt a rush of delight. This could be their lives. She could move to Golden Valley, to his gorgeous home, and they'd live like this: she with her work and he with his. It would be easier for him to be at the farm than work it from here. She knew the pressure he had put on himself and his family by being away from Golden Valley to be with her. She had immense gratitude for that and fully understood the cost to him.

An hour into their morning, he brought her coffee and leaned down to brush his lips against hers.

"I could get used to this," Vega told him, smiling.

"Used to what?"

"This," she remarked, "working together...living together."

Something flashed in his eyes, satisfaction, and hunger. "Yeah?"

She licked her lips, aware she was jumping off a cliff, but he'd catch her, she was certain of it. "Yeah."

He hauled her out of her chair and pulled her into him. "You'll move in with me?"

"Yes," she whispered.

He held her as if she was the most precious thing in his life. "I love you, baby."

"I know, honey and thank god you do." Emotions surged through her, and she held him tightly, like he held her heart and life in his hands, which he did. When Jamie, her ex-fiancé, left her, it had been brutal, no doubt about it, but she'd recovered. If she lost Aurelio, she didn't think she'd recover. Ever.

He set her on her desk and moved between her thighs. He ran his hands up and down her arms. "Say you love me."

"I love you." She was aware of how easily the words slipped out of her, words that usually would struggle to get past her throat, her heart. "Very much, Aurelio."

He smiled wide. "I'm going to wait to ask you that next question. You understand what I'm saying?"

She knew what he meant, and he knew her so damn well, knew that she needed to take it slow. In the past two weeks, she'd already taken massive steps forward. She'd told him she loved him and now had agreed to move in with him.

"I do," she whispered the words à propos for his unasked question.

"But not too long," he cautioned, "My Mama won't be able to stand it, and my sister will nag; and...."

"And?"

"And I don't know if I'll be able to wait too long either to call you—"

"We said we'd take it slow," she interrupted him before he said the W word. Christ on a crutch! Give the man an inch, and he was ready to take it to church and get it wedded and bedded.

He nuzzled his nose against hers. "I can't live without you anymore, Caro."

Tears sprang into her eyes. "Neither can I, honey, neither can I."

He kissed her softly, slowly, like they had all the time in the world, and Vega realized that they did. Joy bloomed inside her. After what Soller did to her, she never thought she'd be whole again; she always believed that she would live with an emptiness inside her.

"Baby." The kiss turned urgent, and laughter bubbled out of Vega.

"What?" he asked amused.

"We get each other hot so fast," she chuckled, "I've never had sex on a desk, you know."

His hand cupped a breast, and she moaned. "Caro, sweetheart, I want to fuck you so hard, but my brother is going to kill me if I don't join him on a call with the FDA."

"Tonight?"

"Fuck that. Give me forty-five minutes, and I'll be in your pants before you can say *fuck me, Aurelio*, in that sexy voice of yours." He put his hands on her hips; lifted and then set her on her feet.

"I didn't know I had a sexy voice."

"I could come just listening to you." He gave her another lingering kiss. "Forty-five minutes."

"I'm sorry, honey. Joey will be here in sixty minutes, and I need each one of them to go through the Solarix contract."

Vega worked for the next hour, feeling supremely lighthearted. For the first time in a long time, the universe felt right.

Her phone rang five minutes before her scheduled meeting with Joey. She was prompt, if nothing else. She directed security at the lobby to send Joey up.

Chapter 43

Sunday, October 14

"You're fucking with me, right?" Drago demanded.

Mateo shrugged. "Well, damn it, Drago, I thought she already told you."

Drago didn't know Vega was working from home, so he had come to her office and found Mateo outside Vega's door, full of information about how Vega had cloned Soller's phone, and he'd just tracked a conversation between him and the unsub.

"Fuck it. What does it say?" Drago demanded, running a hand through his hair. Once they put Kaleb Soller behind bars, he was going on a long weekend to a full-service resort with a good friend and spend his days eating, drinking, fucking, and sleeping.

Mateo led Drago into his office, where he detailed Vega's ingenious yet illicit methods. He described how she clandestinely cloned Soller's phone, a feat accomplished without the Denver Police Department's knowledge. The act, Drago thought sourly, constituted several legal violations: tampering with evidence, obstructing an investigation, among others. Such actions could potentially land Vega significant prison time, not to mention substantial fines.

"There was a message from your...ah...copycat last night."

Drago read the message: Dad, I know you're disappointed, but I'm going to finish your work. I'm going to make Sweet Caroline a butterfly. Goodbye.

"And since then?"

Mateo did some finger magic, and the large screen in his office flashed with messages on an unfamiliar application. Following Kaleb's message to Soller, there were five responses from his father but radio silence from the unsub.

Soller: You're a fucking disgrace. I told you. Prepare. Plan. Patience. You didn't listen and now you've ruined everything like you always did, always do.

Soller: Son, you better not be going after my sweet Caroline without talking to me first. I'll cut your balls off and feed them to you.

"Nice father-son dynamic," Mateo mused.

There were two more messages spaced within two hours. One was right after news broke about Margo Jean.

Soller: Did you put Margo Jean into a coma, you imbecile?

The next followed twenty minutes later.

Soller: Kaleb? Where the fuck are you?

Drago sighed. "We need to let Vega know about this."

"She's working from home," Mateo said. "So, she's fine. Aurelio is not letting her out of his sight until you find Kaleb."

Drago looked around Mateo's office, pursing his lips, and then made a decision. "Can you track Kaleb's location from his message?"

Mateo grinned. "I never thought you'd ask."

Mateo's fingers flew across the keyboard, his eyes locked on the screen as he navigated through layers of digital information. Drago watched, impressed despite himself at the tech wizardry unfolding before him.

"Ah... I'm not going to go to prison for...ah...the stuff I'm doing?" Mateo asked. "Because usually I'm not doing such things in the presence of law enforcement."

"If you go to prison, I'll be in a cell next to you," Drago said dryly. TID would take days to get him what Mateo could in minutes. Right or wrong, legal, or not, he didn't want to have another dead body on a slab at Dr. Chen's morgue if he could help it.

"Alright, let's see where our little butterfly enthusiast has been fluttering," Mateo murmured, his focus unwavering. The large screen displayed a map of Los Angeles, and soon, a series of dots appeared, each representing a location ping from Kaleb's phone.

"Here we go," Mateo announced. "Looks like our guy has a pattern. He's been hitting up areas around Downtown, especially near Skid Row. High homeless population, less surveillance, easy to go unnoticed."

Drago leaned forward, studying the map. "Any recent activity?"

"Just this morning," Mateo pointed at a dot on the map, "at Pico Union. That's a rough area."

"We found Margo Jean around there," Drago murmured. "And Jorja Levey's body as well."

Drago was about to make a call when Mateo held up his hand. "Wait, a second. Wait a second. I have something."

Mateo brought up what looked like the area around Pico Union that looked like warehouses. Drago's heart was about to leap off his chest. Fucking hell, he wouldn't be able to get a warrant based on whatever Mateo was digging up. Unless he lied and said that a CI gave him a tip off. The last thing he needed was to catch Kaleb and lose him because he played fast and loose with evidentiary procedures.

"I know this area," Mateo frowned. "Why do I know this area?"

Drago called Nikki. The hell with it. He'd take the anonymous CI route.

"This is where they have art studios," Mateo exclaimed. "People rent warehouses where they paint, make music, and—"

"Rape, torture, and kill women," Drago finished. "I'm going to get some guys there to see if we find anything. Will you send me the GPS coordinates?"

Mateo's eyes darkened suddenly. "I know how I know this area."

"How?"

"One of our employees told me how she had a studio there, how she did artwork, sculpting, she said."

"Who?" Drago asked.

"Joey Mann," Mateo finally said, "She's a lawyer. She works for Vega."

CHAPTER 44

Sunday, October 14

"I'll get it," she heard Aurelio say when the doorbell rang.

She rose to greet Joey and bring her into her office. Her smile froze when she stepped into the living room, immediately sensing the shift in atmosphere. The sight that greeted her was chilling; Aurelio lay motionless on the floor, a dark pool of blood spreading beneath him. Panic and rage surged through her veins.

She barely had time to process this when Joey, or rather the person she thought was Joey, lunged at her with a knife. Vega's instincts kicked in, her years of self-defense training resurfacing in this life-or-death struggle. Joey was strong, deceptively so, and as they grappled, Vega felt the cold steel of the knife graze her throat.

Adrenaline surged through her, fueling her determination not just to survive but to avenge Aurelio. Their struggle was fierce and desperate. Vega managed to land a few solid hits, but Joey—no, it wasn't Joey, this has to be a man,—was relentless. Was this Kaleb? she wondered with a jolt.

It was the eyes that gave it away. Those eyes, so much like Jacob Soller's, filled with the same cold malice, Vega remembered all too well. The realization hit her like a physical blow, adding a new layer of horror to the situation.

Vega fought with every ounce of her being, driven by fear, anger, and an overwhelming need for retribution. They crashed into furniture, upending chairs, and scattering items in their chaotic dance of violence. Vega grappled for the knife, her hands slick with sweat and blood, her breath coming in ragged gasps.

In a moment that made Vega's heart seize, the knife clanged ominously onto the floor. Both she and her assailant lunged for it in a desperate dance of survival. Vega grappled to gain control, her hands finally finding Joey's hair. But her grip found no purchase, the hair slipping from her fingers like a ghostly whisper. With a chilling revelation, she realized it was a wig, unveiling a layer of deception as eerie as the situation itself.

She tried again and was impeded by the backpack Joey wore, making him bulky. Finally, as Vega's fingers grazed the knife's handle, Joey's hand clamped around the hilt with sinister precision. She swung with a violent arc, the blade sinking mercilessly into Vega's right arm. She collapsed onto the floor, a guttural cry tearing from her throat. Panic surged through her as she frantically scrambled to her feet, her mind fixated on the gun in her office—her only chance of survival in this nightmare.

But before she could move, she saw Joey knelt over Aurelio, pulling out a gun from the small of her back. She held a SIG Sauer P320 in her hand. Vega knew her guns; she grew up in Texas, and she'd seen weapons fired in her life to know the damage they could do. Dallas PD used the exact same gun because it was known for its reliability, accuracy, and adaptability—and because its striker-fired system with trigger safety enabled the shooter to interchange between full-size, compact, and subcompact frames.

She put the gun to Aurelio's forehead.

Why the fuck am I thinking about guns? She wondered shakily. Because this one could blow your lover's head right off, honey. That's why.

Aurelio was sprawled on his stomach. Joey ...had hit Aurelio on the head with something. Was he dead? Vega felt a chill run through her.

No, no, no. He couldn't be dead.

Please, god, please, don't let him die.

She didn't realize she was moaning until Joey whispered, "Shh, Sweet Caroline."

Joey didn't look like herself anymore. The smile she wore changed her face. She'd always looked masculine, but now with her makeup smudged and the wig gone, she looked nothing like the young lawyer Vega had hired.

Vega stood up on shaky feet, one hand clutching her arm that hurt like a mother fucker and even though her eyes were hazy with pain, she recognized the person Joey was. She was Kaleb Soller.

Her heart hammered and she had to calm herself because she knew she couldn't help Aurelio or herself if she went off like an unguided missile.

"Please don't hurt him," she whispered.

"I don't want to hurt him, Sweet Caroline. I don't want to hurt anyone. I want to help you...become a butterfly."

Soller had believed his bullshit, but Kaleb, it was apparent, didn't. He was high, Vega noted. Had she seen that before? Had Joey been high when she came to work?

"Now, why don't we take this out there?" He pointed to the kitchen area with the SIG, and Vega nodded. The instinct to live is a primal one, but the one to protect was just as primal, borne out of love. So, Vega left Aurelio where he lay and walked toward Kaleb Soller, the New Butterfly Killer.

CHaPTer 45

Tuesday, October 15

"We have a problem," Drago called Nikki as he and Mateo ran to get to Vega's house. "Kaleb Soller is in Vega's apartment. I can't reach her on the phone. Get a team out there now; we need eyes and ears."

Mateo was going through his phone as Drago drove them to Vega's place with lights and sirens.

"I'm going to need a computer but...fuck me, I've been looking into Kaleb Soller and now I think can connect some of the dots."

"Why were you looking into...never mind, Vega asked you to."

"I don't know why this didn't pop through during Joey Mann's background check, but it's obvious now Joey's entire identity is made up, but it's a damn good front. If I didn't know, I'd never see it."

"Does she look like a man?" Drago asked. "How could you think a man was a woman?"

"She always seemed a little masculine. I thought she was channeling Elizabeth Holmes with her voice and how she carried herself. Obviously, she's good at disguises. She...he...they should be. Kaleb minored in drama at LSU."

Drago's grip on the steering wheel tightened as he navigated the LA streets with a sense of urgency only a life-and-death scenario could evoke. The sound of sirens pierced the air, a desperate call cutting through the city's usual cacophony.

"Delfino kept saying that he was surprised the profile was wrong regarding the gender of the unsub. But Kaleb disguised as a woman...could have thrown him off," Drago growled, his voice strained with frustration and worry.

Mateo feverishly tapped on his phone, his face a mask of concentration and regret. "Kaleb has been living as Joey Mann for five months now since he/she moved to Los Angeles. He's been blending in unnoticed. It's a perfect cover."

His phone buzzed, and he answered, putting Gomez on speaker.

"What the fuck is going on?" Gomez demanded.

"Loo, we have a clusterfuck situation," Drago began and explained what he could.

"I'm going to get SWAT down there. I can't believe security let the fucking unsub into the victim's fucking apartment," he bellowed.

"I know."

"I thought you did background checks on everyone who works with Vega."

"Ah, Lieutenant, this is Mateo Silva. I work with Vega, and I can tell you that even our background checks didn't flag Joey Mann as anything other than who she says she is. She's good at IT, law, and...changing her identity."

"The profile did say extraordinarily intelligent," Drago barked.

"Nikki is on her way, as am I. Fucking hell, we now have a hostage situation?"

"I fucking hope so, Loo." *Because that meant Vega was still alive.*

As they neared Vega's apartment building, Drago felt a knot of dread tighten in his stomach.

He stopped the car right in front of the entrance even as a security guard came up to them, ready to tell them they couldn't park here. He held up his badge. "You're going to have SWAT swarming down here in a few minutes," he warned. "Now I need to know all entry and egress points of this building. We have a hostage situation. Caroline Vega."

"Miss Vega? Apartment Twenty-four fifty-three, sir," the security guard blurted out.

"You stay out here," Drago instructed Mateo, who raised both hands and stayed where he was. "And...don't fucking call the entire Santos family. I can't deal with them right now."

"You don't have to. You focus on getting her out of there," Mateo told him, "I'll take care of the rest. About staying out here, I'd rather access the building's security and see what I can see."

Drago nodded. TID would be on its way, but who had time for that? "Take him to wherever you keep your security servers," he ordered a guard who immediately took action. "Now, who can block all the fucking elevators except one for the police? The last thing I need is another unsuspecting civilian getting trampled over."

He saw Nikki enter the building, Gomez behind her as well as four cops in uniform. "Well?"

"She's on the twenty-fourth floor," Drago talked as he walked. "I need to make sure no one fucking leaves their apartment until we sort this out."

They moved swiftly, their steps echoing through the hallway as they headed toward the elevators. Drago's voice was firm and authoritative, carrying a sense of urgency that brooked no argument. "I need one of you to stay here and control the elevators. Only police personnel on these, understand? We can't risk any civilians getting in the way."

The guard nodded, tapping away on a small tablet, effectively locking down the elevator system to restrict access. Drago felt a knot of tension in his stomach, a mix of anticipation and dread as they approached Vega's apartment.

As they reached the twenty-fourth floor, the corridor was eerily silent, the usual sounds of domestic life conspicuously absent. He noted the apartments had good soundproofing; for what they cost, they better have.

SWAT was hot on their footsteps, thank fucking god, Drago thought.

They immediately went about setting up their equipment, their presence dominating the space.

Even as Drago briefed the commanding officer, a burly officer with an almost visceral focus, maneuvered a small camera under the door of Vega's apartment.

Nikki came up to Drago, her expression grim. "We've got visual inside."

Drago's heart pounded in his chest as he moved closer to the monitor displaying the feed from the camera. The screen flickered, then cleared, revealing the interior of Vega's apartment. His eyes scanned the scene, taking in every detail: the overturned furniture, the signs of a struggle.

And then he saw the pool of blood and Aurelio. "Fuck."

"Calm down, Horvat, he's still breathing," Nikki told him and they watched the up and down of Aurelio's back. The camera changed angle, and they saw Kaleb holding a gun and Vega holding a bleeding arm.

She'd been cut, but she was alive, Drago thought in relief.

"If we make any sudden moves, he's going to kill her," Drago whispered. "So...let's keep it very fucking quiet out here."

He walked up to Gomez, Nikki in tow. "I need to talk to Delfino to see what the next steps are. Just need five minutes, Loo."

"Go," Gomez instructed.

He and Nikki took an exit to the stairway and called Agent Delfino. Drago quickly laid out the situation.

"He's not there to negotiate, so if you get the chance, you shoot to kill," Delfino instructed. "There is no way he's going to let either Vega or her boyfriend get out of this alive. He'll take them with him."

"Okay."

"Get SWAT ready to kill," Delfino said simply. "And in the meantime, wait for the right moment. Vega's smart: she'll create an opening for you. You just need to be ready to move the second she does."

The team waited, a collective breath held, as the drama unfolded on the camera.

"We have sound," one of the SWAT team techs whispered and held up headphones for Drago.

Every second stretched out, laden with tension. Vega's voice came through steady, her words measured, clearly trying to keep Joey/Kaleb engaged and off-balance. "You don't want to be your father, Kaleb. You could be so much more."

Chapter 46

Tuesday, October 15

Vega's heart raced in her chest, realizing she was at the mercy of another Soller, one devoid of any compassion. She didn't need a profiler to understand that this was Kaleb's final move. It was clear: no one was leaving here alive.

The revelation was a jolt to her system, every instinct screaming at her to fight or flee, but she knew her best chance lay in keeping Kaleb talking until she could find a way to get into her office and to her gun. She could see the wildness in his eyes, a frantic energy that spoke of drug-induced mania and deep-rooted instability.

"Why are you doing this, Kaleb?" she asked, her voice steady despite the fear coursing through her.

Kaleb's lips twisted into a grotesque smile, his eyes gleaming with a mixture of madness and glee. "Sweet Caroline, you're part of my story now. You and my father, you've always been the stars of my movie."

His words were erratic, the ramblings of a mind unhinged, but Vega listened intently, waiting for an opening, a moment to break free and reach her gun.

"It's always been about making daddy proud, hasn't it?" Vega prodded, her tone calculated to keep him talking. "You don't want to be your father, Kaleb. You could be so much more."

Kaleb's expression shifted, a mix of pain and anger flashing across his face. "When I'm done with you, he'll see." He dropped his backpack on the kitchen counter. "I have everything we need to make you into a butterfly. You'll look so beautiful."

He didn't believe his own words, Vega realized. He wasn't a stickler like Soller; he was an ingenue, a pretender.

"You've been planning this for a long time, haven't you?" she continued her voice a soothing lull against the storm of his emotions.

Kaleb's rant grew more intense, his words tumbling out in a torrent. "Do you know when I knew who he was?"

"When?" Vega heard a sound and hoped to god that his drug-addled brain didn't pick it up. Someone was outside her door, right outside. Relief washed through her; Drago was here.

They'd have SWAT here. They'd have snipers. If she could lead Kaleb to where there was a clear shot, maybe....

"When I was ten," he whispered. Joey's red lipstick was smeared around his mouth, and he looked like a cross between a Drag Queen, a clown, and a homicidal maniac. "I saw him with his first. I think it was his first. Long before Lorna Wilson."

Vega sensed his desperation; he was losing coherence. Kristy Reed had been Soller's first known victim, while Lorna Wilson was Kaleb's. However, Kaleb's ramblings suggested a haunting truth: Soller had been preying for far longer than they had ever suspected.

"He didn't tattoo them then. He just liked to do them," his voice dropped to a whisper, "You know what I think? I think he just wanted to have sex, and this was the only way he could get it. I hear he pounded you, real good."

She weighed her options carefully, contemplating the delicate balance required. Her strategy was to stroke Kaleb's ego while subtly undermining his father, pushing him to the brink. She knew she had to tread lightly; the moment Kaleb ceased to revel in his twisted display of superiority, her life would hang by a thread.

"Actually, he didn't. Had to use something like you did with Lorna Wilson."

He scoffed. "I don't need to use something, you can ask Margo Jean. I did her good. But Lorna, that was...that was the way he wanted it. Dad wants to do them, you know? And he doesn't want me to do them."

"That seems a little selfish, don't you think?" Vega tried to think how to get him into her office. If they could just get in, she'd have a chance.

"He never understood my potential. I had to step out of his shadow, make my own mark. He'd always say, *sissy boy, when are you going to man up*," he hissed, his voice contorting, slurring, evidence of how high he was.

A serial killer who was tripping. Great, Vega thought. This couldn't get worse, could it?

"He underestimated you," she agreed, her voice soft, encouraging.

"Yeah, he did! And he still does. I'm the master now. I'm the one they'll remember." Kaleb's eyes were distant, lost in his delusion of grandeur.

"I think the work you've been doing surpasses your father's," she said.

He quirked an eyebrow.

"I can show you." She waved a hand to her office. "I have a murder board there, and you'll be able to see how superior you are. I mean, using a nerve agent like succinylcholine? Now that is innovative."

"Right?" He looked like the young man he was, seeking validation.

They moved to her office; he followed with his gun, his backpack slung on his shoulder. "I hated that metal gurney. I think I'll do you in a bed. I can do the tattoo there, too."

They entered the office, and he looked around. Vega pointed to the wall she'd just covered up and, with his permission, went to pull down the white paper hiding it.

He was enchanted the minute he saw the board as she'd hoped he'd be. She moved away from him and towards her desk as he walked up to the wall.

"Look at how beautiful Lorna looks," he whispered, stroking the crime scene photograph of Lorna Wilson, her back on display with one finger.

Vega thanked the stars that she'd bought a desk that had those drawers that opened softly at a push.

"She certainly does. Will you make me a butterfly that good?" Vega's fingers brushed against the cold metal of her gun. She had to time this perfectly.

He turned to look at her. "Better than he ever could," he said scornfully. "I'll make my own mark."

"They'll remember you, Kaleb," she affirmed, her heart racing.

Kaleb nodded vigorously, caught up in his own world, the methamphetamine coursing through his veins amplifying his erratic behavior.

Vega could see he was feeling charged; he was higher than a kite at this point and double dangerous. His hands roamed over the wall, touching the photos of his and his father's victims.

He watched Vega standing behind her desk and smiled. "They'll all know my name when I'm done with you."

With a swift, practiced movement born of years in law enforcement, Vega pulled out her Glock 19. Her confident fingers wrapped around the grip, the familiar weight of it grounding her as she aimed it at Kaleb.

"You're wrong, Kaleb," she said, her voice now edged with authority. "They'll remember me for ending you."

Before Kaleb could react with his own weapon, Vega, with a steadiness that belied her shaking body, pulled the trigger. The gunshot was deafening in the confined space of the office. Joey/Kaleb halted mid-lunge, a look of shock and disbelief etched on his face.

Vega didn't stop to think. She fired again, ensuring that the threat was neutralized. Kaleb's body first hit against the wall, her murder board and then crumpled to the floor, the life rapidly draining from his eyes. His SIG clattered harmlessly away, its threat extinguished.

Vega stood, panting heavily, her gun still aimed at the motionless body on the floor. Her mind was a blur, a tumultuous mix of relief, horror, and an overwhelming sense of finality. Vega felt a mix of relief and sorrow. Relief that she might survive this ordeal and sorrow for the twisted path Kaleb Soller had walked, one that had led him to this tragic end.

She picked up her phone that lay on her desk and dialed Drago as she rushed back to the living room. "He's dead. Bring a few medics, Drago."

She dropped to her knees next to Aurelio. Her hands trembled as she rolled him onto his back and checked for signs of life. Tears streamed down her face, each one a silent prayer for him to be alright. In that moment, the world around Vega faded into insignificance. Nothing mattered but the man lying before her, the man who had stood by her through her darkest hours. She whispered his name, her voice a fragile thread of hope in the silence that followed the storm.

Then her apartment door burst open. *Shit, I should've opened the door*, she thought, her mind clouded with fear and agony at the possibility of Aurelio not waking up. Her vision, blurred by tears, failed to discern the faces of those entering her home.

She kissed Aurelio's forehead and gripped his hand. "I'll marry you, honey, tomorrow, today, just wake the fuck up."

His eyelids fluttered and opened. He groaned. "I heard that, Caro. And I'm going to hold you to it."

CHAPTER 47

Friday, October 18

Aurelio's head throbbed with the steady rhythm of a drumbeat, a dull echo of the hit he'd taken. Lying in the hospital bed, he tried to focus on the banter around him, but the voices of Mateo, Nikki, Drago, and Gomez seemed to weave in and out like a poorly tuned radio.

"Where's Caro?" he asked.

"She's getting stitches on her arm." Drago put a restraining hand on his shoulder, "Raya is with her, and she said she'd kill me if I let you move."

Aurelio leaned back and groaned.

"How's the thick head, Aurelio?" Mateo chuckled.

"Fuck off, Silva," Aurelio grumbled, wincing as a wave of pain lanced through his skull. "It's not every day you get whacked by a psycho with a knife handle."

Nikki leaned against the wall, her arms crossed. "You're lucky you just have a concussion. Joey...I mean, Kaleb was not messing around."

"Yeah, next time, I'll just ask them nicely not to hit me," Aurelio replied dryly, trying to lighten the mood despite the pain.

Drago, sitting in a chair by the window, snorted. "Next time? Are you planning on making a habit of this?"

"Yeah sure. It's the best vacation I've had since we were in Gainesville a few days ago," Aurelio muttered and then turned to Mateo. "I need to see her, man. I need to...you know."

Mateo nodded and patted Aurelio's hand. "She wanted to change. She didn't want you to see all the blood."

"You talked to Alejandro?" he asked.

"Yep. They're all on their way, as you can imagine," Mateo smiled.

"Can we...ah, not have the reunion here in the hospital?" Aurelio grimaced. He knew his family, they'd all be here en masse, probably more worried about Vega than him if he knew them. Women and children first!

"We're setting you up at our place until you feel comfortable to go to Golden Valley," Mateo informed him. "Vega's apartment is a crime scene, and we need to get it cleaned up before you go there."

"She holding up okay?" Aurelio hated that Vega had to kill Kaleb. She carried so many scars, and now she had to carry the burden of killing someone.

"I think she's doing better than you think she is," Mateo assured him.

On cue, Vega, her arm bandaged where Kaleb had slashed her, stepped into the room, followed by Mateo's wife, Raya.

"Hey, handsome." Her voice wavered as she made her way to him. He sat up, despite the jangling in his head when he did, and grabbed her to him when she got close. "Fucking hell, Caro. Fucking hell."

He held her to him.

"I got a definite *oh Heathcliff, oh Catherine* vibe," Nikki mused. "You know, the way they came together."

"Very Wuthering Heights," Gomez agreed, and when they all stared at him in disbelief, he snorted, "What? You think because I'm a cop, I don't read?"

"You don't read," Drago remarked.

"I read your fucking poorly written reports," he snapped. "And I've started listening to audiobooks. Now that I'm back on the market, need to be more...ah erudite."

"You heard that word on an audiobook, didn't you, Loo?" Nikki asked, all innocent.

"Fuck you all." Gomez good naturedly gave his detectives the middle finger.

Vega sat in bed with him, and they held on to each other as if for dear life. They made a pair, Aurelio thought. He, with his concussion, her with a bandaged right arm.

"Thanks for not bleeding to death," Vega said to him, her head leaning against his shoulder.

"Of course. I am, after all, your knight in slightly dented armor," Aurelio quipped, reaching for her hand, and giving it a gentle squeeze.

Gomez, standing at the foot of Aurelio's bed, shook his head. "You two are something else. Most couples go to the movies for a date night, not a knife fight with a deranged killer."

Aurelio laughed, then winced again as his head protested the movement. "Yeah, well, we like to keep things interesting."

"Anyone got an update on Margo Jean?" Vega asked.

"She's out of her coma," Nikki announced, and everyone cheered. "And she also identified Kaleb as the man who took her. She said that she wasn't worried about letting him into her car because he looked feminine."

"Women can be just as dangerous as men," Drago quipped. "I mean, I've had some vicious women in a car with me."

"That's because you're trying to break up them," Gomez supplied. "You know, our boy here is the King of One-Night Stands."

"Christ, Loo," Drago protested. "The clinic where he stole the nerve agent from identified him as well as Giselle's friend. For her, he'd dressed as a woman called Jackie. Not quite sure what went down there, but he tried to make her death look like a suicide. It was after he killed her that he emailed the clinic a resignation letter on her behalf from her phone."

Aurelio's thoughts turned to Giselle, the nurse whose life was lost in vain, reigniting the panic that had first surged when he saw Joey/Kaleb wielding a knife. Before he could react, he was struck down, regaining consciousness only when he heard Vega's promise to marry him. This declaration filled his chest with a mix of pride and joy, diminishing the overwhelming tide of panic and fear.

"We found Kaleb's studio," Nikki continued. "Or rather, Lee and Martinez, detectives who've been helping us with this case, did. It's a nightmare brought to life by a deranged mind. I wish the fucker was alive so we could prosecute his sorry ass."

"On the other hand, nothing wrong in saving some taxpayer money," Drago said, looking at Vega, "because you know it was either you or him."

She nodded.

"I talked to Delfino when I knew he was in there with you, and he said, kill him on sight. Kaleb was not there to make any kind of deal," Drago finished, wanting, Aurelio knew, to make Vega feel as comfortable as it was possible with her decision to kill Kaleb Soller.

"Oh, and your hunch, Horvat about the security cameras and how Kaleb knew where they were?" Gomez offered, "First glance at his laptop from his studio, TID says our boy hacked into a lot of places. And no one secures the security camera servers—so he had everything easy peasy."

"Will Soller be charged with aiding and abetting?" Aurelio asked.

"We'll leave that up to the DA's office." Drago rose and stuck his hands in his jeans. "I'm so fucking sorry, Vega, that you had to go through this. But I'm not sorry one bit that you killed that asshole."

Vega smiled wanly. "I'm not sorry either."

Aurelio knew what she meant because he knew her in and out. She'd run last time, but this time, she'd stayed and fought. She had the closure she never got before. Maybe now, her healing could properly begin.

CHAPTER 48

Friday, October 18

It was a good thing Mateo and Raya loved to entertain, Aurelio mused, because *everyone* had showed up. Family and friends.

Maria, Alejandro, and their son Silvano, who was right now talking case law with Nick, Drago's partner. He had an IQ at the Mensa level and an unmatched curiosity.

Aurelio's sister Isadora stood with her new husband, Gordon. Her back resting against his chest, his arms wrapped around her, with his hands rested on her pregnant stomach. He'd have a niece or nephew soon…two of them, one Maria's and one Isadora's. Maybe someday he and Vega would have children. They'd never had that conversation. And if she didn't want kids, that was fine as well; they had enough children around them to raise and take care of.

Paloma, his mother, had cried when she saw Vega's arm, and his father had told him that he was a *pendejo* for getting hurt and making his mother worry. Arsenio had tears in his eyes when he hugged his son, so he knew it just wasn't his mother who'd been worried.

Vega's boss, Declan Knight, was there with his wife Esme and their baby, Mireya, who was charming Drago, whose presence along with his partners had been demanded by Paloma. Aurelio wondered if maybe Drago's one-night stand days were coming to an end. There was something going on between the partners even if they hadn't acted on it.

Vega was out by the pool with Mateo. She'd worried that she'd made him do a few (or several) illegal things for this case, and to no one's surprise, Mateo thought that was just grand and told her that she should call on him the next time a serial killer was preying on the city.

Aurelio pulled Alejandro aside. "You got it?"

His brother patted his suit breast pocket. "Yep. It's becoming a Santos-family tradition to propose here in Mateo and Raya's place."

Alejandro had proposed to Maria in Mateo and Raya's pool patio. Isadora had met Gordon for the first time in their home as well.

Aurelio held out his hand, and Alejandro placed a blue velvet box on it. "Congratulations, hermano."

This was his family, which meant that everyone knew he was going to propose to Vega because Alejandro had probably mentioned it to Maria, who whispered it to Isadora, and...really, even Twitter wasn't as fast as the Santos.

"You sure she's going to say yes," Isadora teased.

"She already said yes, I'm just...you know...putting a ring on it."

"She said yes because she thought you were dying," Drago piped in.

He gave Drago the middle finger and walked out onto the patio. Vega was sitting on a chair next to Mateo, a glass of champagne in her hand. As soon as she saw Aurelio, she downed the whole glass, looking guilty as hell. "I know I said I was not going to drink in sympathy to your concussion, but Mateo made me."

Mateo raised his hand. "Yes, it was my fault."

"You're both full of shit," Aurelio muttered and walked to Vega.

Aurelio went down on one knee, and a giggle escaped her. A fucking giggle? Caroline Vega didn't giggle. But, god, he loved that sound.

Mateo slid out of his chair and joined the family to watch what Aurelio knew was going to be a show.

"I want to remind you that you already said yes." Aurelio pulled out the box and held it out to her.

She narrowed her eyes. "How did you get this ring so quickly?"

"I had some help, counselor." He tapped the closed lid of the box. "You gonna open it?"

Vega looked at the Santos family. "Can I trust the person who bought the ring? Will it be decent?"

"I just picked it up; he told me what he wanted." Alejandro held up his glass of champagne.

"Can you guys hurry up?" Isadora whined. "I have to go pee, and I don't want to miss the moment."

"The moment that you're absolutely murdering by talking about peeing, by the way," Raya grumbled.

"Let's not use the word murder," Drago stated.

"Ignore them," Aurelio said to Vega. "Caro, I love you. I've never said these words to any woman who's not my family. And because I'd like to keep that streak going, I'd like you to become my family."

"I love you too, Aurelio. I'd love to marry you, but...," she paused dramatically, and Aurelio quirked an eyebrow, "but nothing. I can come up with absolutely nothing."

She opened the box and gasped. The ring was a masterpiece of craftsmanship, its band forged in elegant white gold. At its heart sat a stunning diamond, radiant and clear, catching the light with every subtle movement. Surrounding the central gem were delicate, smaller diamonds, intricately set to enhance the ring's sparkle.

"Is it okay?" "Hell, yeah."

As he got to his feet, he pulled her up. "I don't want to wait too long to marry you. Will that be okay?"

"Yes. I don't want to wait either. Life is short, isn't it? I want to live it to the fullest and I want to live it with you."

He slid the beautiful yet simple ring on her finger, and just like that, the clouds parted, and the sun shone through.

Chapter 49

A Few Days Later

Nothing dampens your sex life like being concussed while your woman's arm is still recovering from a deep knife wound that needed twenty stitches to be closed, Aurelio thought grumbling.

It didn't help either that they had been staying at Mateo and Raya's place. For what he needed and how he needed it, privacy was paramount. He needed to be at his home with his Caro.

It took three days to leave Los Angeles and reach Golden Valley. Mateo drove them, as neither Aurelio nor Vega could; Aurelio's concussion and Vega's injured arm made driving impossible, and the concussion also meant Aurelio couldn't fly.

They bid Mateo adieu to his amusement at Aurelio's doorstep, asking him to go and bother Paloma. As soon as they were inside his home, Aurelio pushed Vega against the front door, and the purse she was carrying fell on the hard wood with a soft thud.

"I want you," his voice was guttural, and he barely got the words out before slamming his lips onto hers. Finesse went right out of the window, especially when it had been days since he'd been inside her.

He slowed the kiss, and she responded in kind; every suck, nip, and bite was enhanced. She kept one hand on his waist, the one she couldn't lift, and the other went into his hair. His hips held her in place, his erection throbbing against her stomach, keeping pace with his pounding heart.

"Caro, baby, you want me?" He bit her bottom lip and suckled softly.

"I want you very much," she answered, looking into his brown eyes with her blue ones, stormy with desire. She was in as much need as him. Her hands weren't steady, but then neither were his.

He brushed his lips against a satiny cheek, working his way to her earlobes, licking around her diamond studs.

She moaned as he knew she would. She was sensitive there, right there, below her earlobe. He sucked and then bit gently before he licked to soothe the skin. His jeans had gone from comfortable to suffocating a while back, and now his erection was throbbing with need.

"You want me? Show me," he coaxed.

She looked down at his crotch and then slumped down on her knees. He watched her fumble with his belt and zipper. He helped her because she, after all, had only one working hand, and he was past waiting. He wanted to jump headlong into madness with her. Find the comfort of love, of bonding, of connecting.

The tip of his erection was swollen and leaking. A pink tongue licked the precum off him, and his hands immediately went to her hair, holding her closer to his cock.

"Love me, Caro," I murmured, "Keep your eyes on me, baby."

She opened her mouth, and he slid inside, looking into her blue eyes that were telling him how much she loved him. He pumped in and out of her sexy mouth, holding her head. When he hit the back of her throat, her eyes watered. "Is it too much?" His words came out in a suffocated breath.

She shook her head.

"You can take more?"

She nodded.

Watching her pink lips around his cock was as always, intensely erotic. There was something primal in his need to possess this strong, wonderful woman, to have her completely surrender to him.

"You want me to come in your mouth, Caro?" he asked because he didn't have much self-restraint left.

She nodded.

"Then let me fuck your mouth, baby."

She opened her mouth wider in invitation, and he couldn't believe it, but his cock swelled more. "This time is for me," he apologized, "I'll make it up to you next time. I can't hold back, baby."

She looked at him with mischief in her eyes as if saying, no one's asking you to hold back, honey.

He held her head still, pumping in and out of her. He looked into her eyes as he felt his orgasm begin deep in his balls and work its way all the way through his spine to his brain. He exploded, and some of his cum leaked out of her mouth.

She couldn't swallow it all. More cum flowed from between her lips onto her white T-shirt. She looked defiled, and he felt like a fucking rockstar.

She wiped her mouth. "Feeling better?"

He pulled her up and kissed her moist lips, tasting her, himself. He carried her, and she looked like she was in bliss, like it was her who'd just had release and not him. He loved how she enjoyed her sexuality with him, how she never held anything back when they made love.

She lay on his...no, *their* bed and looked at his cock, still at half mast, hanging out of his jeans. He took his pants off and stood naked in front of her while she remained fully dressed.

"Now, I know your arm is not a hundred percent, baby." Aurelio slid up on his bed and leaned against the headboard. "But if I help you along, do you think you could undress...slowly."

She laughed, a joyous sound, something he never thought he'd hear again when Kaleb struck him in the head.

They fumbled with her clothes, first unbuttoning her blouse, which took too long because Aurelio kept suckling her through her bra. She took her jeans off, the ones she'd put on with his help just that morning, and he once again caressed her absolutely perfect ass. Once she was naked, she winked at him.

"Lie in bed, lover."

He scrambled back and watched as she dropped one strap of her bra and then another. "Show me your tits, baby."

She did so, awkwardly. Nothing was easy when one arm was out of commission. Still, she laughed at herself, and he laughed with her because fuck, it was good to be happy after so many days of interminable death and horror.

Her breasts were beautiful. The tips were dusky dark rose and a perfect handful. He knew that, at times, he could suckle her to completion.

He began to stroke his cock as he watched her.

"Enjoyin' the show, honey?"

"I may come again in my hands; I'm loving this so much. Are you wet, baby?"

She nodded.

"Then take your panties off and show me."

She bent all the way down, and all the blood from his head went straight to his cock.

"I love your pussy. I love to see my cum dripping out of you," he whispered, unable to look away from those beautiful lips of hers.

"Aurelio," she moaned, holding her breasts up and bringing them close to him. "Please."

"Not yet. Put a finger inside yourself and show me how wet you are."

She did as he asked and anointed her nipples with her wet fingers. He couldn't help himself and yanked her into bed and began to devour her nipples, sucking, biting, licking until she was begging for release.

"You taste delicious." He crawled between her legs, putting her thighs over his shoulders, going down on her. He barely had a chance to suckle her clitoris when she came, long and hard.

He slid inside her before she had a chance to come down from her high and felt her aftershocks pulse around him. "Every time I'm inside you, I feel like I've come home."

"I love you. Aurelio."

"I know, baby. Let me show you how much I love you." He pumped in and out of her.

"And how will you do that?" she challenged.

He gave her a lopsided grin and a wink, "I'll just make you come until you pass out, baby."

"Who am I to stop you from proving a point." She looked into his eyes as he began to fuck her in earnest.

Nothing had ever been this perfect, Aurelio thought, as he often did when he was with Vega. And he couldn't imagine a time when she'd not make him feel this way.

"Now, come again, baby. Don't make me look bad," he urged, and she laughed because life was fucking awesome.

Thank you so much for reading the series.

With *Twisted Love* we've come to the end of the road with this series. But I don't want to let you go without telling you what happened with **Drago and Nikki**. Read their story: *Night, Night* on my website at www.MayaAlden.com.

ABOUT THE AUTHOR

Maya Alden has a passion for weaving tales of love and desire.

A #1 Amazon bestselling author in a variety of romance categories, Maya pens angsty contemporary romances with a touch of mystery whenever possible.

You can sign up for her newsletter on her website at www.MayaAlden.com; and contact her via email at maya@mayaalden.com or via social media on Facebook (@authormayaalden) and Instagram (@mayaalden_romance).

Made in the USA
Las Vegas, NV
17 January 2024

84370197R00208